Angel,

Wished for **you**

Book boyfriends
are real!

♡ ♡ MD Polichoux

COPYRIGHT

The Blogger Diaries Trilogy

The Blogger Diaries Trilogy is the true story of how I met, fell for, lost, and got a second chance at love with my soul mate. The names of everyone EXCEPT me, Jason, my family, and my best friend have been changed to protect their identities. Full of youthful stupidity, leading to bad decisions and lots of angst, it is a real life story, where inevitably things are messy.

No one can look back at their late teens and early twenties and not think of moments that make them ask, What the hell was I thinking? Every second of this trilogy is true, exactly as it happened.

The first book, 'Wished For You', is a tale of finding 'the one' too early, and then having to let them go.

PLEASE NOTE: This is a true trilogy, meaning the first two books END ON CLIFFHANGERS. But if you take the journey with me, in the end, I promise you a happily ever after you will never forget.
I know I won't.

DEDIC♠TION

For my Granny, who I undoubtably inherited my lack of filter from. No giving anyone a "ride on your foot" or pulling out the shotgun if they don't care for your baby's book. They're entitled to their opinion, even if it's not the same as yours, which is ALWAYS right.

And for Momma, aka Mrs. Robichaux, I don't know how you would've felt about me putting all this out there for the world to read, but I know you would've been proud of me for all my hard work getting here, and for setting a good example for our girls.
Miss you.

PR♠LOGUE

Kayla's Chick Rant & Book Blog
Blog Post 1/23/2007

I'm a happy person, damn it! I'm happy sober; I'm a happy drunk, and I smile until my cheeks hurt. I'm so freakin' perky all the time. I always get invited to everyone's parties; I never get scrolled over when people are looking through their phones to see what's going on. Everyone loves for me to be around because I bring no drama. I'm shameless, and will make a fool of myself to make everyone laugh. I don't say these things to be conceited; I say it to show you how unlike me it is when I tell you...

I cried myself to sleep again last night. I cradled my swollen belly in my hands and rocked myself back and forth praying in a whisper, "Please, God, make him love me. I know you put us here to be together. Just make him realize it. Please!" The last word came out on a sob. I swear I'm not a horrible person, as I laid there crying over another man while I'm six months pregnant with my husband's baby.

I will never say what happened was a mistake. I believe everything happens for a reason. I also believe in soul mates. But what if one person finds their soulmate and the other one just refuses to acknowledge it? Can you be happy with anyone else? Or if once your soul finds its other half, are you doomed to long for them?

These are all questions I've asked myself since I left Texas a year and a half ago, since I left the man I know I'm supposed to share my life with. No, I didn't leave him. He told me to go. He told me there was no reason for me to stay since my semester of school ended. That's when happy, perky, shameless Kayla snapped.

CHPTER One

January 7, 2005

I'm in my 2002 Chevy Malibu, with its cherry-patterned seats, steering wheel cover, and CD holder hooked to the visor. My big brother Mark is in the driver's seat while I sit next to him with my turtle's 10 gallon aquarium at my feet and my lovebird's giant-ass, castle-shaped cage in the backseat. The rest of the car is stuffed to the gills with my TV, clothes, and books. Couldn't leave home without every last one of my Sherrilyn Kenyon's, Julie Kenner's, and the rest of my paranormal romances.

I'm a book blogger, you see. I use my AOL profile website as a sort of scrapbook to keep all my reviews and notes about my favorite authors. It's not just for books though. It's kind of like a diary too. That's why I named it Kayla's Chick Rant

& Book Blog. My mom thinks I put too much of myself on the internet, but I tell her, "I'm not the only one thinking this stuff. I just may be the only one with the balls to say it aloud." I'm from a small town in North Carolina called Fayetteville. Affectionately nicknamed Fayettenam since it's right next door to Ft. Bragg Army Base. I'm on 95 South about to jump on I-10 West, moving to Texas for a semester of school.

Mark flew in to Raleigh and is driving me to his house in Houston, where I'm going to see what it's like to "live outside that shithole vortex" as he put it. I love my big brother. He's the oldest out of the three I've got. I'm the baby and the only girl. Our relationship is different from most siblings, I suppose, because he was 17 when I was born. Yep, I was an accident. I was born the year Daddy retired from the Navy. But Momma finally got her girl!

I think Mark feels like it was up to him to get me out of Fayetteville. Everyone there seems to either marry a soldier and live the military life, or work at a dead-end job. There's nothing in Fayetteville, really, except for restaurants and stores. A shit-ton of them, mind you, but still.

I'm moving in with Mark and his wife, Kim. She's seriously the most hilarious chick you could possibly imagine. I couldn't have picked a better woman for my brother. Kim and I share a love of paranormal romances, so we'll call each other up and talk for an hour about what's going on in some of our favorite series. I'm looking forward to having her around. In a couple of days, I'll be registering at Kingwood College to work toward my degree in English. I want to be a writer, but until then, I took it upon myself to pimp out the authors I'm addicted to, spreading their stories so everyone else can enjoy the escape they bring.

It's not a bad deal. As I sit here, wearing my "Authors Are My Rockstars" t-shirt, you can tell I absolutely love what I do, because a lot of my wardrobe is book-themed. I even have a nightshirt that says "I Sleep with a Different Book Boyfriend Every Night". I get to talk daily with people I adore, like others would their favorite singer. Or even like I used to over Brian Littrell of the Backstreet Boys in the 6th grade. Only it's even better because instead of loving them from afar, knowing you'll never actually get to tell them how much you love them (and marry them in my case with Brian…sigh), I actually hold conversations with them! Any time I want, I can email my favorite author just to see how their day is going, how their next book is coming along, and with a select few, I've really gotten close to, check on how that argument with their hubby worked out. I'll never have to worry about one of my authors not knowing how much I appreciate them… unlike Brian. I was so upset when he got married when I was in the 7th grade that my mom let me stay home from school…true story.

Turtle's cage is taking up the entire floor on my side of the car, so my feet are up on the dashboard, swinging back and forth to the "Disturbed" song playing on the radio. Turtle never got a real name because when I got him in Myrtle Beach, the guy on The Strip told me they only usually live for a couple of months. He was about the size of a fifty-cent coin at the time. Well, five years later and that asshole is still kicking and is about the size of a baseball. Not that I wanted my pet to keel over, but I didn't sign up for this! But when Daddy suggested I just let Turtle free into our lake behind our house, all I could imagine was one of the giant snapping turtles making a midday snack out of the little guy. I just couldn't do it.

So now I get to ride over 1600 miles with nowhere to put my long-ass legs. I'm 5'6, pretty tall for a chick I think, going by the fact I was always one of the tallest girls at my school. All my big brothers are over six-feet tall, one's even 6'5. I have super dark brown hair that hits the middle of my back, and the only green eyes in my family, everyone else has blue. My mom told me that her dad and sister had green eyes, but they both passed away before I was born. I glance over at Mark as he reaches for his fourth Diet Mountain Dew of the day, "Liquid Gold" he calls it. "You know that stuff is just as bad, if not worse than regular Mountain Dew, right?" I ask him.

"Yeah, but it helps me keep my girlish figure, Wench." I don't remember exactly why he started calling me Wench; he's done it since I can remember. But it probably has something to do with all my big brothers bribing me with hide-and-seek to go fetch them drinks and sandwiches while they played video games when I was little.

"You getting tired, Marky? You want me to take over for a while?" I ask.

"Hell no! I didn't fly all the way out to NC to get your ass to just ride all the way back to Texas. You coulda driven yourself if that was the case. Plus, Mom would kill me if I let you drive and something happened. It's up to me to keep the princess safe." He smirks at me. He loves to tease me about being the only girl in the family. "Not to mention, I'm more than a little afraid that your turtle would jump up and bite my legs. You don't look comfortable at all."

"I'm fine. All those years of dance class made me pretty bendy. I'll make sure to walk around next time you stop for gas," I say as I poke him in the ribs when he takes another swig of his Liquid Gold. "You're gonna have to pee soon anyways the way you're sucking those things down."

CHAPTER Two

January 10, 2005

I'm finishing up putting my clothes on hangers in my new room in Mark's house when my cell phone rings. I find it buried under a box of paperbacks on my bed just in time to answer. "What's up, hooker?!" I ask excitedly.

"Nothing much, ho. Just missing my best friend and wondering if the next six months are going to crawl by as slowly as the past three days have since you've been gone," Anni pouts.

"Awwww. I miss you too, boo. I'm almost finished unpacking. Haven't really done much else. I'm going to the school tomorrow to get all registered," I tell her.

Anni's been my best friend for two years now. Funny to

think we didn't like each other when we first met. I worked at my cousin's car dealership as a receptionist when she was hired for the same job. She was from Florida and kind of a bitch, and apparently, thought my always happy and perky personality was annoying. But during a random conversation, she found out I had never ridden a horse, and from that moment on, we were inseparable. The following weekend, she had dragged me to the stables on Ft. Bragg and forced me to ride a damn horse. It was the scariest experience of my entire life. That fucking beast had seriously tried to amputate my leg by running me into a fence, and here I am now...living in Texas. Kind of ironic to be deathly afraid of horses and move to the Lone Star State, right?

"Well, I started the new job at Wiley's last night," she reminded me.

"Oh, yeah! How did it go?" I braced myself for her answer. She'd been having a pretty long streak of bad luck with jobs in the past few months since she quit working at the car dealership. The latest one though, Wiley's, is a restaurant and bar inside of a hotel. With a steady flow of customers, there was no need to worry about it shutting down like the last one she worked at.

"I think I'm really going to like it. My manager, Mike, said that it's different working at a restaurant inside a hotel because not only do you get 'regulars' like a normal restaurant does, you can also get the same people in every single night, sometimes for weeks straight. They'll be staying at the hotel for a contract job or whatnot and come down for dinner or just a drink before bed."

"Well, put on that Anni charm and hopefully you'll get some of them to request you each time they come in. Hike up those giant tatas and rack up them tips, biotch!" I tease her. We chat for a few more minutes before we say our 'I love yous' and 'goodbyes' and I finish up with my clothes and look around my room. All I have left is to go buy a new bookcase to hold all my beloved books since I couldn't fit one in my car.

The next day, Mark rides shotgun as I drive to Kingwood College. We're meeting our brother Tony there since he only lives five minutes from the campus. Mark is making me drive because it makes me physically ill to think about driving to the school on my own. Houston is made up of a ton of freaking highways. We don't have highways where I'm from. We just have our regular old streets, seeing how Fayetteville is maybe thirty minutes across, and that's only because of the traffic lights. My hands are cramping from gripping the steering wheel so tightly. After exiting his neighborhood onto the feeder road, the road that runs along the highways that you exit onto to get to the buildings, I panic. "Marky, don't make me get on the highway. I will freak the fuck out if you make me get up there with all those semis going a million miles an hour right next to each other across six lanes."

"Ok, Wench. Just take the feeder the whole way there. You'll have to leave a few minutes earlier than you would if you actually took 59, but if it scares you that much, just stay on here." Like the great big brother he is, he knows when to tease me and when to be supportive. This is one of those times picking on me would have made the situation dangerous for his appendages.

We arrive fifteen minutes later and I can finally relax. I see my big brother, Tony, standing outside his truck in the parking lot when we pull in. I hop out of the car, take off running, and throw myself at him. I haven't seen him in almost a year. He's a commercial diver; from what I understand, he finds oil under the ocean and his team goes in, drills, and sucks it out. He's gone for weeks at a time with short amounts of time in between trips so it's hard to plan a vacation to come see him. Maybe now that I live here, I'll get to see him more often.

"Hey, kid!" he grunts as he catches me. He's 6'5 and built like a linebacker...or a hockey player I guess he'd prefer, since he's a diehard Flyers fan. Even now he's wearing his John LeClair jersey.

"I missed you, Nony!" Yep, I'm twenty years old and still call him the name I gave him when I was three. I'm told I wasn't able to pronounce the letter T for a while, but even after I could, the nickname just stuck. I drop back down to the ground from where I hung from his neck and the three of us made our way to the administrative office. I'm a total Virgo, super anal, organized crazy person. Tony once took me to The Container Store on a visit to Houston a couple of years ago and I almost wept with joy. As we go through the bustling hallway and enter the office, I have my planner out and ready, and I'm registered for my classes with all my books bought within the hour.

"Shit, sis, that was a lot more painless than I thought it was going to be," Mark says. "As hard as it was to get you to choose between your fifty purses to bring to Texas, I thought it'd take hours for you to pick out your school crap."

I tilt my head down and hide my smirk behind my curtain of long, dark hair. Little does he know I didn't leave behind a single one.

"Want to walk around and find all your classrooms? I took a few classes here just for the shits and giggles so I know where everything is," Tony suggests.

"You're like a gajillionaire; why would you be taking college courses?" I ask him as we make our way to what will be my first class next week: American History I.

"I'm not a gajillionaire." He shoves me playfully into Mark. "I took some classes here just for fun. A couple of history classes, a basic computer class, just random stuff. The cool thing about it is if you're enrolled, you get free access to the on-campus gym. Why not come and check out the cute college girls on treadmills instead of what you get at a regular gym?" He wiggles his eyebrows at Mark over my head.

I smack him in the arm, "Ugh, you're such a Chester."

We walk around for about an hour, find all my classes, the cafeteria, even the gym. We stay at the gym a little longer than I personally thought was necessary to get my key card set up, but hey...not only were there cute girls for my brothers to check out...there were quite a few good-looking guys lifting weights and playing basketball on the indoor courts. Maybe Tony had the right idea after all.

CHAPTER  *Three*

January 12th, 2005

After leaving the school yesterday, my brothers and I went and had some lunch and then Mark took me to Walmart to pick up a cheap bookcase. He helped me put it together and stand it up against an empty wall in my room, before he left me to my Virgo ways. I know I'm not the only person in the world who absolutely loves organizing her books. Or am I that weird? I opened up my boxes of paperbacks and carefully lined up each of my series in reading order. I keep a very neat list of my books in a sparkly pink folder that I stand on one of the book shelves. It's a checklist of all my favorite authors' books in the correct reading order. I have almost all of them checked off, but there are those few that still evade me. I try to find most of my books at used book stores, but some I actually have to go buy at the retail stores because no one wants to get rid of their copy. *Hey, I'm a college chick on a budget.*

The rest of the day went by the same way it had all week. Mark, Kim, and I would eat some dinner, hang out in the living room and watch some TV, then I'd go upstairs to my room and read, until I passed out. I'd been so busy unpacking and getting ready to register for school that I hadn't really had time to think about much else.

Now, sitting in my room by myself, I just finished the latest Sherrilyn Kenyon book. I'm filled with the usual sense of joy for the couple finally getting their happily ever after, quickly followed by a slight swell of jealousy that I haven't found my own. With Mark and Kim both at work, the loneliness I felt in Fayetteville is starting to sink back in. Yes, I had my family and the best friend a girl could ask for, but goodness, how could one chick have so much bad luck in the dating department? The only way to deal with the direction of my thoughts is to hop on my blog and write a Chick Rant post before I write my review for the book I just read. Most definitely my perfect escape.

Kayla's Chick Rant & Book Blog
Blog Post 1/12/2005

In a town full of soldiers, how the hell did I manage to only find the biggest douchebags out of the thousands of men there?

The latest one was David. Let me tell you about good ole David. He waltzed into the car dealership I worked at like he owned the place. He was friends with Ben, who was one of the salesmen, so when he walked in, he went to talk to him about a car he was interested in. He wasn't drop-dead gorgeous or anything, but he had this really happy-go-lucky air about him that I was drawn to. He had light brown hair cut into the military style that is so common where I'm from, and the biggest smile I'd ever seen on a man. He was also wearing glasses with a thick black frame. He had the hot-nerd thing going on. After he talked to Ben, our salesman, the two of them walked up to my desk to grab the keys to the cherry-red Chevy Camaro with the T-top out front.

When I looked up at him to hand him the keys, our eyes

connected; I felt my face heat as his eyes gave me the once over. There was instant chemistry. I could see his eyes were bright blue behind his glasses once he was so close. He slid his fingers against mine as I handed him the keys to the Camaro, letting them linger awhile before folding the keys into the palm of his hand. He gave me that big grin of his and handed me his driver's license to sign out a dealer plate so he could take the car on a test drive. His name was David and according to his card, he was from Kentucky. This was an everyday occurrence there; hardly anyone was actually *from* Fayetteville. People were just stationed in Ft. Bragg, serving their time in Fayettenam.

In an adorable twang that I wasn't used to he said, "Thank you, ma'am," as I handed him back his license and Ben the dealer plate. It sounded different from the southern accent of North Carolinians. I couldn't help but smile back at him since the butterflies in my stomach were tickling the shit out of me. *Nope, I do not have that "play it cool" bone in my body.*

A couple of hours later, David bought the Camaro and was shaking hands with Ben when I saw him make his way over to me. He crossed his forearms as he leaned on to the high front of my receptionist's desk. "Kayla, right?" he asked. I simply answered in the affirmative.

"I have this new car, you see. I'm thinking you should help me celebrate buying my dream car by going out with me Friday evening. Would that be something you'd be interested in?" he asked with that smile.

"Well, that depends. What would we do to celebrate your

new purchase?" I asked him.

"I was thinking we'd go get some dinner, maybe go see a movie since there's not much else to do in this town. But this new car I just got, it has T-tops. What I'd really like to do is just cruise around and see that long gorgeous hair of yours blowing around that pretty face."

Wow. Thinking back, that was actually a pretty good pick up line. Definitely creative. After my brain stopped stuttering, I finally told him it sounded like fun and we made plans for Friday.

The date had been super fun. I had never been in a convertible before; it was kind of exhilarating. My hair was all blown to hell and back but I'd had the mind to put my hairbrush in my purse. After a dinner with conversation that came easily and lots of laughs—David was ridiculously funny —we went and saw *The Day After Tomorrow*. He took me home at the end of the night and gave me a sweet kiss that definitely left me wanting more. David had game.

We dated for a couple of more weeks before we became intimate. But something was...off. Then one Sunday, we had dinner and went back to his barracks room. We cuddled up in his bed to watch a DVD and I did the international girl sign of 'time to get it on' by pressing my butt up against his front. He tensed up and actually scrambled out of the bed. Turning off the movie, he told me it was probably best if we called it a night. I was so confused I kind of just looked at him with a dumbstruck face. "Is something wrong?" I asked.

He looked sheepish as he reached behind him and rubbed the back of his neck. "I don't have sex on Sundays."

"Excuse me?" I was thrown off guard.

"I don't have sex on Sundays. Pre-marital sex is bad enough; I'm not going to have sex on the Lord's Day," he told me, completely straight-faced. Somehow I knew this wasn't some kind of joke. I didn't want to disrespect his beliefs or anything, but damn! Way to make me feel like a tramp! I told him we didn't have to have sex, that I'd like to just cuddle up and finish the movie we started, and he said that was fine. I ended up going home afterwards without even a goodbye kiss.

Things weren't the same after that. Before our 'no sex Sunday' incident, he used to be super funny and make me feel like the prettiest girl on the planet, but since then, he seemed condescending, like he looked down on me. He no longer flirted with me, or made the effort to make me laugh. Shit, he didn't even open doors for me anymore. Apparently, even though it took two to tango, it was *me* who was the sinner for wanting to have sex out of wedlock.

Needless to say, we broke up soon after. But wait! That's not the end of the story about Saintly David. A few months later, after I made plans to move to Texas for my semester of school, he found out from Ben, the salesman, that I'd be moving soon. I received a call from David after not having spoken to him for months, asking if maybe we could date until I left.

"Wait. You're asking me to date you until I leave? As in, you want to break up before I move; you don't want to continue a relationship long distance?" I ask incredulously.

"Well..." he answered stupidly.

"So in other words, Mr. I-Freak-For-Jesus, you want to have me around to fuck whenever you want EXCEPT FOR ON SUNDAYS, knowing I'll just be moving in a couple of months. Fuck you, David. Look up the word hypocrite, you asshat. Don't call me again." I hung up furious and immediately called Anni for a girls' night out. We went to It'z Nightclub. It was a pretty epic night, filled with accepting many drinks from various cute guys, straight from the bartender of course: I'm not stupid. Well, I say that until I ended up going back to hottie number 5's barracks' room. It wasn't bad though. I was woken up with his head between my legs the next morning...it was Sunday.

End Rant ;-)

I snap out of the memory with a chuckle. I click Publish and log out of my blog. I'll write my book review later. I wander around the house for a little while, look at all the pictures Mark and Kim have framed in the living room, pour myself a glass of milk and grab my package of Double Stuf

Oreos—dinner of champions—and make my way back upstairs.

David was just the latest in the long string of dickheads I had dated. Am I ever going to find my soulmate? Am I ever going to find the kind of love like the ones written in the books I obsess over? Surely there's gotta be a guy out there who will think the world of me. I always treat the guys I date like gold, but you see, I'm starting to think that's the problem. I treat them the way I'd like to be treated, and then they end up taking advantage of me. I show how much I care about them, really listen when they talk so I can pick up on little things about them, small things they may mention they want or like so I can surprise them with it.

I lie in my bed for a while daydreaming. Maybe it's me who's the problem. I was a pageant girl when I was younger. It's like I was living two different lives. In the pageant world I was kind of a big deal. I was North Carolina's Miss USA. I sang for talent and almost always won that portion of the competition. I won scholarships and savings bonds, along with the trophies, crowns, and sashes. I had all the best dresses, had a modeling coach everyone wanted who also did my hair and makeup flawlessly.

But then back in the real world, my everyday life, I was kind of awkward. I was always being picked on for being so skinny. I remember a boy even making me run home crying because he wrote me a nasty little poem. "Roses are red. Violets are black. Why is your chest as flat as your back?" I never wore anything but pants, never shorts or skirts, because the one time I did, I was called Olive Oil and asked if

I threw up my food. Everyone is more careful to be nice to people who are overweight, watching their feelings. They never think about the girls who can't put ON weight no matter how much they eat.

So during my early teenaged years, I was super self-conscious. It wasn't until I hit about sixteen that I started getting noticed by guys in their twenties. The guys who realized that after high school, the "hot girls" were the ones who usually gained thirty pounds when they stopped cheerleading. I never once dated a guy from my high school. The first guy I really dated was twenty and a Specialist in the 82nd Airborne. God, Doug was ridiculously handsome in his BDUs. When he rolled up the sleeves of his camouflaged top and showed off his huge biceps covered in tattoos, I didn't stand a chance. I lost my virginity to him after three months of dating. We were serious for about a year before he got stationed in Ft. Richardson, Alaska. We tried the long distance thing but it didn't work out.

After him, I dated a few more guys. No one special in particular, some I can't even remember their last names. I slept with most of them. What are your teenaged years for, right? I wasn't an idiot though. I was on birth control pills, always used a condom, and always careful. That's the one good thing about dating soldiers. You know they're tested practically every week. But one thing was definitely missing when it came to sleeping with these guys, and I'm not talking about mushy shit and feelings. I'm talking about the most important thing of all: I have never once in my life had an orgasm with another person. Yep, I said it. I'm one hell of an actress because each of those fellas ended up thinking they were God's gift to women by the time I finished my porn-star groans and screams of ecstasy.

In reality, I was kind of embarrassed. What the hell was wrong with my vagina? In the books I read, the man can just look at the woman and tell her "Come" and she's writhing on the floor having the best orgasm of her life. Me? If it wasn't for my massaging shower head, I wouldn't even know what an orgasm was. Now don't get me wrong. I've had some really fantastic sex. Like toe curling, eyes crossing and rolling to the back of your head, scream till your lungs get sore sex. But even then...just...couldn't...reach it.

That has to be it. This has got to be the reason that all I ever find are the dickheads. It's not all their fault that they're dickheads. I make them that way! I put them on a pedestal, get them sweet little presents, and scream their names out during sex like I'm in orgasm-city...well fuck! The solution is easy, right?

I will never fake an orgasm ever again.

CH♠PTER Four

About twenty minutes ago, I realized I had been talking to my lovebird, Screwy, for about an hour straight and decided that if I didn't get out of this house, I was going to go insane. But what does one do with no friends and in a giant-ass, unfamiliar city? Well, this chick got on Plenty of Fish. I just completed my profile, uploaded my picture, and now I have access to everyone else's. In my About Me section, I simply put that I was new in town, here for school, and wanted to make some friends to hang out with. I checked the boxes for Friendship and Dating, and lifted a perfectly tweezed eyebrow at the box for Casual Encounter. Did people really check that box? Clicking through the different profiles I learned that, most certainly, people do.

I identified Houston as my city, of course, but quickly

realized that Houston included a million suburbs spanning across God only knows how many miles. I found a picture of a guy I thought was pretty good-looking, but when I typed his location into MapQuest, it said he was more than an hour away. Well that wouldn't work. *Click...click...click...*too old, too short, too far away, Casual Encounter ONLY? That dude wouldn't even need me to turn him into a dickhead.

Is there any way to narrow this shit down? *AH, jackpot.* I narrow my search to within forty-five minutes away, people looking for Friendship and Dating, and between the ages of 20 and 25.

This narrowed my search down to two hundred and eight people. Hmmm, still too many to go through. I found the box that allowed me to only search profiles that had been logged on in the past thirty days. There. Seventy-six people. I read some pretty hilarious About Me sections, but still, I need to get rid of a few more that just don't apply to me. I go to the Advanced Search page and click the boxes for people who are Single (you'd think all people on a dating site would be Single, but nope, there are boxes for Single, In a Relationship, Married, and Swingers), people who do not have kids, and who are straight. Although I'd love to have a gay guy friend, that's not what I'm really looking for.

This time there are only twenty-nine people I have to weed through. Some look pretty promising so I send them a short message introducing myself. I'm clicking past a couple of people who have obviously lied on their profiles and my screen lands on one that makes me pause, tilt my head, and blink like an idiot. "Well, hello there, Spanky83." I read his profile and he seems just as charming as his Paul Walker looking ass portrays in his picture. His blond hair is cut short —maybe just a tad bit receded, but no biggie—and his bright blue eyes made all the more stunning by his dark tan. He's got perfectly straight and blindingly white teeth he's showing off with a friendly smile. Wearing a simple plain black t-shirt and a pair of jeans, he's sitting on a bed, just like he snapped the picture with his webcam spur of the moment just so he'd have one on his profile.

I send him the same message I sent the few other people who didn't look like rapists, and continue looking though the last of the profiles. I check my messages to see if anyone has written back yet and two of them have. But for some reason, Spanky83 just won't get out of my head. Spanky83. That sounds like an email address...or a messenger name. I log on to my AOL account and see if there is a Spanky83 listed in the messenger search engine. Sure enough, there certainly is. His real name is Gavin and he isn't currently online. I send him a quick message saying I saw his profile on Plenty of Fish and was interested in chatting whenever he wanted.

I was about to log off of the computer when my AOL messenger notification went off. Spanky83 had sent me a message.

> Spanky83:   Glad you liked my profile   ;-)
> What's your name?

I do a little happy dance in my seat.

> VampBookBlogger: Kayla, you responded pretty fast!
> Spanky83:   I have notifications sent to my phone.

I'm changing the oil in my truck. Lol!

Truck....he has a truck. Oh, Texas boys.

VampBookBlogger: You can do that? I just have a Nokia flip phone. Just figured out how to text!

Spanky83: Yeah, I have one of those new Blackberrys. I can get email and even get on the internet on it. Crazy what they come up with these days. Had to have it for work.

He has a job that requires a fancy phone. Picture is hot, has a truck, has a job...let's go for it.

VampBookBlogger: I just moved here from NC. Been bored out of my mind since I don't know anybody or where anything is. You have any plans tonight?

Spanky83: Was just changing my oil. What do you have in mind?

VampBookBlogger: Idk, I'm kinda hungry, but need to eat cheap. College chick and all. Wait, have you even looked at my profile yet?

Spanky83: Um. Nope. Hold on...

I giggle stupidly and wait a few minutes before he responds.

Spanky83: WTF are YOU doing on a dating site? Is that like an old picture or something? Lol!

VampBookBlogger: I could ask you the same thing! And no, that's from right before I left NC last week. I'm on POF to meet some new friends. I just always make guy friends because girls don't like me. I'm too perky.

Spanky83: I like perky. How about some Denny's, good food but cheap. Where are you btw?

VampBookBlogger: My brother told me to say I'm where "Beltway 8 is on the ground".

Spanky83: Ah. Ok. That's because Beltway 8 is all a freeway up in the air, it only goes on the ground in one part of the city, before it crosses 59 heading north. I know exactly where you are. So, Denny's?

VampBookBlogger: Sounds yummy.

Spanky83: Just looked it up. There's a Denny's maybe 2 miles from you.

He tells me how to get there and we make plans to meet in an hour. This gives me enough time to put on a little makeup, pull on my dark blue flared jeans, a baby-pink tank top, and a light spray of perfume. I choose Lilu from PacSun. I'm kind of a perfume junky. Mark had wanted me to choose just a couple from my forty-three perfumes and body sprays

—yes, I counted—to bring with me to Texas, but I felt like I was abandoning them, so I packed them all up and snuck them into my trunk when he wasn't looking. With a quick swipe of my brush through my hair, I run downstairs to leave Mark and Kim a note telling them I went to Denny's for some dinner. I leave out the part about meeting a guy there; they'd try to talk me out of it. I'll tell them when I'm back at home without any bodily harm.

I actually find Denny's without getting lost. I'm there a few minutes early so I go ahead and select a table. It's right by the window facing the parking lot, so I'll be able to see when he pulls in. I'll get to check him out a little before he walks up to see if he's as handsome in real life as the picture makes him look. A waitress who looks to be in her fifties with mocha skin, warm brown eyes, and bright red lipstick walks up to me and asks if I'd like to go ahead and order a drink. "Yes, ma'am. Sweet tea, please. Can I ask you a favor?"

"Sure, honey. What is it?" she says in her adorable Texas twang.

"I'm on a blind date. I was just going to ask you if I wave at you, will you call the cops?" I look a little nervous, I'm sure.

"Of course, honey! You wave and I'll have a cop here so fast it'll make your date's head spin. But let's just hope he turns out to be a gentleman." She winks at me and bounces away to get my drink.

I'm fidgeting in my seat. I'm really starting to spaz out now. My heart is pumping and my hands are starting to sweat...my tummy is even beginning to get that nervous bubbly feeling. So not good. What the hell was I thinking? Only my naïve ass would move to the fourth largest city in the US and say "Awww, I'm lonely. Let me just jump on the internet really quick and meet a stranger for dinner. No biggie!" I should have called Mark and told him where I was going instead of just leaving the note. What if he finds it too late? What if I'm already raped and murdered and dumped in some ditch somewhere where alligators will eat my body? There will be no evidence; everyone will think I'm just missing and keep on looking for me for years and years hoping I'll turn up. By the time the waitress returns with my drink, I've worked myself up so much I just blurt out, "Are there alligators in Texas?"

She looks at me like my eyes are looking a little squirrelly and rests her hand on my shoulder. "Sweetie. I ain't gonna let nothin' happen to you. He makes any sudden movements and I'll tackle him my damn self."

This makes me burst out laughing and some of the tension leaves my body. I sip my sweet tea and before I can work myself into a frenzy again, I see a bright red truck pull into the parking lot. It's been lowered to just a couple of inches off the ground and the windows are tinted to the point where it's probably illegal. I watch as it swings into a parking spot and the door opens.

I sit up a little straighter and practically press my nose to the window as a man unfolds his over six-foot-tall frame from the lowered truck. The picture on his profile was spot on. He could be a stunt double for Paul Walker, especially with the way he just drove that truck. His blond hair looks like it was gelled back this morning but has loosened a little, maybe from running his hands through it a few times. He still has a killer tan and I can see how bright blue his eyes are all the way from here. He shuts his door and walks—no, prowls—to the door of the restaurant.

Before he opens it, I call to the waitress, "Scratch that! He can have his way with me if he wants!" and we both giggle as he steps inside.

CHAPTER *Five*

He glances around the restaurant and when he spots me, his face brightens. He walks over in that smooth way I noticed a second ago when he was walking from his truck, and flashes me a sexy grin with those perfectly white teeth and eyes so blue they almost don't look real. "Oh, thank God," he says as he slides into the seat across from me.

"Um, thanks?" I smile back at him; my heart is thumping so hard I'm sure he can hear it, or at least see it through my pink tank top.

"Oh, sorry. It's just that I've met quite a few women on that website and none of them ever look like their picture. I was seriously starting to think about deleting my profile; now, I'm really glad I didn't." He makes a show of letting his eyes wander over me from the top of my dark hair down to my waist where it disappears under the table. I know he sounds like a pig, but I'm instantly turned on. I've always had a thing for assholes, after all.

Our waitress comes over to the table and turns her back to him, looks at me and makes an O-face and fans herself. I keep myself from busting out laughing as she turns back to him and asks him what he'd like to drink. "A coke, please, ma'am." And there it is...that Texan accent that instantly melts my panties right off my ass. I manage to keep myself from drooling as he opens up his menu. "I don't know why I even bother lookin' at this thing. I always order the same thing every time."

"And what is that?" I ask, genuinely curious. "I know this is going to sound kind of crazy, but I've never actually been to a Denny's before."

"The hell is wrong with you, woman? How have you gone...wait, how old are you?" he interrupts himself.

"I'm twenty," I say, completely amused. I knew that would get a rise out of him, just like when I say: "I've also never seen *Terminator* or been camping before."

"I know you said you just moved here, but from what planet?" he jokes.

"I'm from North Carolina. Land of the Waffle House and a few IHOPs, but no Denny's. At least in my town."

"And you've never seen *Terminator*...or been camping. What, they don't have Blockbusters or tents in North Carolina?" *He's a witty one, isn't he?*

"I don't really know why I've never seen *Terminator*, but I've never gone camping simply because no one's ever taken me," I shrug.

We joke back and forth as we give the waitress our order and wait for our food. I ordered a Grand Slam with fried eggs over medium, bacon, white toast with an obscene amount of butter, and pancakes. He ordered the club sandwich with French fries, and specifically asked for a giant bowl of ranch, even indicated how giant by making a big circle with his hands. His very large hands...that were as tanned as the rest of him, and looked to be rough and calloused like he used them pretty often and not just to write with. A shiver goes through me and I ask, "So what do you do, Gavin?"

"I'm a finance student during the day and work at a high-end furniture store in the evenings. What about you?" he asks.

"I'm an English major about to start at Kingwood College next week, and a blogger." I shrug. Most people think I'm a nerd when I tell them about my blogging.

"What kind of blog do you have?" he asks, seeming genuinely interested.

"Well, it's kind of a mix. I'm a book blogger; I'll read a book and then write a review about it. I'll interview the author. I'll find pictures off the internet of celebrities that I visualize playing the part of the main characters, and I'll make collages with quotes from the book. But not only the book stuff, I also make posts about stupid stuff I think other people might like to read. Just random rants or raves, mostly girl stuff I think others might feel but not have the guts to talk about. I'll post something and then the comments people leave are almost always of women going crazy, saying, 'OMG,

I thought I was the only one!'" I realize I just went off on a tangent and blush a little. "Sorry, I like blogging." I smile shyly. Now he'll definitely think I'm a dork.

"Don't apologize. That's pretty awesome. A hot chick with a brain...who woulda thunk." His amazing eyes sparkle at me. "What kind of books do you read?"

Now I feel like my face is on fire. On the internet, I'm anonymous; nobody knows my real name and I can be as explicit and raunchy as I want. My blog is like my alter-ego. There are a few people I'll talk openly with, the way I do on my website, but normally, I like people to think I'm just a sweet girl who likes to read. But the way Gavin is gazing intently into my eyes with a look on his face that tells me he wants to get to know the real me, I go for it. "Well, mostly I read paranormal romance, like the vampire that falls in love with a human and in the end he turns her and they live in their HEA, or happily ever after. In order for me to like a book, it has to have an HEA. But recently, I got into BDSM romances. They are few and far between, but when I actually find one, I usually inhale it in one day." I watch his face trying to judge his reaction.

"BDSM, as in like, whips and shit?" he asks as the waitress brings our order out. My eyes grow to the size of saucers as my face jerks up to see if she heard what he'd said. What a spot in our conversation to walk in on. She gives nothing away if she did, so I decide to pretend we weren't just talking about naughty books with elements of dominance and submission. The grin he gives me when he realizes my embarrassment completely distracts me. I forget all about the close call and focus on not drooling on my pancakes.

"So what do you like to do for fun?" I ask lamely.

"I like to fish, work on my truck, play computer games, and I play pool a lot. Me and my best friend are kind of addicted to pool. We go to a bar called Legends Billiards on our side of town almost every night." He picks up a section of his sandwich that's been cut into quarters and dips the entire thing in the cereal-sized bowl of ranch dressing she'd brought out. I watch as he shoves the whole thing into his mouth and starts to chew, his clean-shaven cheeks pooching out with all the food inside.

I raise an eyebrow at him, but he doesn't seem to notice and continues to keep chowing down like a starving man. I pick up my fork and tear little holes in the tops of my fried eggs, allowing the yolk to ooze out, then I dip my buttered toast into them and take a bite. Heaven. My granny always fixes my eggs like this for me. No matter how hard I try, I can never get eggs into a pan to fry without the yolk breaking, which totally ruins them for me. I try my best to ignore Gavin as he picks up five fries at the same time, dips them in the ranch, and devours them all.

"I've tried to play pool a couple of times at one of my brother's shows. He's a drummer in a band back home. They always play at a place called Jester's Pub and it has a few pool tables. I suck at it though." I nibble on my piece of bacon as he proceeds to grab a piece of his own that had fallen out of his sandwich, uses it like a spoon to scoop up more ranch dressing, and shoves it in his mouth.

This guy is a pig, I think to myself. I can't be choosy though; I have no friends in Texas yet, and he is totally hunky. I figure I can overlook the fact he eats like one of the hogs at the farm we passed by on our way home from seeing my school campus. There are random grassy acres surrounded by barbed-wire fences all over the place here, all filled with various colored cows, and even a few horses milling around. You wouldn't imagine so, but it looks completely normal to drive past a high-traffic area with restaurants and stores, and right next door are a few acres of open field with the large animals hanging out like it's no big deal. I guess they've grown accustomed to all of us noisy humans with our honking horns and backfiring vehicles.

"Maybe if you ever come to my neck of the woods, I'll take you to play," he says, leaning back in his seat and taking a giant gulp of his Coke. As soon as he sits the condensation-covered glass back down on the table, he lets out a belch that makes me jump from its tremendous volume.

I'm barely able to keep my nose from wrinkling in disgust as I reply, "That sounds like fun. I haven't really been anywhere since I moved here, except to check out my campus. I'm ready for school to start next week; I've been bored out of my mind."

We finish up our dinner, which I manage to keep down, even with his horrid dining manners, and after he pays the check—score one for him on that, at least—we walk outside and stroll to his truck. He pulls out a pack of cigarettes and uses a shiny silver Zippo to light it, then whipping it in the air between his fingers to close the lid.

He uses the handle to drop the tailgate of his lowered truck, and then turns around to plop down onto it, patting the metal next to him for me to sit. When I do, he offers me his cigarette with a raise of his eyebrow, seeming almost like he's testing me. I take it from him, take a long drag, blow it out, and then give it back to him with a smirk. I don't smoke regularly, but I do socially. I gave into peer pressure while hanging out with Anni and her roommate, and after that, since I hung out with them practically every day, it just became the norm.

"Do you want to go somewhere? I know of a couple pool halls up here on your side of town. It's still pretty early," Gavin asks.

"Sure, I'll follow you," I reply, and after we finish sharing his cigarette, I make my way over to my Malibu and hop in.

CHAPTER Six

Kayla's Chick Rant & Book Blog
Blog Post 1/16/2005

Good evening, everybody. My name is Kayla, and I'm a ho. How did I come to this conclusion, you might ask? Well, after meeting Gavin for the first time at Denny's after only speaking to him over AOL Instant Messenger for two-point-five seconds, we went to a little hole in the wall pool hall down the road from Mark's house. All the tables were taken, so we didn't get to play, so we just hung out at the bar and played on the touchscreen video game for a couple hours while we chatted. Conversation came easy with him. He's equal parts good-natured gentleman, and pigheaded misogynist. A conundrum, I know.

He managed to win me over a little by making me laugh the entire time, so at the end of our date, when he walked me to my car, I didn't slap him when he said, "Okay, so in the personality and looks department, I've decided I definitely like what I see, but the final test is a goodnight kiss. You cool, or are you gonna be one of those 'I don't kiss on the first date' bitches?"

By now, I'd come to the realization his word vomit wasn't meant to be mean; he just really didn't think before he spoke, or he really didn't believe what he was saying was rude, like it didn't dawn on him at all.

I had been admiring that amazing smile and those achingly beautiful eyes all evening, so I decided it wouldn't hurt just to throw caution to the wind and kiss the guy. I had never kissed someone so tall before, so it made me feel extra small and feminine as I stepped up to him and reached up high to wrap my arms around his neck, giving him the go-ahead to lay one on me. As he leaned down, he dipped me a little, showing he had experience kissing with such a height difference and knew how to make it more comfortable for the chick.

And boy could he kiss.

All the food-smacking, huge belching, and choke-on-my-drink-worthy things that came out of his mouth throughout the night went right out of my head as he worked my lips and tongue like a champ.

When it ended, he stood me back up straight and held me steady as I wobbled a little, and then grinned as he said,

"Yep, you pass to the next round."

I told him, "Uh, yeah. You too," and then laughed when he threw his fist in the air *Breakfast Club*-style.

We made plans for me to drive down to his end of town the following day, where I'd meet him at the high-end furniture store he works at and then follow him to his house to hang out.

This is where the I'm-a-ho part comes in.

After chatting with him all day long on Messenger, I met him at his work as planned, where he introduced me to all his coworkers, and then proceeded to show me all the mattresses in the showroom, informing me which ones were 'the best for fucking'. Apparently, you can't have one that's too soft, because you can't get any leverage when your knees sink too deeply into the memory foam, but a pillow-top mattress is fine, as long as the underneath part is firm. I managed to keep a straight face until he tackled me onto one and started bouncing with his knees on either side of me, saying, "See? This one is perfect!" sending me into a fit of giggles.

See what I mean? He'll do something that makes me think, 'What the hell is wrong with this guy?' and then turn around and do something cute and funny.

When I followed him back to his house—actually, his grandparents' house, who he's lived with since he was little—we grabbed some fast food to eat in the middle of his bed while we watched an action flick on his big screen. I felt really comfortable with him after having talked to him all day online, and he was just so stinkin' good-looking, so when we were done eating, we got under the covers and cuddled up to watch the rest of the movie.

I'm sure you can imagine what happened next...

NO! Jeez! Not that! Gah...

That wasn't until the next night.

Yep, the following night, while his grandparents were out of town for the weekend, I gave it up to my first Texan.

Disappointed doesn't even begin to describe what I felt.

The saying is most definitely false.

Everything is NOT bigger in Texas.

And I don't mean he was just a little below average. Oh no, *nonononononono*...we're talkin' three inches...*erect*.

How?

First, how in the hell did this really great looking tall-ass dude get stuck with such a little...doodle? And second, how do I always pick these guys? I need to start a running list of epic failures, seriously.

So it goes without saying that my first real orgasm was not had. But you'd be proud: I didn't fake it. He didn't seem to care much that I didn't get one, though, which kind of pissed me off. I mean, in my big plan, I figured if I wasn't pretending to get off, then the guy would work harder to get me there...right? *Right?*

Bueller?

He certainly enjoyed himself though, and I know this, because instead of sending me off with an 'I'll call you', or whatever else guys say after they get laid and don't plan on seeing a gal again, he asked if I wanted to come down to hang out the next day.

In which we tried again.

And failed.

Le sigh...

Afterwards, we went onto his back patio and had his after-sex cigarette, in which I gratefully joined in. I was in a tizzy. Although I wasn't getting my big finish, the guy could still kiss, and all the heavy petting left me in quite a state. I was wound so tight after two days, you'd think the seam of my jeans would do the trick, but alas, it looked like I was going to have to take matters into my own hands when I got back home...literally.

We spent a good couple hours just talking and joking around, working our way through half a pack of cigarettes as he told me about his best friends Robichaux and Adam. They've apparently been giving him a hard time for spending all his free time with me instead of their usual nightly routine of playing pool or poker. After he gets off work, he'd usually go hang out with them, but for nearly a week now, he's been holed up with me.

Maybe I should get a job...note to self.

So here I sit writing this blog post, because I can't sleep since I'm excited for my first day of school tomorrow—much different from when I was in high school, when I'd dread leaving my summer reprieve from being taunted and teased for being too skinny. God, those bitches were so hateful. Nobody batted an eye if they heard me being called anorexic, even after seeing my mom, who'd had four kids and was still as thin as me. At fifty-seven, she still has a rockin' body.

I'm still pretty self-conscious, especially over my skinny legs and small breasts, but being out of the school-age environment and being around people like Anni, who couldn't give a rat's ass about what I look like, has helped me get past all the bullying I went through and come out of my shell.

Also, hot-ass soldiers at dance clubs...they helped boost my confidence a little, too.

God bless the troops ;-)

Well, I have to get up for class in less than four hours. At least it should be an easy one, my next English credit in a long line of them, and after that is my Art Appreciation class.

Then I'll be heading down to Friendswood to see Gavin again.

Is it crazy that I drive forty-five minutes each way every day to hang out with the only friend I've made in Texas so far? Maybe, but it beats hanging out alone in my room with my turtle and bird.

CH♠PTER
Seven

January 17, 2005

My first day of college in Texas went well today. We really only did getting-to-know-you exercises and went over our syllabi, which left me plenty of time to run by a couple of the car dealerships right off the freeway between the campus and Mark's house. I put in applications for receptionist positions, and one gave me an interview on the spot because of my experience. They said they'd let me know if I got the job by the end of the week.

Sitting on the footboard of Gavin's queen-size bed, we're trying to decide what to do tonight. Hanging out in his room and making out is fun and all, but I didn't move to a big city to stay cooped up all the time. I could've done that in a soldier's barracks' room...tee...hee.

"Well, you keep talking about this Robichaux guy all the time. What is he doing tonight?" I ask.

"Probably working on his truck," he mumbles.

"Well, we could go keep him company while he's doing that, if you want," I shrug.

"You'd want to go hang out with my friends? Even if we're just sitting around?" he asks, looking a little befuddled.

"Sure, why not? You forget—I have three older brothers. I know guys just like to chill and shoot the shit most of the time. I don't mind at all."

"Well, shit, okay. Lemme call him real quick," he says, picking up his Blackberry.

After a few seconds, Gavin says "Robi-ho, whatcha doin', homie?"

I smile to myself, enjoying the banter I catch listening to one side of their conversation. Apparently, his best friend is installing some newly upholstered seats into his truck, but should be done pretty soon, and we can all go to the pool hall Gavin has been telling me about since the night we met. Their friend Adam is also there, so I'll get to meet him as well.

After Gavin takes a few minutes to change from his work khakis into a pair of jeans and spritzes on a little cologne—making my eye twitch a little, because the original Ralph Lauren smells horrible—he grabs a black leather cylindrical case that's about three feet long out of his closet and slings the strap over his shoulder.

"What's that?" I ask curiously.

"Oh, it's my new pool cue. Wanna see?"

"Sure," I answer with a nod.

He balances the case on the edge of his bed as he unzips one of the ends. He carefully pulls out the fatter of the two wooden halves of a pool stick, showing me the shiny red-lacquered finish. "This is my new baby; spent a pretty penny on this bitch and have already had to get it re-tipped."

I have no idea what he's talking about, so I just nod and comment on how pretty the color is. He slides it back into the case, zips up the end, and we head out his bedroom door. He kisses his grandma's cheek and tells her he'll be home late. I give her a wave as we make our way out to his truck. I cringe as he turns up his country music full-blast when we turn right at the stop sign, taking us deeper into the neighborhood instead of out to the stop light like we normally do. I don't have to suffer through the twangy music for long though, because within two minutes, we are turning onto a long driveway.

I look around the perfectly cut front yard, up to the nice one-story grey brick house, and then over to the two-car garage at the head of the driveway, where the front end of a truck is up on a jack stand. A really tall hefty guy with light brown hair and a ton of freckles stands near the hood of the black older-model truck holding a giant flashlight for the person lying under the cab.

"Robichaux! What you doin' under there, man? I thought you were installing your seats," Gavin calls as we walk up the driveway.

A deep voice with a thick Texan accent comes from

beneath the vehicle. "My fuckin' starter went out after I put the seats in. I knew it was on its last leg, so I already had the part ordered. It'll just take me a few more minutes to get it in."

Some banging and lots of cursing later, the mystery man rolls himself from under the truck and stands up, wiping his grease-covered hands on his worn jeans. They were obviously not bought that way, the small rips and shredding perfectly aligning with his knees. As my eyes make their way up, they pass over a sweat-drenched used-to-be-white wife-beater plastering itself to a well-built chest, side-to-side to admire the tattoo-covered, muscular tan arms smeared with black grime, and then finally up to a handsome face holding the most gorgeous dark chocolate-brown eyes I've ever seen, topped with almost-black hair cut short, almost military in style.

"Mother fuck," he and I say at the same time. It startles me, and I trip over my flip-flops as I continue my way up to the garage. Gavin reaches over and steadies me, telling me to watch out for the cracked concrete, not noticing the way I'm practically drooling over his friend. "This piece-of-shit wrench I got at Walmart doesn't fit the nut," he gripes, and I realize he hasn't even noticed me yet.

"Jason, this is Kayla. Why don't you just have your dad help you?" Gavin introduces me and asks.

"I don't fuckin' need my dad's help. I can do it myself," Robichaux—apparently also known as Jason—says, completely ignoring my existence.

He barely even glances in my direction as he turns and

walks to the back of the garage where a row of red tool organizer cabinets are lined up against the wall. He pulls open a few of the drawers, visibly frustrated as he slams them shut, looking for a tool that's evading him. He finally spots it, holding the wrench in the light to read the size etched into the metal, mumbling a "There you are, you little shit," as he prowls back to his truck. He plops his amazing ass back onto the rolly thing and pulls himself back under.

I absently notice when Gavin walks over to the big guy holding the flashlight and pokes him in his side. "What's up, homie? This is Kayla," he says and hitches his thumb toward me.

"I'm Adam," he says simply, holding the flashlight steady when we hear Jason growl, "Dude—light."

"Nice to meet you," I reply, my attention focusing on where the bottom half of two filthy jean-clad legs and scuffed brown leather work boots stick out from beneath the truck.

I vaguely hear Adam telling Gavin what he and Jason had been doing all day, working on his truck, working on something called a Healey, and also helping his dad put together a new above-ground pool that they'll have to finish tomorrow. After about ten minutes of just standing around, and not really paying attention to anything but the grunts and curse words coming from under the Chevy, we all breathe an audible sigh of relief when we hear Jason call, "Fuck! Finally!"

He pulls himself out, careful not to bump into the jack, stands, and wipes his hands on his jeans, adding more grease to the already-stained denim. He uses the inside of one of his forearms to wipe the sweat from his brow, and the other on his upper lip. The whole time, I just gawk at him, his every movement hypnotic in its masculine grace, time seeming to slow down as I take in everything about him. He walks to the back of the garage to pull a few blue shop towels from a roll and wipes his hands more thoroughly, reaches into his front pocket, and pulls out a red and white pack of cigarettes. He flips open the lid and pulls one out, along with the lighter tucked inside the box. As he flicks his Bic, he cups his hand around the flame, the glow alighting his face brightly for a moment before he pulls his thumb away, extinguishing the lighter. He slides it back into the pack, then stuffs it back into his pocket as his other hand lifts to pull the cigarette from his mouth, a long steady stream of smoke blowing out from between his almost-femininely plump lips. My mind immediately imagines what it would feel like to have that pucker pressed against mine, knowing the taste of his Marlboro Red and the Shiner Bock sitting next to the truck would taste sexy as hell coming from him. Anyone else, it would most definitely be gross. He seems to savor the cigarette as he takes another drag, and when he pulls it from his lips this time, his eyes lift to mine. The contact sends a jolt through me, jarring me from my fantasy, and I catch a subtle frown and shake of his head as he looks over at Gavin, so small I actually question if I saw it at all.

"So you still want to go play some pool?" Gavin asks cheerfully.

"Yeah, just let me go get cleaned up," Jason replies as he walks over to the jack and lowers his truck. He strides to the driver side and opens the door, lifts himself into the seat, and then looks as if he's saying a silent prayer to himself as he cranks the ignition. The black Chevy roars to life and I take a step back, both at the loud rumble of the vehicle, and because I see a heart-stopping smile spread across Jason's face for the first time, completely altering his features. No longer brusque or even kinda scary looking, he looks young and playful as he does a silly victory dance in his seat and sings, "That's my beeoootch!" He hops out after he turns it back off, takes one last drag of his cigarette, runs the lit end along the cement of the driveway, pinches it to make sure it's completely out, and then tosses it into a trashcan as he makes his way into his house through a door inside the garage.

Staring after his retreating back long after the door closes behind him, I don't snap out of it until Gavin asks if I want anything to drink before we go. "We have a few minutes before we leave. Robi-ho takes forever to get ready," he says, sharing a grin with Adam, who I forgot was even there.

"Why do you call him that?" I ask. "I heard you say that on the phone, too."

"Robichaux, Robi-ho...it rhymes; plus, he's a certified manwhore, hence the 'ho' part," he replies.

"Very clever," I say sarcastically, following behind the two guys as they head through the same door Jason had used.

"Momma!" I hear Gavin call ahead of me, and walking through the laundry room and into a kitchen with an attached dining area, I watch as he wraps his towering frame around a tiny woman, who probably barely reaches five-feet tall.

"Hey, dude," she says, embracing him back hard, "you kids going out tonight?"

He lets go of her, but keeps one arm around her shoulders. "Yeah, going up to Legends. This is Kayla, by the way." He nods in my direction.

She steps out of his grip and reaches for me, pulling me into a fierce hug. For such a petite lady, she sure is strong. "Nice to meet you, Kayla. We're huggers around here."

"Oh, I don't mind. I love hugs, and it's nice to meet you too, Mrs. Robichaux," I wheeze out the last part as she squeezes tightly before letting me go.

"What's a pretty girl like you doing hanging out with this bunch of crazy boys?" she asks.

"Well, I just moved here a couple weeks ago from North Carolina, and Gavin kind of took me under his wing," I reply, smiling up into his happy face. He obviously adores this woman.

"Isn't that sweet," she coos, reaching up high to pat him on his back, but at the same time, giving him a look of warning. "Now you be good, Gavin, and show her what a gentleman is like."

"Yes, ma'am." He gives her his mischievous grin, receiving a pointed finger poked into his firm chest from Jason's mom.

"I'm serious, young man. She looks like a good girl, so don't go corrupting the poor thing or I'll have your appendages, you hear me?" The look on her face is completely serious, but when he gives her a sincere 'Yes, ma'am' this time, she reaches up and pats his cheek before turning back to me with a smile. "And you let me know if he's a pig, Kayla. Gotta keep these boys in line."

"I will. Promise." I look up at Gavin and giggle as he mocks Mrs. Robichaux behind her back, purposely doing it long enough for her to spot him when she turns around, getting a pinch on his butt for that one.

"Hey, now!" He hops away from her, chuckling. "Where's Mr. Robichaux at? Gonna tell him his woman is getting a little handsy."

"He's out back in his shop," she replies. "Grab y'all some drinks and take one out to him, will you?"

"Alrighty." He walks to the fridge in the laundry room and grabs a couple bottles of Shiner, and looks up at me in question.

"Um, I'm not twenty-one yet. I'll just take some soda or something," I tell Jason's mom.

"Nonsense. This is my house and I say you can drink whatever you want, as long as you are here. If you don't like beer, I have my white zinfandel, and we also have Steve's Crown if you'd like that," she says.

"I'd love some of your wine then, thank you." I smile at her, and then watch as Gavin pulls out the giant bottle of pink Barefoot Zin from the refrigerator. He makes a show of lugging the huge wine bottle into the kitchen, pretending to struggle to lift it up to counter, and sets it down, dramatically collapsing onto the dining table behind him.

"Boy, if you go breaking my table trying to show off for a pretty girl, I will beat your ass," she hustles over to him, swatting at him until he rolls himself off and onto the kitchen floor.

He looks up at us as we stand above him, wipes his brow like he's sweating from a workout, and says in feigned exhaustion, "Damn, I know they say size matters, but did you really have to buy the *biggest* bottle in Texas, Momma?"

"It takes that much to deal with you guys every day. If I didn't buy the big one, I'd be making daily runs to Potter's." She puts her hands on her hips, glaring down at him.

"You talk so big, but I've never seen you drink more than one little glass at any given time. You know you love us," he calls her out.

Just then, we hear a door open and close, and in walks a handsome older man in olive green cargo shorts, a grey pocketed t-shirt, and a khaki-colored cap. He doesn't even seem fazed by the scene before him, Gavin on the floor looking up at the two women hovering above him, giant bottle of wine and a few beers on the counter next to us. If this was my house, and my dad walked in on this, he might not have anything to say about the people playing around, but he'd raise hell about the drinks. The only alcohol my daddy has ever drank is communion wine, even with the twenty-some years he spent in the Navy. He's definitely who my brother Mark got it from. The rest of us—Tony, Jay, and I —must get our enjoyment of drinking from my mom, who I've caught staring longingly at pretty, fruity margaritas and daiquiris before, but who can't drink them because they'd mess with her heart medication. She even ordered a virgin drink when we went to visit Kemah Boardwalk a couple years ago, saying she needed the sugar...*uh-huh*.

The man grabs one of the beers off the counter, uses the hem of his t-shirt to wrap around the cap, and twists it off, coming to stand over Gavin too. "Whaddya do this time?" he asks, taking a swig from the bottle.

"Your wife asked me to grab her wine, and now I'll have to drink a recovery shake in order to not be sore tomorrow. That's Kayla," he points at me, "and this is Mr. Robichaux," he tugs on the cargo pocket of Jason's dad's shorts, earning a gentle kick to his hip.

"Steve," he says, taking my hand and shaking it firmly. His green eyes are stunning, and I kind of melt a little when he smiles at me. Mrs. Robichaux is a lucky lady. "Where's the rest of your crew?" he asks, looking back down at Gavin.

"Jason is taking a shower and getting ready—we're going to Legends to shoot some pool—and Adam is probably watching TV or something."

I had forgotten about Adam again. The guy is so quiet, even stealthy for a dude his size. We all turn our heads toward the living room, and sure enough, there he sits. He looks over at us from the couch, gives us a wave, and then goes back to watching his show.

Gavin reaches his arms up into the air, waiting for any of us to grab his hands to help him up. I take hold of one, Steve grabs the other, and as we pull him up, Mrs. Robichaux takes the opportunity to tickle his sides, digging her fingers into his ribs and making him wiggle and jump out of our grasps.

"You see? Handsy! And he was here to witness it this time," he says, playfully and gently pushing her toward her husband.

Steve wraps his arm around her and gives her a quick peck on her forehead before walking over to a cabinet and pulling down two wine glasses. "You want some too, Momma?" he asks his wife.

"Yeah, I'll have a little one," she replies, and she opens up one of the drawers and pulls out a corkscrew. Gavin tisks at her and takes it out of her hand, sliding the bottle across the counter toward himself and uncorks it for her.

We laugh and enjoy our drinks for a few minutes, the Robichauxs making me feel like we've known each other for ages, when Jason finally strides into the kitchen attaching cufflinks to his long-sleeved, button-up shirt that's black with tiny white pinstripes. He's paired it with some dark-washed jeans and cowboy boots. The light above the dining table reflects off the silver cufflink as he holds his arm up to check that it's securely fastened, and it draws my attention to the small silver hoop in his left earlobe. I've never found earrings attractive on a guy before, but it looks sexy on him, and adds to the bad-boy vibe he puts off.

When he walks past me to give his mom a brief peck on her cheek, the cologne he's wearing wafts up my nose and directly down to my core. I actually feel light-headed for a second, and I'm sure it's not from the little bit of wine I've drank. It has to be the most delicious smell I've ever inhaled in my entire life. I want to ask him what it is, but don't think it'd go over too well in present company. I even consider doing a recon, saying I need to go to the restroom to see if he keeps it in there. As my little daydream escalates to me smuggling the mystery cologne into my purse and flashes forward to me in my room pulling it out, sniffing it, and whispering "My precious," in a severely creepy voice while I stroke the bottle. I'm snapped to attention when Gavin claps his hands together and says, "Let's go!"

I clear my throat and walk over to the sink, wash my glass out, and put it in the rack on the counter. When I turn to follow the guys out the door, Mrs. Robichaux grabs me in another hug and urges, "Be careful and have fun. They're good boys, but they can get a little rowdy."

"Yes, ma'am," I reply with a smile, and agree when she tells me to come back soon. I catch up with the guys and head to Gavin's truck, already feeling the loss of Jason's presence as he hops in his own with Adam getting into the passenger side, wishing we could all just ride together. Being enclosed in his truck's cab would give me prime opportunity to covertly look at him...and smell him. *God, I'm such a creeper.*

CHAPTER Eight

We arrive at Legends Billiards about half an hour later, after having several mini-heart attacks as Gavin and Jason raced each other down 45 South, exiting onto the feeder, and then burning off at every stoplight. We swing into the parking lot and circle the building, which looks like an old-timey saloon with its covered front-porch decorated with rocking chairs and wood-burned signs. Hopping out of the truck, anxious to be in Jason's company again, I smile as I listen to the two of them bash each other's racing skills and call each other names. I look back and see Adam just trailing behind quietly, looking down at his wrist as he taps a new pack of cigarettes against it.

We walk around the corner of the building and onto the wooden porch, and I can't help my giggle when I hear the loud hammer of Jason's boot heels as he heads toward the door. When he pulls it open, I thank him as I walk inside, catching the smirk on his face even though he doesn't actually look at me, still refusing to make eye contact for some reason. We pass by an old arcade game as we stroll up to the bar, and the guys order drinks, Gavin asking me what I'd like. When I tell him just a Sprite, he shakes his head and says, "Try again." When I give him a questioning look, he turns to the bartender and tells her, "Malibu and pineapple, please." I'm both pleased he remembered my favorite drink and thrown off-guard since I'm not twenty-one yet, wondering what he's thinking buying me an alcoholic drink, but when the bartender hands me my drink without carding me, I stop my mind's questions and just go with it.

Jason orders a 'rack of balls', gets his own drink, and then leads the way around the corner of the bar through room after room of different sized pool tables. We pass a jukebox pumping country music over the speakers, and then finally come to the longest room of the building, which holds about ten eight-foot pool tables with plenty of room around each to line up the perfect shot without bumping into anyone at the next table. As a group, we head to an open pool table near the center of the room, and sit our drinks down on a ledge-like counter sticking out from the wall with two wooden stools underneath it. I pull one out and watch as Jason and Adam head over to the opposite side of the room, picking which stick they're gonna play with. Gavin sits his leather bag on the pool table, and unzips it to start screwing the pieces together. Jason chooses one from the wall, then walks over to the opposite end of the table as Gavin, and rolls the cue across the green felt, eyeballing it closely.

Without thinking, I ask him, "What are you doing?" I swallow a gulp of my fruity drink when his eyes shoot up to mine, the light hanging above the table casting shadows over his face, making his already dark features look ominous and mysterious.

His next words are the first he's ever spoken to me. "Making sure my cue is straight. No one likes a crooked stick."

My mouth gapes open for a second, and he gives me a heart-stopping wicked grin, but he quickly recovers and goes back to his ever-present scowl. It doesn't last long though, because when I get over my initial shock at his dirty joke, I throw my head back and let out burst of laughter, and I catch him hiding his own snicker as he reaches into his pocket for his pack of cigarettes and lights one behind his hand.

He snatches his cue from the table, apparently deeming it straight enough, and then begins to rack the balls from the triangle frame he grabs from the top of the light fixture above his head. Adam doesn't bother checking his stick on the felt, just grabs one in his beefy hands and then comes to sit on the stool next to me, silently pulling his own cigarettes out of his shirt pocket, lighting one up to watch Gavin and Jason play the first game. After the two of them use the little cube of blue chalk sitting on the side of the table to coat the tip of the cues, Gavin tells him, "You're breakin'. I just had this bitch re-tipped."

Jason sighs, shakes his head, and walks around to the end

of the table closest to me, and I hear him inform Gavin, "You're the rack bitch tonight, then." When Gavin shrugs and stands back, Jason takes hold of the white ball, sets it on the felt a little off center of the triangle of colorful balls at the other end, places his cue on the table and aligns it. Leaning down low, he's practically lying on the pool table. From this angle, I have a great view of his amazing muscular ass in his dark jeans. His right hand holds the back end of the stick loosely as he pulls it back and pushes it forward several times, before he exerts a burst of force into the cue ball, sending it hurling into the racked ones on the other side. They scatter like a swarm of ants when you throw a stick on their anthill, and when they finally settle, rolling to a stop, they're all completely dispersed around the entire table, a few even falling into various pockets. Jason walks around the perimeter, glancing into all the holes, and when he seems to find what he's looking for, he looks up and says, "I'm stripes."

He takes a position on the opposite side of the table this time, so he's facing me as he leans down low over the table. I take in a deep stuttering breath as I watch the look of complete concentration on his face as he lines up his shot. His cigarette is pressed between his full lips at the side of his mouth, his dark eyes framed with his jet black eyelashes dart back and forth between the cue ball, the striped one he's about to hit, and the pocket he's aiming for, and again, that strong masculine hand holds the back end of the pool stick loosely as he moves it back and forth before he takes his shot. Everything about him screams pure sex to me, and indecent visions of his hand wrapped around a different stick as he strokes it up and down pop into my head.

The loud crack of balls hitting together startles me out of my fantasy, making me jump, and when I shake my head to clear it, I see they've already started another game; this time, Jason plays Adam. I look up as Gavin walks over to our table and plops down onto the stool Adam had vacated. He lights one of his cigarettes and throws his pack and lighter up on the table, and then checks the tip of his cue. "You gettin' a grasp of the rules? You looked like you were concentrating pretty hard on the game; you wanna play?"

I clear my throat, glad it wasn't obvious I had actually been drooling over thoughts of his friend masturbating in a pool hall...*da fuck?* "Y'all play differently than I learned the few times I played before," I tell him, trying to further cover my tracks. What is this pull Jason had on me? So far, he's been nothing but a douchebag, practically ignoring my existence since I met him two hours ago. Is he anti-social? Or does he just instantly not like me for some reason unknown to me? I'd never had a guy utterly disregard me before.

"We've played so often we've pretty much made up our own rules. We take a few from nine-ball and some from WPA, and mix them with our own little twists, but we always play by that set," he explains. Again, I have no idea what he's talking about, so I nod and finish off my drink. "Here, let me get you another one," he says, and starts toward the bar.

I reach out and grab his arm, stopping him so I can ask, "What's the deal? How are we able to drink here?"

He gives me his mischievous grin and tells me, "Well, I celebrated my twenty-first birthday here last year, and at the time, Jason had a fake ID that said he was twenty-one, too, when he's actually not turning it 'til the end of this month. We always come here, practically every night, and we've gotten to know all the bartenders and servers who have worked here for years, so they never check for our IDs anymore, and assume all our friends we bring with us are twenty-one too. Except for Adam, who they know isn't twenty-one yet."

I look over at Adam, and sure enough, he's just got a Sprite in his hand as he waits his turn while Jason takes his shot. I forcefully jerk my eyes away from Jason's concentration face before naughty visions start playing in my head again. "So you want the same drink, or you want to try a shot?"

"Oh, I don't do shots; they remind me too much of liquid medication, which I've refused to take since I was four. *Ick.* Just the same drink would be good, thanks."

I smile up at him, and he shakes his head, saying, "You're such a girl. Come on, it'll put hair on your chest."

"Um, should I be worried that you *want* to put hair on my chest?" I ask with fake concern, tilting my head as I look into his bright blue eyes, which are twinkling playfully.

"You should ask him about the time he auditioned to be in a porno," a deep voice says, sending a thrill through me as Gavin steps to the side revealing Jason standing right behind him, sipping on his dark-colored drink, his eyes still on the pool table as Adam takes his turn.

"Dude! The fuck?" Gavin exclaims with a laugh, obviously not really fazed by his friend outing him.

"You auditioned for a porno?" I ask in disbelief, crinkling up my nose and thinking, *I thought men in pornos had to have big cocks.*

"Ha! I'm gonna go get us some drinks, and if you take a shot, I'll tell you all about it," he bargains.

"Ugh, shit. Okay, but make it one that at least tastes good. I don't like to taste the alcohol in my alcohol," I give in.

"Hold my stick," Gavin demands with a goofy leer, and after I take hold of his cue, he makes loud groaning noises, shudders his whole six-foot-plus frame, and moans, "Ahhhh yeah, baby. You grab my stick sooooo good. Just like that." I laugh and shake my head at him. Righting himself, he walks off, with every few steps, stopping to fake some aftershocks as he makes his way to the bar.

I turn back toward Jason to ask what he's drinking, but he's already moved to the other side of the pool table. A blanket of disappointment shrouds me when I see it's not even his turn to shoot yet. It's clear to me now that he's purposely avoiding me, but I still have no idea why. I grab my purse off the back of the stool, determined to see how he will react to me. I walk straight up to him blocking his view of Adam's shot, and ask, "Where's the bathroom in this place?"

He visibly takes in a deep breath, expanding his muscular chest just below my eye level. I'm so close to him that I breathe in that delicious cologne again, and when he blows out his breath in a heavy sigh, I feel it against the bare skin of my upper chest exposed above my hot-pink tank top, hardening my nipples instantaneously. It has a built in shelf bra, so with my non-existent boobs, there was no need for me to wear a real one, but now I wish I would have, because his gorgeous almost-black eyes are drawn automatically to my breasts like a magnet. I immediately take back that regret though, because as he slowly raises them up to meet my own green ones, a heated look crosses his face before he's able to hide it. I smirk on the inside, my inner-self doing a happy dance seeing that I do, in fact, have an effect on this hard-to-read man, but on the outside, I only raise an eyebrow at him in question.

With a jerk of his head, Jason tells me, "It's in the back corner by the arcade games."

"Thanks a million," I tell him with extra enthusiasm, making sure to whip my long dark hair in his direction as I turn to make my way to the restroom. Before I exit the room we're playing in, I glance back and catch him staring at my ass.

Boom! I finally let my face grin out the girly glee I have been holding in as I walk toward the games I see in the corner, where he'd told me. After using the facilities, I take a minute to freshen up in the mirror. I apply a little bit of shiny lip gloss to my "DSLs" as my best friend Anni calls them— short for dick-sucking lips—and use my fold-up travel brush I keep in my purse to get out a few knots in my hair. Finally, I lean close to the mirror and pull my upper lip between my teeth to make sure I don't have any bats in the cave—don't even act like you don't do it—and then check my teeth. Seeing I'm all clear of both offenses, I head back to the guys.

When I get to the table, they're all standing around the stools and I see there are three shots sitting on the counter.

They are a milky brown color, like a café au lait, and when I pick one up to sniff it as I sit down on my stool, it smells like butterscotch. "What's this called?" I ask, holding it up to get a closer look at how the opaque liqueur on top looks like it's forming a mini tornado where it meets the clear liquid on the bottom.

"It's called a Buttery Nipple...a total girl shot, so you should like it," Gavin teases.

"Ugh, okay. Let's get this over with," I reply, and he and Jason pick up the remaining two shots.

"Here's to the storks that bring good babies, the crows that bring bad babies, and the swallows that bring no babies," Gavin says loudly, holding his shot glass in the middle of us, up in the air, and then they both take down the drinks in a heartbeat. I bring the glass to my lips, breathing in the sickly-sweet fumes coming off the liquor while my pulse rises, nervous as all hell to gulp down the unfamiliar beverage. They stare at me for a second, and Gavin starts taunting me, pissing me off more than anything, and it's not until Jason quietly reminds me, "Gotta take the shot if you want to hear about his *big*"—dramatic fake cough —"audition," that I finally take a deep breath, close my eyes tight, and shoot the drink.

I swallow the thick liquid, open my mouth wide, and let my tongue hang out, making a very unladylike noise before Gavin hands me my Malibu and pineapple juice while calling me a pussy. I take a swig through my straw while glaring at him. He smiles that mischievous grin, and then begins his story.

"So I'd broken up with my ex a couple months earlier and decided I didn't want anything serious for a long, long time... but that didn't mean I had to be celibate. So what did I do? Got on the wonderful World Wide Web and searched for some casual encounters, of course."

I internally roll my eyes as I think about my search on Plenty of Fish when I had specifically weeded out the assholes who had checked that box. "Anyways, one page led to another, and I found an ad for porn auditions. I thought, why the fuck not? So I emailed the contact and set up a time to meet them. The night I went—"

I interrupt him, "Wait a second. Did you do any research to make sure this person was legit?"

He scoffs and says in an I'm-not-stupid tone, "Yeah, I looked up the company name they had on their site, and it was an independent label based here in Houston, and as an extra precaution, the night of my appointment, I told Robichaux and Adam where I was going, and told them if they didn't hear from me in an hour, to come looking for me," he replied.

I took a swig of my drink, feeling the nice warm buzz in my belly from the shot, and nodded for him to continue. "So when I get there, it's a rundown, cheap hotel off Airport Boulevard, that—I kid you not—has an hourly rate. I walk up to the room I'm supposed to meet the contact at, and who opens the door? This fat, hairy Mexican dude who's about five-feet tall and wearing just plain old jean shorts and a t-shirt. I'm kinda confused for a second, but then the dude asks if I'm Gavin, so I know he's the fucking contact, and I walk in

—"

"Hold up," I interrupt him again, "seeing *that* answer the door, you still go inside the hotel room?" I know my face is horrified, and when I glance from Gavin to Jason, I can see Jason's trying his best to contain laughter. I tear my eyes away from the way his are dancing with mirth and focus on Gavin as I take another big gulp of my drink.

"Okay, in my defense...I had taken some...happy pills before I went," he says, like that would explain his stupidity.

"What, like some kind of antidepressant or something?" I ask, not understanding how that would make any difference in his poor decision making.

"No, like HAPPY pills...as in Mr. Happy pills...I took my granddad's Viagra. I figured if it was a porn audition, I was gonna need some extra go-go to...you know...take whoever I was auditioning with to Poundtown," he says, nudging Jason with his elbow and wiggling his eyebrows up and down.

My eyes widen and I gasp, inhaling the sip I was taking down the wrong pipe. I choke for a second and panic when I can't catch my breath, and as Gavin just stands there laughing his ass off at me, Jason reaches behind me and pats me firmly on the back. When I'm finally able to cough and get some oxygen into my lungs, I look up into his face through my tear-filled eyes and he asks with eighty percent concern and twenty percent amusement if I'm okay. "Yeah," I croak, feeling his hand still resting in the center of my back. The heat from his palm spreads through me, and as my breathing returns to normal, my body instinctively leans toward him.

His eyes move from mine, down to my lips, and then back again, but the spell is broken when Adam declares he needs another Sprite and walks off toward the bar. *Damn, I forgot that dude was even there again*, I think as Jason jerks his hand away from my back and reaches into his pocket. He pulls out his cigarettes, lights one, and says out of the corner of his mouth, "Go on, fucker. You're getting to the best part."

"Yeah, so as I was saying, I had taken the pills and had a hard-on that wouldn't quit, and I still figured that either the chick I'd be banging was in the room, or would maybe show up after the interview, so I went inside. The guy told me to sit on the bed, and he sat down at a table where he had a video camera set up. We talked for a few minutes, him asking me if I had any experience in the porn industry and stuff, and then without hardly any preamble, he tells me to take off my clothes and lay on the bed." Gavin reaches over our empty shot glasses to grab his own cigarettes and lighter off the table. When he lights one up, I reach out and grab it out of his hand, turning it around and putting it in my own mouth. He quirks an eyebrow at me, but then grins and lights another one for himself.

I pull it from my lips, holding it between my pointer and middle fingers, and make a motion with that hand for him to keep going with his story, blowing out a long stream of smoke while feeling the nicotine mix deliciously with the alcohol coursing through my body. As Gavin speaks again, I glance at Jason, who isn't standing as close to me as he was, but is now watching me carefully. I take another drag as I direct my attention back to Gavin, trying to look like all my focus is on his story, even though I'm one, hyper aware of Jason's eyes on me, and two, can't really feel my face anymore, because I'm now definitely tipsy, so I'm not sure what my expression is. *At least I did my booger check in the bathroom,* I think and giggle, which is okay, because I believe Gavin just said something about the hotel room being hotter than a witch's titty. *Okay, focus, Kayla. Pay attention to the story you gulped down a fucking shot to hear.* With another puff of my cigarette, I zero in on what he's saying.

"...so I'm sweaty as fuck in this sleazy hotel room, naked on the bed with this creepy Mexican dude over in a chair by the TV with his camcorder, and then he tells me, I shit you not, 'Jack off until you come on yourself.' I'm all, 'Uhh, where's the girl?' and he's like, 'No girls until after you audition and get called back,' and then I'm all, 'Well, fuck.'"

He pauses to take a drink of his beer and I urge him, "So did you get up and leave?"

To my utter shock, he shakes his head, but has the decency to look ashamed...but only a little, and he continues, "He pushed the button on his little camera and tells me 'Go,' and I said fuck it and started jerking off. I mean, I was already hard because of the pill, so I might as well get it over with and hopefully get called back so I could fuck some porn stars, right? So I'm going to town, getting all into it, trying to make it good for the video, ya know? But after a few minutes, I'm no closer to coming, and my dick is so hard it's starting to hurt. I'm worried on the inside, but don't want it to show on the outside, because I wanted to look good and all...anyways, it took me like thirty fucking minutes to get off, and when I came, I almost cried right there, naked on the bed with my load on my chest in front of a dude videotaping me jerk off, because my dick was completely rubbed raw, and when my hand finally let go and the salt from my jizz and the air hit it, it felt like I lit my cock on fire."

At this, I completely lose it. I throw my head back and laugh so hard tears stream down my face. I'm happy to hear the two of them laughing with me so I don't look like an idiot dying laughing by myself, and when I catch my breath again, I finish the last of my drink and set the glass on the table, ungracefully shoving it against the other glasses and bottles on the table in order to make room for it. "So then what happened?" I ask as I flick my ashes onto the floor. It feels wrong to do it, but they're both doing it, and I don't see any ashtrays nearby. Plus, I'm a little too far gone to really care.

"Well, after I finally found the strength to move, I hobbled over to the bathroom and cleaned myself up, and grabbed some ice from the ice bucket sitting by the sink. I put it in one of the plastic wrappers that the cups in hotels are covered in, and when I put my pants back on, I put the makeshift ice pack on my junk. The dude told me he'd let me know if they were interested, and I left. Never heard from him again."

All I can do is shake my head, not only at him, but at myself as well. *You really know how to pick 'em, don't you, Kayla?*

I listen to Gavin and Jason banter back and forth, trying to one-up each other with crazy stories, but I don't think anything can top the porn audition. I watch them play a few more games, and before I know it, it's nearly 2am and the bar is closing. I feel a sudden sense of disappointment thinking about the night ending, but then Jason turns from the table where he's collecting all the balls and asks his friends, "IHOP?"

"Fuck yeah, man," Gavin answers, and Adam just nods.

I'm drunk enough that I'm completely uninhibited and ask the quiet giant, "Do you talk...like...ever?" I stand from my stool and grab onto his arm to keep from plopping back down as the room spins. He just smiles and hands me off to Gavin, who wraps his arm around my waist, and after grabbing my purse from where I hung it on the back of the chair, he hangs it around me like a necklace. I giggle and look up at him, whispering conspiratorially, "Your friend doesn't talk. Did you know that?"

He grins down at me and replies, "We keep him around for muscle," and then slaps Adam on his shoulder good naturedly.

We follow behind Jason as he takes the set of balls up to the bar, and the guys each pay their tabs. I thank Gavin for my drinks, and he tells me he was just getting me drunk to take advantage of me. I don't know for sure, but I think he's only half-joking. We make our way to the trucks, and this time, the drive isn't nearly as scary. In fact, I shout for Gavin to drive faster, encouraging him to "Beat Jason's ass!" as we speed up 45 before taking an exit that eventually leads us to an IHOP.

CHAPTER Nine

We're loud and admittedly obnoxious as we enter the empty restaurant, but as we pick a booth in the smoking section, Jason and Gavin both call out, "Kevin!" and a tall, lanky man with skin the color of dark chocolate pops his head around the wall with a big grin on his face. I slide in on one side, and Gavin sits beside me. Adam sits across from me, and Jason slides in last.

"How y'all doin' tonight?" he asks as he comes over to us with a bounce in his step. "And who is this purdy girl you've got wit' ya?"

"I'm Kayla. Nice to meet ya, Kevin," I say before anyone has the chance to introduce me. "I need cheese fries. Do you have cheese fries? I've only gotten breakfast food at an IHOP before, but I could really use some cheese fries."

Gavin laughs and tells him, "She's a little tipsy. We went to Legends."

"Y'all are always up at that pool hall. Did you win any money this time, man?" he asks, pointing his question at Jason.

"Nah, wasn't betting tonight, just played for fun," he replies.

"Gotcha, gotcha. Alrighty then, so the hotty wants some cheese fries. Is that it for you?" he asks me.

"Ranch. I need lots of ranch with them...and some pancakes. Can't come to IHOP and not get pancakes. Oh! Coffee. I definitely need some coffee if I'm gonna make it back home tonight," I ramble.

Kevin chuckles and then takes the guys' orders. When he leaves, they tell me they come here every night, whether it's to sober up some before they go home after playing pool, or to pull a cram session, studying for tests at school. I find out Jason is going to school for Business, but hasn't been in for long since he chose to get a couple of jobs right after he graduated high school instead of starting college immediately. Kevin brings us a full carafe of coffee and a bowl full of individual creamers, takes a moment to fill a mug for each of us before leaving again.

I reach over and grab a handful of sugar packets, and Jason asks, "Hand me some pinks, would ya?"

I look up at him, and as my eyes lock with his, I burst into a fit of giggles. His face shows a mix of confusion and humor as I continue to laugh at his question. I'm not really sure why it's so funny, but in my fuzzy head, it was the most hilarious thing in the world for this tough looking, tatted-up dude to ask me for some 'pinks'. I can't stop the word vomit when I catch my breath and ask, "I've got something pink for ya," and immediately slap my hand over my mouth, my eyes widening in horror as I look from Jason to Gavin.

There is a moment of awkward silence, where I don't know if Gavin is going to laugh it off as a drunken joke, or if he is finally going to pick up on the fact I'm...I don't know what to call it...crushing? Yeah, we'll go with crushing...on his friend. I mean, I don't have anything to feel guilty about. Gavin made it perfectly clear from the beginning he doesn't want anything serious, but still. We are kinda, sorta dating, so even if we aren't an exclusive couple, it still feels...wrong to like his friend. And I don't even *like* Jason! I don't know what I'm feeling. He's an asshole—a very hot, funny, and smart asshole, but an asshole nonetheless.

Thankfully, Gavin throws his head back and lets out a burst of laughter, allowing me to let out the breath I'd been holding. I look back over to Jason, and he visibly relaxes, holding out his hand for the sweeteners he asked me for with a raised eyebrow. Instead of handing them to him though, I lean diagonally across the booth and look closely at him, getting within a foot of his face. His brow furrows as he has no choice but to look at me. I tilt my head to the side, studying his masculine but perfectly shaped black eyebrows.

"Do you pluck your eyebrows?!" I ask incredulously. There is no fucking way this...*man*, who screams alpha from every pore on his body, plucks his eyebrows. But they're perfect, not a stray hair in sight, and it's impossible that slight arch is natural. I can't imagine Jason sitting in front of a lit magnified mirror with a pair of tweezers in-hand. My brain doesn't even process the vision; all I get is an ERROR message crossing behind my eyes as I wait for his reply.

"No, I go get them waxed," he answers unfazed.

Gavin scoffs...like, actually scoffs, and asks, "Dude...you get your eyebrows done?" A look of disbelief crosses his boyish face.

"Yeah, I go to the little Vietnamese chick at the nail place by the Kroger. If I didn't, I'd look like the dude who works at the gas station," he responds, swiping his pointer finger down the center between his eyebrows. "Now, can you please hand me some pinks?"

With a grin still plastered to my face, I reach over and pluck a few sweeteners from the holder next to the line of different flavored syrups, and then place them in his outstretched hand. My fingertips barely graze the center of his palm, but it's enough to send a bolt of lightning all the way up my arm, causing me to jerk back and elbow Gavin right in the gut. I feel my face heat as he rubs his belly and asks me if I'm okay. "Sorry," I say lamely, "something tickled my foot. I hope there isn't a bug under there." I look beneath the booth, trying to play off my fib. I top off my act with a dramatic shiver and fold my legs under me Indian-style.

A few minutes later, a woman who looks to be about my mom's age peeks her head into our section. "You boys doin' all right?"

"Hey, Max. Yeah, we're just trying to sober up a little bit before we go home. Need our food to soak up some of the alcohol," Gavin tells her as she comes over to our table.

"Well, it'll be out in just a few minutes. Just waiting on French fries to get done," she explains.

"Oh! Those are mine," I say and bounce a little in my seat. "Do y'all know everybody who works here?" I ask the guys.

"Just the night shift. Max and Kevin are here every night when we come in," Gavin answers.

"These boys could keep me in business themselves," she jokes, patting Jason on the shoulder. He gives her a small smile before taking a long drink from his coffee mug. "It should be done in a sec. I'll go check on it."

"Thanks, Max," Jason says, and she walks away.

"So did you end up meeting that chick off POF the other day?" Gavin asks Jason.

Jason takes a sip of his coffee before answering, "Yeah, but she didn't look anything like her picture."

I try to ignore the twinge of jealousy that blossoms inside my gut, but then it explodes into something else when he continues, "She was too skinny. She must've lost weight after the picture was taken or something, or maybe she had photoshopped herself."

"Wait...what?" I ask, shaking my head in confusion. When he said she didn't look like her picture, I had imagined just the opposite. I figured he meant the girl on the dating website had put on some extra pounds since the photo was taken, not the other way around. And he was disappointed by this?

"Ho-bichaux here is a chubby chaser," Gavin says, grinning across the table at his friend.

"A what?" I can't wrap my head around what they're talking about.

"He goes hoggin'," Gavin quips unhelpfully.

"Still not getting it," I say, starting to get annoyed that they don't outright explain it to me.

"He only dates fat chicks," Gavin says slowly, using a voice he'd use on a kindergartner.

My mouth drops open and my eyes go wide, and I turn my head from Gavin to the sexy man sitting across from him, the one I've been drooling over all night, the one I've been imagining doing sinful things to since I met him hours ago, the one who I now know I'll *never* have a chance with.

Somehow in my tipsy state, I remember to school my expression not to reveal any type of disappointment, only surprise in what's been revealed. "Like, *only* big girls?"

"Yeah, and the bigger the better," Jason says, refilling his coffee mug. He holds out his hand, and still blinking at him dumbly, I place a couple of sweeteners in his hand. "My screen name on POF is NoMax4Me."

I make a mental note to search for his profile when I get home. I hadn't seen him while I was browsing, and I'm pretty sure his picture would have stood out to me. I would've definitely messaged him.

"Is it just like a fetish or something? Like dudes who fantasize about women's feet?" I ask.

"I guess you could call it that," he says, and before I can ask him anymore questions, Kevin returns with all of our food.

I make it home safe and sound around five in the morning after filling my belly with tons of carbs to soak up all the alcohol. Instead of going straight to bed like I know I should, I head straight to the extra bedroom next to mine, where I plop down in front of my brother's computer. I hurriedly sign into my Plenty of Fish account, and in the search toolbar, I type in NOMAX4ME.

His picture immediately pops up. It's a goofy one, not a picture of him trying to come off as tough or sexy. He's sexy in his playfulness. He's in the same black, long-sleeved shirt he wore tonight, and he's not looking at the camera. He's seems to be giving someone off the side 'Blue Steel'—the pouty-lipped, funny expression Ben Stiller models in *Zoolander*. I can't help but giggle, and when I click on his profile, I'm so giddy I don't know where to look first. I decide to start from the beginning so I don't miss anything.

NOMAX4ME

Age: 20

Birthday: January 25, 1984

His birthday is next week! I have to remember to tell him happy birthday.

> Sign: Aquarius
>
> Eyes: Brown
>
> Hair: Dark brown
>
> Height: 6'
>
> Weight: 185
>
> Looking For: Casual Encounters Only

And there we have it, folks. It all makes sense. The reason I didn't come across his profile is because he's got it set for exactly what I weeded out. Alas, I forge on.

> Smoker: Yes
>
> Drinker: Yes
>
> Wants Kids: Someday

This answer makes me smile. I allow myself to picture him holding a baby, and can almost hear my ovaries sigh, 'Awwww.'

> About Me: I always hate this part of a profile. If you'd like to get to know me, then message me. As you can see, I put Casual Encounters as what I'm looking for. I'm not looking for a relationship. Take that at face value. You will not change my mind, so don't contact me thinking you'll be the girl who reforms me.

Oooooh, testy, testy. Sounds like something may have happened in the past and he's still bitter about it.

Or maybe he's just a dick.

Yeah, or that.

> Interests: Drinking, smoking, playing pool, playing poker, making money.

Wow, he really did nothing on his profile to try to sell himself. There's no way in hell if I had read this, I would've contacted him. He sounds like the exact type of guy I would have avoided. Oh, wait, I did avoid him—when I set my browsing criteria to comb through the douchebags.

He wasn't one though. I mean, sure, he wasn't the friendliest person in the world, but there was something about him...something that seemed...sad.

By this time, my eyes are starting to cross; I'm so exhausted. My coffee fuel has official ran out and made this body sputter to a stop, the last five minutes having ran on fumes. I make my way into my room and I'm asleep before my head even hits the pillow.

CHAPTER Ten

Kayla's Chick Rant & Book Blog
Blog Post 1/23/2005

Well, I started my new job a couple days ago. It's ridiculously easy. Instead of being out in the open to greet customers as they come in, like at my cousin's car dealership, I'm in the back office. I'll be working the evening shifts since I go to school in the mornings, and that means I'll have the entire office to myself, since all the other office personnel get off at five. All I have to do is answer the phone, direct the caller to the correct person, and file completed car sales in alphabetical order. The manager knows there is a lot of down time, so he said he is completely okay with me doing my homework here. Guess

I'll have lots of time to read!

Anni messaged me the other day telling me to make an account on a website called Myspace. I had heard of it before, but never really paid any attention to it. Apparently, it makes sharing your pictures with family and friends really easy, and she thinks it would be good for my blog. So I made my free account if y'all want to check me out and add me to your friend list. I really like how you can change the background of your profile, and being able to comment of your friends' pictures is really fun.

In other news, I've been back down to Friendswood a few more times to hang out with the guys. I haven't done the deed with Gavin ever since the second time failed, and I think he's getting the hint I'm not really interested in him as more than a friend, the kind *without* benefits. I just don't want to burn any bridges with him, because I really do love spending time with all of them. I'm scared if I tell Gavin I don't want anything more than his friendship, he won't even want that. I know I'm probably a bitch for using him to hang out with Jason—who, by the way, is still Mr. Broody, but has started speaking to me a lot more—but I can't shake this pull Jason has on me.

Jason's twenty-first birthday party is on Tuesday. It's weird to have a party in the middle of the week, but when you're a college kid, I guess it doesn't really matter. I wanted to get him something, but I also don't want it to be blatantly obvious that I have such a big crush on him by buying him something extravagant, not that I could afford anything that great anyway. But I found him this really cool lighter that looks like a deck of cards, and when you slide the top card to the side, it ignites the lighter. They had a few different ones, and I happened to get lucky and grabbed the last one with the ace of spades as the top card. He has a thing for spades. He even has a huge tattoo on his right bicep of one with the words *Lucky Spade* inked in script. The gift is small, but hopefully, he'll appreciate the sentiment.

CH♠PTER

Eleven

1/25/2005

I lean against the wall of Jason's hallway, waiting impatiently for the person to finish using the bathroom, who has been in there for a good fifteen minutes. I'd use the one off the kitchen, but with all of these crazy boys running around, most of who are intoxicated for Jason's big party, I thought I'd play it safe and use the one at the back of the house to avoid being pranked when I'm most vulnerable.

Finally, I hear the lock being turned and the door abruptly swings open, revealing an annoyed looking Mr. Broody. When he spots me waiting in the hall, his face softens slightly, and I smile at him. "You okay? I was about to go find help to see if you'd fallen in," I tease.

"Yeah, was just hiding out for a while. Sorry. There's two other bathrooms, you know," he tells me.

"Yeah, but it felt weird going into your parents' bedroom, and there was no guarantee I'd get to pee in peace with all your drunk friends running around the other one."

"Good call," he says, stepping out of the doorway.

My full bladder has been completely forgotten as I stand here talking with the birthday boy. I haven't spent any time alone with him before, and the tension I feel between us is almost palpable. "You sure you're okay?" I ask. "Why were you hiding in your bathroom?"

"I just needed to get away for a while. There are so many people here; I just needed to get where it was quiet. Don't get me wrong. I'm happy people came, but I just get anxious sometimes," he explains. He reaches his muscular, tattooed arm up to rub the back of his neck with his hand, then brings it up over his short cropped hair and down his face, blowing out a long stream of air.

I hate seeing him so tense at his own party, so I do the first thing that pops into my head to make him feel better. I take the two steps separating us and wrap my arms around his waist, surprising the both of us as I give him what I mean to be a supportive hug. He stands stiffly for a moment, probably wondering what the hell I'm doing, but then I feel him physically relax and place one of his arms around my shoulders.

We stand there for what seems like hours, but what I'm sure is only a few minutes, as I try to send him good vibes through our embrace. I don't want to let go—one, because I don't want it to be awkward when we finally do, and two, being in his arms feels amazing. I can hear the thud of his heart in his chest, and I feel so protected and...at home wrapped up in his hold. When his grip loosens, there is no weirdness as we step away from each other. Instead, he looks a lot calmer than he had before my sudden need for a cuddle.

"Thanks," he says, "I guess I needed that."

I giggle and tell him, "Sorry, I'm a hugger. I thought it was a shame for you to look so unhappy at your birthday party. Oh! I have something for you. It's small, but when I saw it, it reminded me of you." I pull my purse open that's hanging on my shoulder and take out the tiny wrapped box, handing it to him. He holds it up to his ear and shakes it, making me laugh. "You don't have to guess; just open it," I encourage, making a shooing motion with my hands.

"Now?" he asks, already starting to work at the wrapping.

"Yeah, now. I know I've only known you for a week, but I couldn't come to your party and not bring you something for your birthday." I shift from foot to foot as I watch him remove the small white box from the blue paper I'd found in Mark's spare bedroom and then crumple it up in his hand. He steps backward into the bathroom, and tosses the paper out of my line of sight, I assume into a trashcan.

I find myself holding my breath as he works the lid off of the box, and then sigh as I see a rare smile cross his handsome face. He turns the box upside down in his hand, and the lighter falls into his palm. He absently hands me the empty box as he turns the rectangular-shaped metal over on each side, visibly trying to figure out what it is.

"Slide the ace to the side," I hint, stuffing the box back into my purse.

When his eyebrows furrow and he does as I told him, the lighter ignites with a distinct *click* and he jumps a little, making me giggle again.

"Holy shit! That's awesome," he says, sliding the top card over and over, making the flame light and extinguish repeatedly. "I've never seen one like this before."

"Me neither," I say quietly through my big grin. I'm sure my face is going to split; I'm smiling so hard, feeling overwhelmingly proud of myself that I could make this guy with such a tough exterior react to a gift like a little kid with a brand new toy. I watch him play with it for a few more moments before my bladder makes itself known again. "Well, I'm glad you like it, but I've really gotta go potty now," I say and move around him to go into the bathroom. As I go to close the door, his hand shoots up to stop it from shutting. I look up at him through the narrow opening, startled by his action.

"Thanks, Kayla. This was really thoughtful," he tells me sincerely.

"You're welcome, Jason," I reply breathily, looking into his dark chocolate eyes before he finally pulls the bathroom door all the way closed.

I stand with my hand pressed against the cool wood for a few moments as I listen for his footsteps to make their way down the hallway, but they never come. I wonder what he's still doing on the other side of the door, if he too is recovering from the innocent but intense exchange we had in the quiet of his house while his party raged out in his closed double bay garage.

Finally, I hear the movement I've been waiting for and then drag myself over to the toilet to handle my business. As I wash my hands, I glance around the counter top, peaking at Jason's different products from his shaving cream to his... *cologne!*

I quickly dry my hands and then carefully pick up each bottle of cologne he has neatly lined up against the backsplash, bringing them up to my nose for a quick sniff, looking for the one that was so intoxicating the first night I hung out with him at Legends. And then I find it. I feel my eyes cross as I inhale the scent that instantly soaks my panties. I remain breathing in the delicious smell like a creeper for a ridiculous amount of time before I'm snapped out of my stupor by loud laughter making its way up the hall toward me. I pull the black bottle away from my face and look down at it to read the label: *Realm*, and below it in a white rectangular box: *Contains Real Human Pheromones.*

And there we have it.

A couple hours later, I'm in a huge circle of people sitting around in lawn, camping, and dining room chairs out in the garage. The doors are closed and there are a couple of space heaters running, the night being a little chillier than usual. Not a single person in the group is without a drink, including me. Mrs. Robichaux and I are the only ones with glasses of wine, but I'm no less tipsy than the rest of the people who are drinking beer and mixed drinks.

Before she had handed me my second glass, she'd made me call my brother to let him know I'd be sleeping on her couch tonight. Wednesdays, I only have US History I, but seeing how the professor never took attendance and said our only grades for the entire semester would be our midterm and finals, which will both be five-page papers on any topic of our choosing, I figured it'd be all right to skip class in the morning.

Jason is opening his presents from all his friends. Most of them are bottles of liquor or six-packs of beer, but there are a couple gifts that are quite...inventive. His mom hands him a gift bag full of tissue paper, and when he pulls out the folded fabric inside, we see two t-shirts. When he unfolds one to read the front, it's a picture of him and Gavin on the front with the words *The Seagulls* at the top, and then *Eat, Sleep, Shit* across the bottom. We all laugh as he tosses one of the shirts at Gavin, who proceeds to strip out of his jacket and hoodie to put it on.

"Put yours on too, dude," Mrs. Robichaux tells Jason, holding up her camera to indicate she wants to snap a picture of the two of them wearing their new shirts. He sets the gift bag on the floor beside his chair and stands up.

That's when my world stops turning.

It happens in slow motion. Jason's arms crisscross in front of him before grasping the bottom hem of the long-sleeved Henley he's wearing. As he begins to lift it, his undershirt clings to it, rising along with it, as inch by delicious inch Jason's taut and tan stomach is revealed to my wide eyes. I catch a glimpse of a tribal tattoo around his belly button, and then a light smattering of chest hair before the Henley and undershirt are tugged apart with a crackling of static electricity as he pulls the white cotton back down into place.

I start to feel dizzy and immediately think it's the wine, but then I realize I haven't exhaled and inhaled any fresh air in a while. I expel it with a whoosh and then gasp quickly, feeling instantly better. Jason looks over at me and gives me a smirk, apparently knowing I'd just watched him like my own personal peep show. Gavin is too busy striking ridiculous looking poses in the center of the circle to notice me drooling over his friend like the Looney Toons' wolf over Jessica Rabbit.

When I look back up at Jason, he's pulling the new shirt on, and then he joins Gavin in the middle of the group to pose for some pictures.

"What's up with the shirts, Miss Barbara?" Jason's friend, Michael, asks.

"When we went to Steve's cousin Phil's house in Louisiana last summer, these boys had too much fun. He lives on a huge piece of land with swamps and a lake, and Jason and Gavin became 'The Seagulls', because all they did the whole time was just eat, sleep, and shit. That's it. They occasionally left the house to hunt alligators and fish, but then they'd come back and start the cycle all over again—eat 'til they'd almost pop, fall asleep with their full bellies, and then wake up only because they'd have to shit," she answers, and the garage erupts with laughter.

After we all settle back down, Michael hands Jason the last

present. When he unwraps it, he throws back his head and laughs harder than I've ever heard him laugh before. I lean forward in my chair to see what's gotten this reaction out of him. He balls up the wrapping paper and throws it into the trashcan next to the door, and when he lifts up the gift, we all see it's a package of Depends, adult diapers. His laugh is infectious and has me joining along with him, but I'm confused over the present. Is it an inside joke?

I don't have to wonder long because Michael tells the group, "The last time Jason and I drank together, he told me he's gotten so drunk before that he will pee in all sorts of interesting places. I figured if he has some Depends, he won't have to even worry about getting out of bed. Just let it flow, brother." He laughs and smacks Jason on his back good-naturedly.

"Like what kinds of interesting places?" I can't help but ask.

"Well, let's see. There was the bathtub," Michael says.

"And that cigarette butt container outside Legends," Gavin offers.

"The fountain in front of that mansion by the high school," Jason adds.

"That asshole John's gas tank," Adam speaks up.

We all turn to look at him, surprised by the sound of his deep voice joining into the conversation, and then what he said registers and we all burst out laughing again.

"So yeah, my gift should save his ass from an indecent exposure charge. You're welcome, buddy," Michael says with a chuckle.

CHPTER
Twelve

After playing drinking games and listening to people tell more funny stories either about Jason, drinking, or Jason drinking, the crowd shrinks little by little until all that's left is Jason, Adam, Gavin, and me. We make our way inside to the living room, where the couches have already been opened out into double beds. We pile into them, Gavin and me in one, Jason in the other, and Adam in Jason's dad's recliner, and then we scroll through the list of movies on demand. The three guys agree on *The Grudge* after I tell them it scarred me for life.

I'm so glad I don't have to drive home tonight as I'm heavily intoxicated having finished off Mrs. Robichaux's giant bottle of white zinfandel. It's also because the first and only other time I saw *The Grudge,* when it was in theaters, I was so terrified that I kept seeing those scary asshole ghosts in my rearview mirror. I ended up calling my mom and making her talk to me the entire way home...that was, until I'd lost reception and my phone cut out. I had screamed bloody murder and pulled into a brightly lit gas station, thinking, *This is the part in the movie when the girl always dies.* I didn't move until my phone started working again and I reconnected with Mom.

She talked me down the rest of the drive home, telling me this cute story about how *The Exorcist* came out when she and Dad had only been married a couple years. She wanted to see it, but he blatantly told her no, saying it was too scary for her. As a big "fuck you"—her words, not mine—she went anyway thinking he couldn't tell her what she could and couldn't do. And she said it scared her so badly, she about peed herself. By the end of the story, I was walking into my parents' living room laughing my ass off, but when I went to bed, my terror was back as I thought about the part in *The Grudge* when the demonic-looking Asian bitch crawled underneath the covers at the end of the bed. I seriously didn't sleep for like a week straight.

And now, here these asses are, making me watch it again.

Soon, though, Gavin gets up and says he's going to go home since he has classes in the morning he can't miss and he won't be able to get enough sleep on the uncomfortable fold-up bed. He makes a joke about being spoiled by his amazing mattress he bought himself from work before leaning down to give me a hug, bumping fists with Jason, and then heading out the door.

I find it weird the guy I'm semi-dating left me at his best friend's house to sleep without him, instead of just spending the night with us, but apparently, he must not be worried...or care...that something could possibly happen between Jason and me.

A short time after that, Adam also says he's ready to go home, and leaves after giving us a quick wave. Jason's parents have long since gone to bed, so I'm left alone with the darkly sexy man I can't seem to get out of my head.

I'm not even paying attention to the movie. Instead, I'm intensely aware of Jason's every movement, every sound, and every breath as he lays only a few feet away from me on the other sleeper sofa. Out of the corner of my eye, I watch him as he stares at the screen, his eyes making minute movements as he watches Sarah Michelle Gellar wash her hair in the shower, discovering a ghost's arm coming out the back of her head and screaming wildly.

Suddenly, Jason reaches for the remote and pauses the movie, getting up and making his way around the furniture. When he reaches the back door in the corner of the living room that leads to the patio, he turns and asks, "Want to smoke?"

I nod and follow him as he opens the door, grabbing my purse from the top of the upright piano against the wall. He leaves the overhead light off, saying it would attract bugs, so we use only the light coming from the lamp sitting on the other side of the living room's window.

I can't help but smile when I see him light his cigarette with the lighter I bought him, and he tilts his head to watch me as I pull out one of my own to light mine. He holds his hand out, not bothering to speak as he blows out a long stream of smoke, and I place the cool metal into his palm. He turns it over and sees mine has the queen of hearts as my sliding card.

"They had different ones?" he asks, still turning the lighter around and around as he holds his cigarette between two of his fingers.

"Yeah," I say quietly, taking a drag.

"You got me the ace of spades?"

"Yeah," I breathe out, along with the smoke I'd inhaled.

He nods, putting his cigarette between his lips.

When he doesn't say anything else, I work up the courage to ask him, "Will you tell me about your tattoos? I got you the ace of spades because of the big one you have on your bicep, but I know you have more."

He takes his time, savoring the rest of his cigarette before putting the butt out in the ashtray in the middle of the table. Without looking at me, he pulls up the right sleeve of his black Henley, pointing at the small scorpion on his forearm. "Most people wonder if I got this because I'm a Scorpio, but I'm not; I'm an Aquarius through and through. I got it because I like scorpions, plain and simple. Some people think it's a crawfish, maybe signifying my Cajun family, but no. I had the artist make the tail straight instead of curved because I had to have it symmetrical. If it was curved to one side, it would have made me insane. I'm OCD when it comes to that shit."

I make a mental note to ask him about the Aquarius

comment later as he unbuttons the two buttons of his shirt and pulls the fabric down so I can see the cross with the initials and date over his heart. "I got this is for Granny, my dad's mom, when she passed away. She was my absolute favorite. When I would go and stay with her, she'd make me a big-ass breakfast and give me a full glass of milk and full glass of orange juice. She'd tell me she didn't care how much I ate, as long as I finished off both drinks."

His reminiscent story makes me smile, picturing him as a little dark-haired child sitting at the breakfast table, wanting to eat all the bacon and pancakes, but having to finish off all that liquid first. I watch as he slides the neck of his shirt off his shoulder, turning his body to show me the series of triangles put together to form one large triangle, with more initials and numbers. "This one is for my buddy, Wes, from high school. He was a Marine and died over in Iraq," he says emotionlessly, and then pulls up the sleeve on his left forearm to show me the small tattoo of crosshairs he has there. He doesn't explain it, but I assume he got it because he loves to shoot guns. He spins his chair, giving me his back, and he lifts his shirt all the way up, making my breath catch at the sudden exposure of all that beautiful skin. Across the top of his back is his last name, Robichaux, in a bold font, and then he turns to face me, saying, "And then the most painful one I've gotten, the one around my belly button."

I try my damnedest, but I can't help the giggle that bubbles up from inside me. I slap my hand over my mouth, tears coming to my eyes as try to contain my laughter, and I see a small smile tugging at his lips. "Yeah, yeah, I hear you.

Laugh all you want," he tells me.

In a strained voice, I ask, "Why the hell did you get a tribal tattoo around your belly button? I don't know for sure, but that's probably as bad as if you would've gotten a tramp stamp!" I throw my head back and let loose an all-out belly laugh, grasping the arms of the chair as it rocks with my sudden movement, reminding me of the alcohol using my veins as a lazy river.

"Well, I was dating a stripper, and she told me it'd be sexy, so being the highly intelligent person I am, I got it to make her happy," he explains.

My laughing immediately stops, and if I was on the outside looking in, I'm sure it would have been quite comical to see my face go from gleeful hilarity to stonewall grumpy in two-point-five seconds. The sudden, overwhelming rush of jealousy I get makes me feel queasy. *First, thick girls, and now strippers? Fuck, I stand no chance.*

I guess a small part of me still thought that even though he liked girls with plenty of curves, I might still be able to win him over with my...*flat chest and awkwardness?* God, I'm such an idiot! If I'm not dating the cream of the crop—insert sarcasm here—then I'm falling for a guy who wants nothing to do with me.

Wait.

Falling for?

Dude, serious as a fucking heart attack, you need to calm it with the 'falling for' bullshit. You've known this guy for a week. Sure, he's everything you want all wrapped up in a deliciously tattooed package, but you barely know the guy. Suck it up, girlfriend. He's just not the one for you.

He's observed me having this entire conversation with myself, watching me closely, almost gauging my reaction to what he revealed about himself. I don't have a poker face, so I'm sure he's seen every single one of my emotions play across my features—humor, shock, jealousy, and possibly that little bit of hope dying. It's like he's been in my head along with me, and it surprises me when he asks, "What do you look for in a guy?"

I tilt my head, and respond with a question of my own, "Why do you ask?"

"I'm just wondering why you're dating Gavin. Why the fuck would a girl like you have anything to do with a guy like him?" He takes another drag off his cigarette and ashes it on the ground beside his chair.

A girl like me? "Well, that depends. What kind of girl do you think I am?" I can't believe I just had the balls to ask him that. Yay wine!

"From what I've gathered, you're a sweet, naïve, overly-trusting girl, who probably has very little experience with the opposite sex. I think you're settling for my best albeit moronic friend, because you don't think you can do any better. Plus, you'd rather be taken and unsatisfied than single. Am I right?"

"You're a dick," I scoff. My heart wants to linger on the part he said about me being sweet, but the rest of it hits something inside me, making me feel a mix of embarrassed, ashamed, and dumb.

"True, but I'm right, am I not?" He rocks back and forth

in his chair casually, waiting on my answer.

"All except for one thing," I say more to myself than in response to his question.

"And which part was that?" he asks, cocking an eyebrow and leaning forward to absorb what I'm about to say.

"I have more experience with the opposite sex than you think." I don't know how, but I manage to look him dead in the eyes while I throw this out there, and whether he had meant sexually when he'd stated his theory, he knows for certain that's exactly what I'm talking about because of the tone of my voice.

He leans back in his chair slowly, making the springs squeal under his muscular weight. He reaches for his pack of cigarettes and uses the end of the one he's finished smoking to light the next. After a few minutes of me wondering if that's the end of our conversation—right when it was getting interesting—he looks up at me with those chocolate-filled orbs and takes my heart to a whole new level of erratic pounding by saying, "I'd be interested in hearing about this so-called experience you have."

I gulp. Do I really want to tell this intimidating, gorgeous, obviously highly sexually experienced man about my ridiculous bedroom blunders? I can't think of anything more embarrassing than revealing all the shit I've been put through by guys ranging from boys who have no knowledge of the female anatomy, to men who think they're gods...even when they only last a total of thirty seconds.

But for some reason, I want to confide in Jason. I want to tell him my tragic tales, purge all the horrid memories. He makes me want to let it all out, with a real person, who might be able to say something that'll make me feel better. No one knows all the crap I've done, or what I've let be done to me, not even my best friend Anni. Sure, she knows about the never-orgasmed thing, but she doesn't know the lengths I've gone through trying to get it.

Oh, God…if I tell him anything, it won't make any sense unless I tell him *that* part, the part that makes me feel like a freak, like there's something wrong with me.

All or nothing, Kayla.

Am I willing to tell him every detail about my sexual history, this beautiful stranger sitting in front of me, waiting patiently for me to decide if I'm going to confess all my sins to him?

Yes. Tell him. He'll make it better.

I don't know where that voice comes from, but I listen to it, praying it's the right decision.

"I've been having sex since I was fifteen and have never had an orgasm." I say this to my lap. I couldn't bring myself to watch his reaction. I don't want to see it when he laughs at me, or looks at me like I'm broken.

But he does neither. Instead, I'm thrown for a loop when he says, "Fucking idiots." I glance up at him, seeing him shaking his head. "What kind of dumbasses have you been sleeping with who haven't taken the time to make you come?"

Suddenly, it feels like my scalp has been set on fire, and the liquid flames pour from my head, down to the very tips of my toes. I've never felt such an intense feeling before, and I can't actually identify it. It sort of feels like relief, mixed with a little surprise, with a dash of discomfiture, topped off with a whole lot of turned-on.

I can't speak, so he takes the opportunity to ask, "Like, you've *never* come, or never with another person?"

"Um...I have by myself, but never with anyone else," I confess.

He rubs at his plump bottom lip, contemplating what I've said, drawing my attention to that kissable mouth of his. It's not helping douse the heat rolling along my skin, stoking it instead. I realize I'm playing with my own bottom lip when he brings me out of my trance by asking, "Then it's not you. You don't need to feel bad about yourself for the dipshits you've been with. If you can come while you pleasure yourself, then it has nothing to do with your body. I mean, a surprising percentage of women don't have the ability to have an orgasm at all. Period. Not while they masturbate, not while they have sex, nothin'. The female orgasm is ninety percent in their head. You obviously either can't concentrate enough during sex to get there, whether you're distracted, thinking about other things, and/or the guy isn't doing a good enough job of keeping your attention."

I stare at him for only God knows how long. It's the most I've ever heard Jason say at one time, plus, it makes a whole hell of a lot of sense. When I finally find my voice, I ask quietly, "How do you know all that?"

"I didn't start having sex until I was seventeen. I was a very awkward looking teenager. So when I finally did, I wanted to make sure I was good at it. Girls will overlook you not being the best looking guy in the world if you can make them have multiple orgasms." He smiles. I can't help but laugh. He continues, "I read anything I could get my hands on, from Cosmopolitan magazine, to internet articles, even anatomy books. I learned everything I could beforehand, because I knew when it finally happened, it better be fucking good, because if it was bad, whoever it was would go back and tell her friends, and I'd never get laid again. But if it was good, if she told anyone, then they'd want to see it for themselves."

"So what happened?" I prompted.

He gives me a wicked smile. "Add a zero to the end of your number of sexual partners."

I think for a minute, my eyebrows furrowed in confusion, but then when it dawns on me what he's saying, my mouth drops open in astonishment. "Are you freaking serious?! You been with over a hundred women in," I do a little math in my head, "four years?! How is that even physically possible?"

"Making up for lost time, I guess." He shrugs. "It wasn't as hard as you may think. You see how much Gavin and I go out. Even if I would've picked up just one girl every single weekend, it would be way more than that. But I've tried dating here and there, and I never cheat if I'm exclusively dating someone, so that held back my number a little. But then when you add in the times with multiple partners...and that stint as a single guy in a swingers' club..." he trails off, smoking his cigarette, looking like he's deep in thought.

Cue the infamous record scratching to a halt. Add in the real life crickets chirping in the yard around us.

My mouth opens and closes like a guppy. My internal reaction is what shocks the shit out of me though. One would think, seeing how I'm apparently the most jealous person in the history of ever when it comes to this guy that I'd be green with envy over the great amount of women who have gotten to experience the sex on a stick that is Jason Robichaux. But instead, it actually makes me feel better. In my twisted brain, if his number is that high, it means they meant nothing to him. They were just at the right place at the right time, a warm body for him to dip his willy.

Ugh, gross, brain.

There are so many questions I want to ask him, but the first thing that flies out of my mouth is, "Will you tell me about the swingers' club?"

The excitement in my voice must alert him I don't find his history repulsive. He smirks a little as he puts out his cigarette in the ashtray, and then interlocks his fingers, places them behind his head, and leans far back in his chair. "What do you know about swingers' clubs, little girl?" he teases me in an extra deep voice.

"I'm actually quite fascinated with them, *old man*," I mock his tone. "Has Gavin told you anything about me? About my blog or anything?"

"Oh, he's told me all sorts of stuff about you, but hasn't mentioned anything about a blog," he says conspiratorially.

I flush. "Oh, God, I don't want to know. Moving on. Okay, well, as if you couldn't tell, I'm a giant nerd. I have a blog, where I review books and I also rant about random chick stuff. The books I review are...colorful. Most of them are paranormal romance but when I can find a BDSM romance, I devour it like pecan pie. There aren't very many out there. It's a taboo subject that most authors don't even want to bother trying their hand at, but damn," I sigh wistfully, fanning myself and grinning at him.

My enthusiasm makes him smile. He shifts in his seat, facing me fully, looking like he's settling in for a conversation he's really interested in. "First of all, you say pecan funny," he tells me, pronouncing it puh-CON instead of PEE-can like I do. "Your way sounds like something you use when there's not a toilet available. Yankee."

I gasp dramatically. "I am NOT a Yankee! North Carolina is like two states below the Mason Dixon line, sir, so don't you give me that shit."

My face heats as he laughs. He laughs! I made this tough as nails hottie laugh! It feels like a great accomplishment, and I bask in the deep rumbling coming from him. "Okay, I'll give you that one, for now," he says. "About the swingers' club, what do you want to know?"

I wiggle until I'm sitting higher in my seat, excited to grill him about his adventures. "Oh, lawd, where to start? Umm… okay, let's start at the beginning. How did you get into it?"

He thinks for a second, and then tells me, "I was friends with this couple who invited me to a party. At the time, I didn't know it was going to be a swingers' get-together, but when we got there and I saw what was going on, I said fuck it. I was a single guy surrounded by couples wanting me to join in on their sexcapades. Everyone made it known that it was a safe environment, so when men would approach me asking if I'd bang their wife while they watched, I thought, why not? I mean, who was I to get in the way of someone's fantasy, ya know? At the time, I figured I was only nineteen. If I was going to do something dumb and reckless, I might as well do it then, while I was young. That's what those years are for, right?"

I nod and he continues, "I mean, looking back now, it's not something I'm proud of. Probably not one of the brightest decisions I've ever made. What if mid-thrust the husband changed his mind and attacked me, literally with my pants down? What if their STD tests weren't up-to-date like what was required?"

I add, "Yeah, or what if the condom broke and you got one of the wives pregnant?" I make an eek-face.

"Well, at least that's one thing I didn't have to worry about," he says quietly, more to himself than to me.

"What do you mean?" My eyebrows draw together. "Was everyone required to be on birth control or something?"

"I'm sure they were, but that's not why." He lights another cigarette, and after blowing out the long stream of smoke, he admits, "I can't have kids."

"What makes you think you can't have kids?" I ask. It's suddenly like pulling teeth trying to get answers out of him.

"I don't *think* I can't have kids; I *know* I can't. Something happened to me when I was little, and after they ran some tests, they found out I wouldn't be able to. But that's a whole other story entirely. Back to what we were talking about before. Is there anything else you wanna know about the swingers' club?"

His answer makes me pause. I'm surprised he put 'someday' as his answer on his dating profile if he can't have any himself. If he can't get a girl pregnant, but he wants children in the future, then it makes sense that it would be hard for him to talk about with a virtual stranger. So, I leave it alone, allowing him to change the subject back, asking, "How long did you do it?"

"I only went a couple of times. Whenever I would get home, I'd feel shitty about myself, so I didn't think it was a good idea to keep going," he confesses.

"Okay, it's your turn," I say perkily, wanting to change the mood back to the funny way it was before. He looks at me a little confused, so I explain, "I asked you a question, now you ask me one. We can make it like a game of twenty questions."

"Okay, how about my original question—why is a girl like you dating a guy like Gavin?" he asks.

"Technically, I'm not dating Gavin. I've gone out on dates with him, and we hang out, but it's not like I'm Gavin's girlfriend. We've made it perfectly clear to each other we don't want anything serious," I explain.

"But you've had sex with him, right? Or at least, that's what he told me."

"Ah, another point in the reasons-why-Gavin-sucks column. Unfortunately, yes I did. And if y'all are as close as you seem to be, you probably already know why I say 'unfortunately'."

"That I do, but I'm surprised you even went that far with him. Usually the poor guy just opens his mouth and loses all chance at getting into a girl's pants." He chuckles, shaking his head.

"Wow, some best friend you are. Harsh much?"

"He knows this about himself, but still refuses to do anything about it. He believes there is a girl out there for him who will accept him just the way he is, disgusting manners and all," Jason tells me.

"I'm kind of embarrassed I allowed myself to sleep with him. I mean, I am on my quest for the magical O, but I should at least have standards. Loneliness and horniness is no excuse for settling for a pig," I mutter.

"Hey, don't go feeling bad about it now. What's done is done. Look at it this way; what if you would have slept with him and he gave you your first orgasm? It would have been kinda worse, right? I mean, you wouldn't want the man who turns your sexual world upside down to be a douchenugget outside the bedroom would you? It's better this way," he says firmly.

Nodding, I giggle. He somehow knows exactly what to say to make me feel better about the situation. "Very true."

"Okay, your turn," he prompts.

"Hmmm," I tap my pointer finger against my chin, enjoying the fact he's as into our little game as I am. "What got you into big girls?"

"Have you ever heard that saying 'Big girls need love too'?" I nod. "Well, that's how it started out. See, like I said, I wasn't the best looking dude back in the day. I was skinny, I hadn't grown into my ears, and I had this big nose—"

"I like your nose," I blurt, and then my eyes widen when I realize that was my outside voice. I squeak, "Continue."

He smiles and lets me off the hook for my interruption. "Well, the first girl to ever really come on to me was a girl of the extra curvy persuasion. She's who I ended up losing my virginity to. Since that was my first experience, I kind of just stuck with what I knew."

"So it's not that you aren't *attracted* to smaller chicks?" I ask, and I can't hide the hope in my voice.

His face falls as he picks up his pack of cigarettes, and doesn't look at me while he lights it with the lighter I got him and answers, "I haven't come across one I've been attracted to yet."

It's like he's sucker-punched me right in the gut. All hope lost once again. You would think I'd have learned by now, but the more I get to know about Jason, the more I want him to like me. Everything he's said that would have normally turned me off a guy—hearing his sexual stories, the things he's done in the past, the womanizing—for some reason has the opposite effect. I like that he's so honest with me. And I like the feeling of being open with him, too. I have no reason to hide anything from him. I mean, we aren't dating. Hell, it looks like I would never get the chance to date him, seeing as I'm most definitely not his type. Plus, who would he tell my secrets to? Gavin? Big fucking deal. I let the gut-check ease away, conceding that if I don't stand a chance with him, at least I've made a friend. A really hot, dreamy, tattooed, lickable friend, whose face I'd like to sit on, but a friend nonetheless.

"Your question," I remind him.

"What is your favorite fantasy?" he asks.

"Shit," I say, really, *really* not wanting to admit the naughty things I think about while taking care of myself.

"Shit? Like…" He makes a motion with his hand near his butt, indicating something coming out of it.

"NO! Oh, gross, no!" I shiver with revulsion.

"I know, I'm just messin' with ya. Although, your Gavy-boy has a thing for golden showers," he tells me in a stage whisper. I look at him with a horrified expression. "Oh, he hadn't told you about that one yet? That's normally a conversation starter for the moron. 'Hey, girl, you want to come back to my place, where we can pee on each other?'" He laughs as he watches me cover my mouth, feeling rather vomity at the image filling my head. "Yeah, I guess you can add that to your reasons-why-Gavin-sucks column."

I only have a split second to think about why Jason would be trying to give me reasons to not like his friend before he reminds me, "C'mon, woman. Let's hear it. Favorite fantasy."

"I'm not drunk enough for this," I joke.

"On it," he says, hopping up from his chair. Before I have a chance to stop him, he's already closing the backdoor, leaving me to my own thoughts.

Am I really going to confess my deepest, darkest fantasy? I could always just make one up, tell him it's something else, like a threesome with two dudes or something. Every girl dreams of that, right? But another part of me feels guilty for even thinking about withholding the truth. He's been so open and honest with me about the things he's done; I can't turn around and lie.

I'm psyching myself up to reveal my dirty little secret as

he comes back outside carrying a glass of pink wine in one hand, and a beer bottle in the other. He hands me the wineglass before sitting in his chair again.

This time, it's me who reaches for the cigarettes. I take a long swig of my wine before taking and even longer drag off my cigarette, and as I exhale the smoke, I let my confession come out with it. "I have a rape fantasy."

He cocks his eyebrow at me. "That's it?"

I look at him completely befuddled. That was not the reaction I was expecting. "What do you mean, 'that's it'?"

"Well, one, the way you were acting, I thought it was going to be something way crazier than that, and two, that's it, as in, that's all you're going to tell me?" he asks.

I tilt my head to the side, wondering if this is real life. How can one man be so...cool? Nothing ruffles him. It's like nothing I could say would cause him to have a judgey response, which makes it easy for me to talk to him.

"Wow, umm...I've never told anyone about that before, because, well...rape is bad. Very, very bad. It's not something a normal person would be turned on about, I don't think." The pitch of my voice on the last word makes it sound more like a question. I think my subconscious wants his...not necessarily his approval, but for him to tell me that my fantasy is okay, not so...weird.

"Get ready for this. I'm about to blow your mind," he says. "I've gone to a therapist for several years—"

"Gasp! That does blow my mind," I joke.

He playfully sticks his tongue out at me, completely breaking his bad-boy image, like when he did his silly happy dance when he fixed his truck the first night I met him. "Anyways, I have a thing for psychology. I'm kinda fucked-up if you haven't noticed, and I've always tried to figure out what the hell is wrong with me. And during this journey of self-discovery—which I'm still on, by the way—I've gained a mindful of useless information. Well, useless in my case anyways, but not in yours, because I've got you figured out," he informs me.

"Do you? Let's hear it, Dr. Robichaux," I tease.

"Huh, I like the sound of that," he says. "Say it again."

"Dr. Robichaux," I say in a sultry voice.

He grins and does a little shimmy, like I've given him chills. I glow from the little bit of innocent flirtation. "Okay, back to blowing your mind. You think too much. You are all up in your head, trying so hard to get your orgasm, chasing that motherfucker, but when you try so hard, it makes it unreachable. You gotta relax, just feel, concentrate on the sensations. Your rape fantasy makes perfect sense. You fantasize about a man just coming in and taking you, forcing pleasure on you, taking it completely out of your hands. It's not you chasing the pleasure anymore, it's being given to you against your will. I'm guessing in your fantasy it's not how nonconsensual sex would happen in real life, correct? I mean, it's not some thug who beats the shit out of you and hurts you, right?" I shake my head vehemently.

"Right, so how does it normally play out?" he asks.

Oh, God, he wants me to tell him the whole story I've worked up in my head? Shit, shit, shit. Okay, I can do this.

I take a big gulp of my wine and settle into my seat. I zone myself out, pretending I'm just writing one of my blog posts. I'm anonymous. Nobody knows who I am. I can say whatever I want to say and not have to worry about any repercussions. I clear my throat and begin.

"I'm living in my own apartment all alone. My dream bachelorette pad. It's a pretty night, so I've left my window cracked a little bit to let the fresh breeze come into my room. I'm drying off after a shower, getting ready for bed. All I have on is the towel I've wrapped around myself as I brush out my wet hair. I don't hear it when he opens my window all the way, because I've turned on my blow dryer. He watches me as I flip my hair from one side to the other, making sure I get it all dry. I can't go to bed with damp hair, because I'll wake up with a sore throat. He's patient while he stares at me through the crack in the bathroom door. He's biding his time, waiting for the perfect moment before he pounces. When I turn off my dryer, he holds his breath, not making a sound that would alert me I'm not alone in my one-bedroom apartment.

"I run my brush through my hair one last time before putting everything away in my drawers, and as I open the door all the way, I'm looking in the direction of the light switch as I flip it off, not forward, where the predator awaits his prey. He stands to the side of the doorway, so when I walk out and toward my dresser, where I've laid out my clean panties and t-shirt to sleep in, I'm completely unaware of his presence. Not until I reach out to take hold of my underwear, does he choose to finally make it known he's there. He wraps one arm around my towel-covered waist and clamps his other hand over my mouth, making my scream of surprise and terror almost inaudible.

"He's big, much taller than me, his arms like steel bands around my small frame. And as he whispers in my ear that if I don't stop struggling and screaming, he'll kill me, I go completely still and quiet, even as he moves the arm around my waist to separate the edges of the towel I won't be wearing for much longer."

I continue the storyline in my head, imagining my attacker as he walks me to the wall beside my dresser and forcefully presses me against it...

I'm pulled out of my head by Jason clearing his throat. When I look up at him, he's grinning, and a surprised laugh bursts out of me when he reaches down and adjusts himself in his jeans. "Keep going...I'm almost there," he says, closing his eyes as if he's concentrating on reaching his own happy ending.

I throw my head back and laugh. When I catch my breath, I tell him, "You get the picture," and finish off the rest of my wine.

"Awww, you're gonna leave me hangin'? That ain't nice. Blue balls are bad for a man," he drawls.

"Well, I'm pretty sure blue balls would be bad for a woman too if she had them," I say snarkily, holding up my wine glass and tilting it back and forth, silently asking for a refill. He tips his beer back and finishes the rest in one big swallow, then takes my glass from me and moves to the door.

"When I get back, it's your turn to ask a question," he demands, and I nod before he closes the door behind him.

I feel lighter, like a weight has been lifted off my shoulders at having told someone about what I'd thought was a dirty secret fantasy. Or maybe it is as bad as I originally thought it was, but I've just so happened to find the one person who understands me, and is as sexually messed up in the head as I am. The thought makes me both happy and bummed. Happy, because I'll have someone to talk to who I know won't judge me or think badly of me for my weirdness, but bummed, because it'll will never go farther than a friendship.

CHPTER Thirteen

February 4, 2005

I make the drive down to Friendswood after getting off work at closing time, so I don't arrive at Gavin's until about 9pm. He's waiting for me by his truck as I pull into his cul-de-sac, and I immediately hop into his passenger's seat, eager to head over to Jason's. The past few nights, they've been teaching me the rules of Texas Hold 'em, playing a few games before going to play pool at Legends, but we've planned to just make it a night of poker tonight.

Mrs. Robichaux gives me her usual squeeze as I walk into her kitchen behind Gavin, and I look up to see Jason coming out of his hallway carrying a silver box with a handle and latches. "Look what I got today," he says as he approaches us.

He holds the shiny case in one arm as he uses his other hand to flip the latches and lift the lid. Inside are rows of different colored poker chips, a couple of pairs of red dice, a few packs of cards, and a larger bone-colored chip with the word Dealer engraved in black.

"Sweet," Gavin says, and walks off to grab a beer out of the back fridge.

"Shit, more rules to learn?" I ask Jason, running my finger down one of the rows of white poker chips.

"Nah, it'll be easier now that we have the different colors to use as bets, instead of trying to teach you with can tabs and cigarette butts," he replies, and I don't know for sure, but the way he says it makes me think he went out and got the set just for me. A wave of warmth comes over me as I consider Jason thinking about me when I'm not around. I look up and smile into his gorgeous brown eyes, and after a second that feels like forever, he clears his throat, breaking the spell, and shuts the case back up to hold it by the handle.

"I got y'all a citronella candle today for the mosquitos out on the patio, so they shouldn't eat you alive tonight during your big tournament," Jason's mom teases, patting him on the back as she goes to the fridge, where Gavin stands, chugging down his bottle of beer. When she wraps her arms around his middle to give him a hug, he lets out a giant belch and then grins down at her. I can't help but roll my eyes, and when I look back up at Jason, he's looking at me curiously. My smile returns, but his attention makes me feel self-conscious, so I glance back at Mrs. Robichaux when I hear her opening the refrigerator.

"I got us a new wine, Kayla," she says. "The lady at the store said if you like sweet but not dry, then you'd definitely like this." I walk over and take the green bottle from her, reading the label. It's called a Moscato, which I've never had before, but I'm always willing to try new drinks, as long as they aren't beer. They keep telling me it's an acquired taste, but I don't think I'll ever be able to drink enough of it to 'acquire' it.

Gavin snatches the bottle from my hands and takes it to the counter to use the corkscrew to open it. It makes a loud popping sound as it's pulled free from the neck, and I see the liquid inside rise and bubble at the opening. At my confused expression, Mrs. Robichaux explains it's a carbonated wine, also called 'sparkling', very similar to champagne. He grabs us two wine glasses from the cabinet and fills them to the brim, the bubbles actually arching above the rim of the glass, but miraculously not overflowing.

"Here you go, miladies," he says, handing us the drinks. Jason's mom and I cheer before lifting them to our lips carefully, so we don't spill the fizzy fluid, and take a tentative sip. The sweetness and carbonation combine on my tongue, creating a flavor explosion in my mouth that is delicious and energizing. I lick my lips, letting out an audible moan before taking a less cautious drink. I feel eyes on me, but when I flick my gaze between Gavin and Mrs. Robichaux, I see they've moved to the pantry to get some snacks ready for our poker game. I turn my head and discover it's a chocolate stare boring into me from the archway leading into the living room. I catch Jason's heated expression for only a moment before he schools his features, turns, and disappears; the sound of the backdoor slamming shut follows a few seconds later.

It seems Mr. Broody is back. A wave of sadness hits me, missing the Jason from the night of his birthday party, but the logical part of my brain reminds me he can't be that same Jason when we aren't alone. Feeling a little light-headed, I realize I've stopped breathing and inhale some much-needed oxygen. I shake off the tingling feeling his devouring eyes left inside me as much as I can and turn to help Gavin carry the snacks they've unearthed.

We make our way outside with our armloads of goodies and drinks, and I see Jason has set the case open in front of him on the round, glass table as he sits in one of the spring-loaded chairs. Without looking up, he tells me, "Okay, pay attention so you'll know what to do if you ever want to be dealer."

"Yes, sir," I reply militarily, letting him know he's being bossy. I feel a little giddy when his lip twitches. After setting down a bag of potato chips, a bucket of French onion dip, and my wine glass, I remove my crossbody bag and hang it on the back of my chair, and then give him my full attention.

"The whites count as one dollar, the reds count as five, the blues count as ten, and the greens count as twenty. You get fifteen whites, seven reds, three blues, and one green to start out with. This is what you get when you buy-in for a hundred bucks. Obviously, we aren't playing for money, but just so you know, if you lose and run out of chips, you can buy back in; it just depends on who you're playing with," he explains as he removes the chips from the case and stacks the different colors in front of each of us. He tells us to 'ante up', tossing one of his own white chips into the center of the table, and Gavin and I follow suit.

After we all have the appropriate numbers, he then takes out a deck of cards and begins shuffling them. His hands are almost hypnotizing as he halves them, holds each stack in-between his thumbs and ring fingers while pressing the center with his middle ones before sliding the mixed edges together. He repeats the process over and over, alternating between a simple shuffle and bridging at the end, creating an arc with the cards as they fly together with a sound that's almost soothing, mesmerizing.

I finally snap out of my stupor as he hits one of the edges of the deck against the table loudly, making sure they're smooth across before he deals them out. We each get two cards that are face-down, and then in the middle of the glass, he deals one face-down, and three face-up, placing the rest of the deck to the side. We pick up our hands, being careful not to let either of us see what we have, and glance back and forth between the cards we're holding and the ones in the center of the table.

"Okay, Kayla, check, bet, or fold?" Jason asks, reminding me that since I'm sitting to the dealer's left, I have to make the first move.

"I'm going to check," I state, because I don't have anything between my hand and the cards on the table that would make even a pair.

"I bet five," Gavin says, throwing one of his red chips onto the pile of white ones we anteed. He leans back in this chair, rocking on its springs and taking on a bored expression as he plucks his bottom lip with his fingers.

Jason takes a red chip from behind his hands resting on the table and throws it on the pile, looking up at me and asking, "Bet or fold?"

"I fold," I reply, and put my cards face-down on the burned ones in the middle.

"Pussy," Gavin teases, but I don't bite. I'm watching the two of them closely to see if either of them has a 'tell', which would let me know what to look for in the future to detect if they're bluffing.

Jason nods once, burns a card, and then places one face-up at the end of the other three showing. Gavin leans forward to look at the card, and then looks at the ones in his hand. He glances up at Jason before taking two reds off his stack and tossing them on the growing bet, and leans back to pluck at his lip again.

Jason reaches behind him to scratch the back of his head before betting a blue of his own. "I'll see your ten, and raise you ten more," he tells him, raising one of his perfect, masculine eyebrows in challenge.

I'm studying them closely, but I can't tell if any of their movements are just unconscious fidgeting, or if they're signs that would give them away. Gavin sighs and looks between the cards, and then decides to meet Jason's bet, throwing in two more of his red chips.

"Pot is good," Jason says, and then burns a card before dealing the last one of this round. Again, Gavin leans forward to take a good look before deciding to bet his last two reds. He doesn't relax this time, instead placing the cards in his hand down on the table to await what the dealer will do.

Jason grins, and then bets another one of his greens. "Come on now, fucker. Gotta pay to play," he taunts his friend.

"Fuck," Gavin growls, and then puts in one of his greens before taking back the two reds he'd put in previously. "Turn 'em over. Whatchu got?"

"I have a pair of twos. You?" Jason asks.

"I ain't got jack-shit," Gavin huffs out with a laugh.

"Dude, this is why you always have to buy in like five times every time we play. You've got no game!" Jason shakes his head, scooping all the chips he won to his side of the table and then gathering up all the cards to shuffle for the next hand.

I reach behind me to my purse hanging on the back of my chair and pull my pack of cigarettes out. Jason reaches over to the boombox sitting against the wall of windows and grabs the ashtray on top of it, placing it on the table for us all to use. We're outside, but we'll still need somewhere to put our butts, and after the few weeks I've been spending with these guys, I know we'll have to dump it a few times before the night is over. We all light up before Jason deals the next hand, and just like when he was playing pool, I find him incredibly sexy as his cigarette hangs out the side of his mouth while his hands are otherwise occupied.

We play for a while, each of us winning a couple of times, me doing a happy dance each time I manage to beat them.

Gavin's had to 'buy-in' a couple of times, paying Jason with a few cigarettes, since we aren't playing for money. Jason's chip stacks and mine are both quite large, him having a bit of a lead on mine because of the huge pot he just won off Gavin.

He deals out the cards, and when I lift mine up to see what I got, I consciously keep my face unreactive as I discover I'm holding a pair of sevens. I look down at the cards displayed on the table, and see there is another seven sitting between a queen and a two. My face stays completely devoid of emotion, but inside I'm jumping up and down and shaking my ass like a crazy person. I light myself another cigarette and then pull off two white chips to toss in the center with our antes. I want to start small so I don't scare them away from betting, but I also don't want them to bet too much and make me chicken out, since I'm still new at this game and not too great at spotting other hands like straights and flushes. I had learned my lesson a few times tonight, thinking I had won with a three-of-a-kind, only to find out I had lost a large sum of my chips to a full house.

Gavin meets my bet, and Jason does the same, burning the next card and flipping over another. It's a ten of spades, and I dramatically sit up straight in my chair, wiggling a little to make them think I'm excited over the card that was just shown. I pick up a few of my red chips and toss them in the middle. "I bet fifteen," I say perkily, and look over to Gavin.

He lifts his eyebrow at me and then looks down at the cards on the table. "You got a pair of tens, do ya?" He calls my bet, and then adds twenty, making me evil-cackle inside my head. I look at Jason, who is staring me down. My breath catches a little at being the center of his attention, but I force myself to concentrate on the game. He meets Gavin's twenty, and then waits to see if I'll put in the chips to call the pot square. I do, and what happens next absolutely blows my mind.

Jason burns a card, and then turns over the last one of this round.

It's the fourth and final seven of the deck.

I've got a four-of-a-kind.

I've won the fucking game.

I make myself pout, wanting them to think I've only got a pair of tens. There are two sevens on the table, so if I didn't have the other pair, I'd have to worry that either one of the guys had one, giving them three-of-a-kind, which both of them are thinking at this very moment. With them believing I have the tens, I play off my newbie status and place my bet. "I have four of these blues, which look kinda silly between these tall stacks of whites and reds, so I'm gonna go ahead and get rid of them," I say cutely, tossing them in the center.

"You know that's forty bucks, right?" Gavin asks.

"Yep," I reply, popping the 'p' before taking a drag off my cigarette and then ashing it on the ground.

He shrugs and meets my bet. Jason, however, studies me closely. I try my best not to fidget under his dark stare, and I hide my nerves by giving him a wide grin and asking, "Ya folding?"

He cocks that sexy brow up at me and shakes his head. "Fuck, no. You may have a pair of tens, but there's a pair of sevens on the table. Have you thought maybe I have one of the other sevens, or maybe I have a queen? So many ways you could lose this hand, baby girl," he says in that delicious Texan drawl.

My panties immediately become wet. He called me baby girl. I can't even come up with a snarky reply, because those two words are bouncing around my brain like Forest Gump's game of solitaire ping-pong.

"I'm all in," he says, and I barely hear the bet through his Matthew McConaughey sounding-induced stupor he's put me in.

"I'm sorry, what?" I ask, shaking my head to clear it.

"I'm. All. In," he states slowly, punctuating each word with a slide of a pile of his chips to the center of the table. His cockiness both turns me on and causes me to fully come out of my fog.

"Fuck," I groan, keeping up my act. I've got him. I've won the game. He has a few more chips than me, so even when I take the pile, he'll still have a few left over, but there's no way he'll come back from such a hard hit.

"I call," I say, and look over at Gavin. He's three sheets to the wind and couldn't care less right now. He also goes all in and flips over his cards.

He's got nothing. *Shocker.*

"Okay, baby girl, let's see that ten," Jason says, watching me closely. Whether it's because he noticed my reaction to the last time he called me the pet name or because he's really interested to see my cards, I don't know, but this time, I'm too excited to respond to the endearment.

I flip over one of my sevens.

I watch the confused look come over Jason's face, his dark brows lowering over those gorgeous chocolate eyes.

And then the final nail in his coffin.

I turn over my second seven, lean back in my chair to flirtatiously take a drag off my cigarette, and then blow the smoke across the table into his face. I bite my bottom lip to keep from giving him a shit-eating grin as he shifts his eyes between my face and my cards. He's completely befuddled.

"Well, hot damn!" Gavin shouts loudly. "She fucking got our asses!"

That breaks what little control over the gurgling excitement inside me, and I finally allow my face to split into a smile that hurts it's so wide. I watch as Jason glances between his hand, all the cards on the table, and up to my beaming grin, and then hop up from my chair and do a silly victory dance as he throws his two cards down on top of the pile. I'm in the middle of doing 'The Running Man' when I see him shake his head and start divvying up the chips. He has just a couple of small stacks of the little circles of clay left when he slides my winnings to my side of the round, glass table.

Eventually, I end up losing all my chips, Jason slowly winning them back hand after hand, but I will never forget my epic win with four of a kind

CH♠PTER
Fourteen

February 11, 2005

Over the past almost two weeks, I've spent at least four days a week over at the Robichauxs' house. It's been a mix of poker nights and playing pool, not just at Legends, but at a couple of other pool halls too. We've had a barbeque, a movie night, I've gotten drunk off my ass again and spent the night on Jason's couch—after playing another fun round of twenty questions, of course—and they also somehow talked me into going to a strip club. That was...interesting.

If I hadn't known Gavin was *not* the guy for me before, I definitely would've then; seeing the creepy, hypnotized look on his face while he watched the gyrating bodies of the cracked-out looking strippers would have clued me in.

Jason had taken it upon himself to be my bodyguard for the night. The men at the tables and lounging on the couches scattered around the club thought it was amazing for a pretty college-aged chick to be in the audience, not up on stage hanging from a pole, and seemed to think I was fair game, a steady line of horny men dropping by our table to offer me a drink, or to chat me up, or one who blatantly asked me to join him at his truck to fuck—his words, not mine. This dude almost got a fist to the face from my apparent knight in shining armor. After that, Jason took me by the hand, pulled me along with him as we made our way through the tables of men in various stages of drunkenness, and reached Gavin, who was standing over by one of the small podiums with a stripper who was currently upside down on a pole.

He didn't acknowledge Jason's existence, even when Jason shoved him on the shoulder, as his empty eyes followed the girl's saggy, stretch-marked covered tits as they slid down on either sides of the pole. After another attempt at gaining Gavin's attention to no avail, Jason gave up, growling, "We're leaving. I'm taking Kayla with me. I don't know if Adam is leaving or not, but since we all drove separately, it doesn't fucking matter. Deuces."

He turned abruptly, tugging me along with him once again. I looked back once, only to see Gavin's face being buried between the stripper's unfortunate-looking funbags as she pulled his head to her by the back of his hair.

Also, last week, I had the pleasure of playing witness to Jason meeting someone off Plenty of Fish. Before she showed up at Legends, Jason said he'd only been talking to her for about three days over messages on the site, and this would be his first time seeing her in person. When she arrived, the full-figured blonde wrapped herself around him like he was her long-lost lover, and I had to fight the urge not to wrap my hand around her hair and slam her face as hard as I could on the wooden edge of a pool table.

After a couple games of pool, I looked over and she was playfully poking him in the ribs. It took all I had to talk myself out of snapping a pool stick in half over my knee and poking her with the jagged end. A couple of drinks later, she sat beside him and crossed her leg over his, and I allowed myself to imagine crisscrossing my legs around her neck and choking her out with a scissor lock.

Needless to say, it wasn't a very fun night for me, but after watching her crowd him on their side of the booth at IHOP while he was trying to eat and he looked up at me and gave me a 'kill me, please' look, I knew this heifer didn't stand a chance. After our late-night meal, he gave her a one-armed hug and sent her packing with no invitation back to his place.

Tonight, though, I have a date with a woman. Not just any woman, one feisty-ass woman who barely reaches five-feet tall and likes to drive her BMW convertible at an obscene speed. Mrs. Robichaux was tickled pink when I asked her if she'd like to go with me after we saw a commercial on TV one night for the movie *Hitch*, starring Will Smith. I knew the guys wouldn't want to see it, and the look of relief on Mr. Robichaux's face when he heard me make the offer to his wife told me he was happy he wouldn't have to be dragged along to see the chick flick either.

When I arrived at their house tonight, I was surprised to see the tiny silver car in their driveway. They usually kept it in the garage behind their house. When I walked into their living room after hearing Mr. Robichaux yell from his recliner, "Come in!" Mrs. Robichaux was coming out of their bedroom, putting the backing on her earring.

"Look at you, lady!" I cried, and she did a little circle for me to see her pretty outfit consisting of a three-quarter-sleeved shirt with a brightly colored abstract pattern and black dress pants. It had been deemed 'girls' night' after we made the plans, so I dressed up too. I was wearing flared white pants and a black lace top with a hot pink cami underneath.

After grabbing her purse off the couch, she leaned over her husband and gave him a big kiss on the lips, purposely leaving as much lipstick on his face as possible. Obviously used to her antics, all he said was, "Y'all have fun watching your shit-flick," before moving his attention back on his game of solitaire on his laptop.

She started simultaneously tickling and pinching him all over his legs, belly, and arms, saying, "I'll show you shit-flick!"

"Quit, woman," he said in an unaffected voice.

"I'll get your appendages!" she yelled playfully, pinching the inside of his thigh. This made me burst out laughing; having heard and seen this routine a couple of times since meeting them, it still made me grin like a fool watching them flirt with each other, even after being married for more than thirty years.

So here we are now, me gripping the door handle like my life depends on it as Mrs. Robichaux zips in between cars and semis on 45 South going a hundred and twenty miles an hour, switching gears like a racecar driver and laughing at my look of absolute terror. Her behavior surprises the hell out of me. She is one of the top dogs at NASA, in charge of everything that gets put on the space shuttle before it's launched. She's anally organized, always in control, and as I peel myself from the leather seat and contain the sudden urge to kiss the ground beneath my feet, I ask her, "What the hell was that?!"

Laughing, she admits, "That's my fun. I always have to be so serious all the time at work, and I got my fast little toy to help me let off some steam."

I nod, my legs feeling shaky after holding myself so tense the entire drive to the movie theater. Mrs. Robichaux is so excited to be out on our girl date that she buys practically everything at the concession stand. She tells me to order whatever I want, but when I only order a hot dog and a Sprite, she scoffs and prompts, "And what as your side?"

"Um, nachos?" I ask.

She nods. "And what for dessert?"

"Uh...chocolate-covered almonds?"

"Good girl," she says, and then turns her expectant gaze on the acne-covered teenaged boy behind the register.

After she orders everything under the sun, they have to put all our candy in a large popcorn bag and balance our food and drinks in carriers. I'm so glad I didn't attempt to wear heels, because I know for a fact I would have bit it, falling flat on my ass and ended up covered in relish and nacho cheese. That would've smelled lovely.

When we find two seats together in the stadium-style rows of cushioned chairs, I carefully lower my ass into one and maneuver our drinks into the cup holders in the armrests. We distribute all our goodies between the two of us and settle in for the movie.

"Thanks for suggesting this, Kayla. This has been a lot of fun, and we haven't even watched the movie yet," she says with a grin.

"Thank you for all the food and for coming with me. My mom and I go to our dollar theater all the time back home, probably about once every two weeks. Thanks for filling in for her. I miss her like crazy."

"I think of it this way. If Jason were going to a semester of school in another state, and he made a friend, I would want the friend's family to take him in and take care of him like he was their own. It's a pretty scary adventure you're on, having never lived anywhere but the town you grew up in. It would be the same for Jason. When we adopted him—"

"Wait, Jason's adopted?" I interrupt her, surprised.

"Well, yes, sweetie. Didn't you notice he looks nothing like me or Steve?" she asks with a little smile.

"I guess I never really paid attention. I could've chalked it up to him getting his dark features from grandparents maybe? But now that you mention it, no, he looks nothing like you," I say with a giggle.

"Steve and I tried for seventeen years to have a baby. We did every treatment under the sun, and never once even conceived. So then, we decided to adopt. Jason's biological mother was a sixteen-year-old girl in Beaumont, Texas. Basically, when he was born, he came out of her and was placed in my arms. We brought him home to the house we still live in now. So if he were to go off to college somewhere, he'd be in the same position you are, trying to make all new friends in a place you don't know. When I realized you would be coming around often, instead of just the once or twice like the floozies before you, I told myself I'd stand in for your momma, because I'd want the same for my Jason. So if you need anything, anything at all, you just let me know," she finishes with a nod.

I wrap my arm around the tiny woman and squeeze, saying lowly, "Thank you, Mrs. Robichaux." I don't have time to ask about the 'floozies', because the lights go down in the theater and the previews start, but I can't help but feel warm inside over what Jason's wonderful mother had told me.

CHAPTER Fifteen

February 18, 2005

"*Constantine* came out today," I say excitedly, jumping up and down and clapping my hands. Jason looks up at me from where he's sitting at the patio table, smoking his cigarette and looking perfectly broody in his black t-shirt and dark-wash jeans. I don't know how he can stand being in short sleeves right now. It's super chilly today, and I've got on a hot pink hoodie with my flared jeans. I stop my hopping and pout my bottom lip, asking, "Please, please, please? It looks soooo good. Let's go see it. We play pool all the damn time. Let's do something I want to do for once." I barely contain the urge to stomp my foot like a toddler, but it's true. Any time I make a suggestion to do anything, it's always shot down, outvoted by all the dumb boys.

Mrs. Robichaux leans forward in her chair to grab her scissors from the table to clip the thread she's using to sew a button back on Steve's shirt. I see her nod before she tells the guys sitting at the table, "Y'all should be ashamed of yourselves. Here this sweet girl is in this big city she's never explored before, and y'all make her go to the same old pool hall nearly every night. Why don't you take her around to see some stuff? I bet she'd love Kemah Boardwalk."

I narrow my eyes when I see Gavin start to shake his head, but then Jason cuts in and says, "Fine. This is your night then. Pick three things you want to do and we'll do it all tonight, but don't expect this to happen again anytime soon."

I ignore his grouchiness and focus on what he's agreeing to. I get to choose what we do tonight! Oh, my gosh, what to pick? I think for a minute, and then say, "Okay, I'm dying to see *Constantine*, so let's see that first. And then I want to go to Kemah...but I don't know what to do after that. Can I reserve the last thing for if I spot something during the evening?"

"Sure, why not. I guess I better go get ready," Jason says, sighing heavily before standing and making his way around the table. He stops and leans down over his mom to kiss the top of her head and then goes inside.

Gavin doesn't look happy. Apparently, he doesn't like a change in routine, but I'm sure he'll get over it. The movie looks freaking awesome. Adam, who hasn't said a word, as usual, looks like he couldn't care less what we do. He just goes with the flow, seeming just to enjoy everyone's company.

A few minutes later, surprisingly fast for Jason who decided just to throw on a soft, thick wool button-down shirt on top of his t-shirt, Jason, Gavin, and I pile into the single cab truck, while Adam opts to just hop in the back. Jason reaches behind his head without looking and slides open the window, like it's a normal thing for his buddy to chill in the truck bed. When he sees my questioning look, he says simply with a shrug, "He likes to stretch out. Dude is like 6'3."

"Yeah, but won't he be cold?" I ask.

"Yo, man. You cold back there?" Jason asks.

"Nah, I'm good," Adam says, and Jason looks at me expectantly. I make a sound of acknowledgement and he starts the truck. He fumbles around with the radio for a bit, slapping Gavin's hand away when he tries to put it on a country station, and I grin at him in gratitude. He knows I hate country. He lands on my favorite top-forty station, and then backs out of his driveway.

"Seriously?" Gavin asks, looking over my head at Jason as Jessica Simpson's "With You" comes on, a look of horror on his face. He goes to change the song, but again, Jason slaps his hand away.

"Driver picks the music, dick," Jason tells him, and to my utter amazement, he starts humming the song. No, not humming...*meowing*. I can't control the laughter that bubbles out of me as his meowing grows louder, really getting into Jessica's song. I'm actually impressed he keeps a straight face as he hits all the high notes; even Gavin shakes with silent laughter beside me. I grimace when his voice cracks as he tries to meow the note she holds near the end of the song, but it's so hilarious I have to cover my face I'm laughing so hard. You've heard of an ugly cry; well, on the other end of that scale is an ugly laugh, where you lose all sense of how red your face is, how large your nostrils are flaring, and you can see every molar in the back of your mouth as tears slide down your cheeks. I'm there. I'm at my ugly-laugh point. No sound is even coming out anymore as I try to stop laughing in order to catch my breath.

It hurts! Oh, God, it hurts so bad!

Next, Kelly Clarkson's "Since U Been Gone" comes on, and right on cue, Jason's meowing starts up again. I'm starting to panic from lack of oxygen, and I'm actually worried I might pee if he doesn't stop. How freakin' embarrassing would that be? Oh, my God, how mortifying it would be if I peed myself laughing in his truck, his 'baby'. I have to calm down. I try to block out Jason's caterwauling, taking deep breaths in through my nose and out through my mouth, and when he sees me reach down and physically hold my crotch to keep from making a mess out of myself because of his antics, he does something I've only seen him do on one or two other occasions: he throws back his head and bellows with laughter.

I glare at him through my smile, trying to admonish him for laughing at me, but my attempt is weak, not able to put any real sting behind my look because hearing his reaction makes me glow. It's *me* who made him laugh that hard. Yes, it was because of something super embarrassing—damn my mom for blessing me with her weak bladder control—but it's me who got him to give up that hard exterior for a few minutes. "Shut up," I growl, punching him on the arm, then shaking out my hand after a couple of my knuckles crack on contact with his rock-hard bicep.

"Please don't pee on my new seats," he teases.

"As my mom would say, 'You made me laugh so hard, tears ran down my legs!'"

He chuckles, and by the time we reach the movie theater, I've thankfully regained control of my bodily functions.

After getting our tickets and concessions, we're still a little early, so we're able to get some good seats together. Gavin heads the line, I'm right behind him, Jason follows me, and Adam brings up the rear. Each of us holding a drink in one hand, and candy or popcorn in the other, we sit our butts at the edge of the folded seats, lean back and lift our feet off the floor, and then plop down when they unfold. No matter how old I get, that never gets old, and it looks like I'm not the only one who does it.

We each try to guess the answers of the movie trivia questions on the big screen in front of us, filling the time before the movie starts, and as I get every question right, the boys have different reactions. Gavin starts to get huffy, acting upset when he doesn't get the answers right, and Jason looks impressed. Even Adam leans forward to look around Jason to ask me, "How do you know all this stuff?"

"Well, one, I have an addiction to celebrity gossip, and two, you know how I told y'all I rate the books I read and write reviews? Well, I come by that hobby honestly. My dad has done the same thing with movies since before I was born.

He has notebook upon notebook of movie titles with one-to-five little dots beside them, which are his ratings, one being poor, and five being outstanding. The man gets the Los Angeles newspaper at the beginning of every year and goes through the section that tells about all the movies coming out for the entire year, decides which ones he'll see and which ones he'll 'waste', and then keeps track of all of it. He sees like 3 movies a week. If you want to know how good a movie is before you go see it, you ask him. He could be one of those movie critic dudes on TV," I tell them.

The next question pops up on the screen, and before the multiple choice comes up, I call out the answer. Jason and Adam both chuckle, and Gavin sulks, deciding his hot dog is more fun than playing movie trivia with me. I evil laugh on the inside, thoroughly enjoying having a night to do what I like doing. *My, how the tables have turned.* Instead of me being the clueless one, trying to learn how to play cards or play pool, feeling like the lost puppy tagging along with them, I'm finally in my element, having fun using my brain full of useless information.

A little while later, the previews finally start. I grin as Jason reaches over and steals one of my chocolate-covered almonds, and then bite my lip as he tilts his bag of buttery popcorn in my direction. I take a few pieces, and feel his eyes on me as I lift my hand to my mouth, eating them and then licking the butter from my fingers. I try to be as natural about it as possible, knowing I'll look completely stupid if I try to do it all sexy-like. I pretend I don't know he's watching me as I pour one of my candies into my hand and then toss it into my mouth, mixing the salty of the popcorn with the sweet of the chocolate. I can't help but close my eyes and moan as the yummy goodness hits my taste buds.

I hear Jason clear his throat and then shift in his seat, and I smile lightly, opening my eyes to watch the opening scene of the movie I've been dying to see. Several things happen pretty soon into the film, making me gasp and look over at Jason each time to see if he noticed it too. First, the priest's necklace is the same trinity knot I have tattooed on my wrist. I grin widely at him and do a dorky little dance in my seat, pointing at my wrist to show him what I'm all excited about. He shakes his head at my giddiness, but I see the corners of his mouth tilting up slightly. Next, Keanu Reeves dramatically fights to pull his forearms together, putting two halves of a tattoo together to form a symbol that looks eerily similar to the crosshairs tattoo on Jason's left forearm. My jaw drops and I look over at him with wide eyes.

He sees my expression and furrows his brow before reaching his right hand over to pull up his left sleeve to look at his tattoo. When he looks at me again, he has a curious smile on his face, and I playfully grab his wrist to lift his hand, then give him a high-five. He shakes his head at me again, and then we settle back to watch more of the movie.

Ten more minutes into the film and all four of us are squirming in our seats. Constantine is a heavy smoker, lighting up every five minutes. Gavin leans over me to whisper to Jason, "Fuck, dude, this movie is killing me. I'm niccing like a motherfucker."

Jason frowns at him, holding his finger over his plump

lips in the international sign to shut the hell up. Gavin sits back with a huff, and his knee starts bouncing next to me. It's shaking my seat, so I reach over and press my hand to his leg, trying to get him to stop the movement. He stops for a few seconds, and when I remove my hand, it starts up again. I let out a heavy sigh and glare at him, and when he looks over at me, I move my eyes down to his knee, and then back up at his face, lifting my eyebrow at him.

He sits up abruptly, and then stands. I move my feet out of the way as he makes his way past our group, shuffling his large form sideways down the aisle, apparently heading for a smoke break not even a half-hour in.

The movie is fantastic. It's action-filled and sexy at times, and as we relax and really get into the plot, we unconsciously shift positions in our seats. Suddenly, Jason's leg is resting against mine, and even through both of our jeans, I feel the electricity of his touch. It drags all of my attention from the huge screen in front of me to the few inches of my thigh where his presses against it. I consciously reprimand myself for being so silly, letting the simple, innocent touch have such an effect on me, but I can't help it. It tingles there, making my skin feel hot, and I close my eyes so I can focus even more closely on it.

It's not until I feel Jason scoot back in his seat that I shake out of my dreamy state. I look up to find Gavin making his way back over to us before scooching past me and plopping down in his seat, noisily sighing and making a show of how happy he is he stole a nicotine fix.

When the movie ends, the four of us stand with the rest of

the crowd, and the second we hit the exit door, we all reach for our packs of cigarettes, and we laugh when we see several others doing the same thing. When they notice, everyone makes comments about how hellish that movie was to sit through for smokers. Too bad real life isn't like the end of the film, when the Devil reaches into Constantine's lungs and pulls out all the tar and lung disease.

We get into Jason's truck, and I'm both disappointed and grateful I'm not serenaded by his meowing skills. It's not too long before we are crossing over a tall bridge, and in the near distance, I see the lights of Kemah Boardwalk. I glance around and see the marina holding hundreds of both speedboats and sailboats, and I dance in my seat as the amusement park rides come into view. There are tons of restaurants to choose from, along with smaller concessions, like the ice cream parlor and the candy shop. I tell the guys I'm hungry, and they all grunt in agreement.

After parking and walking toward the middle of the boardwalk, we head to the Aquarium Restaurant. As we're seated and given menus, I discover it's pretty expensive, but what catches my eye is under the appetizers. I order the crab wontons with the mango sauce, and then watch the colorful fish swim around the giant aquarium in the center of the restaurant as the guys order their food.

When our dinners come, they are like works of art, and I can't wait to dig into mine. Jason's leans over to me, exaggeratedly looking at my plate, then at me, and then back at my plate. I smile and ask, "Would you like to try one of my wontons?"

He shrugs and replies, "If you insist," making me laugh as he holds his plate out to me.

"Do you want some sauce on it?" I ask.

"Fuck yeah, I want the sauce," he scoffs, and I grin as I dip the wonton into mango drizzle before placing it next to his fried catfish.

Having ordered cream cheese puffs from Chinese restaurants, I know the contents inside the folded, crispy outer shell is blazing hot, so I gently pull the pocket apart, allowing steam to come out. I take one half and dab it into the sauce before lifting it to my mouth to blow on it for a few seconds, and then take my first bite. Heaven. "Oh my gawwwwd, it's so freakin' good," I moan.

I look up and see Jason hiding a smile, and then glance at Gavin, who is currently devouring his seafood pasta like someone is going to steal it from him. Adam takes his time cutting up his steak, and I remember he's allergic to seafood, having had a hamburger during the crawfish boil we had at the Robichauxs' a couple weekends ago.

After Jason finishes off his catfish, I watch as he tries the wonton I shared with him. He bites into it, having let it cool off first, and I see him nod and furrow his brows. "Good, right?" I ask.

"Hell yeah. My favorite food in the world is crab," he tells me.

"Really? Me too! My mom and I once finished off like ten pounds of snow crab legs at an all-you-can-eat buffet in Myrtle Beach," I say with a giggle.

"I don't get them very often because my family and these

fuckers don't care for crab," he states, using his fork to point at his friends, "but when I do, I put 'em away, too."

Gavin replies by taking a long drink of his beer and then letting out a giant belch, making the patrons at the table next to us look over and glare at him. I shake my head and look down at my plate in disgust. What the hell was I thinking ever dating this guy? Desperation is a terrible thing. I vow right then and there to never date a guy just because I'm lonely ever again. It's a vow I'm pretty sure I'll break, but I make it nevertheless.

I want to leave room for some fudge from the candy shop, so I ask Jason if he wants my last wonton. He grabs it and swirls it through the remaining mango drizzle on my plate before popping it into his mouth, using the napkin that was lying across his lap to wipe his lips. I've eaten out with Jason a couple times now, and I'm always impressed with how good his table manners are. I've asked him about it before, and he told me his parents taught him early on everything from the proper way to set a table to how full to pour wine into a glass. They have special dinners with important people quite often because of his mom's status at NASA, and not to mention, the people from his dad's impressive career at a chemical plant.

After paying our separate checks, we make our way out of the restaurant and up the stairs to the little shops along the boardwalk. We find a table to sit at for a while to enjoy an after-dinner cigarette, and then I tell them to wait for me while I run into the candy store. I buy myself a brick of walnut fudge, and then hurry back to the table outside.

"Okay, now what do you want to do?" Jason asks me.

"Let's go over to the rides," I say excitedly.

"All right," he replies, and we all walk back down the stairs, and stroll to the other side of the boardwalk, walking along the water so we can see the small boats leave the marina for some night fishing. When we finally reach the amusement park, I'm nearly jumping out my skin with giddiness. I love going on rides. My whole family is addicted to rollercoasters and adrenaline-pumping rides. There are hardly any amusement parks left in the United States that we haven't visited, some several times over. I've lost count of how many times I've been to Carowinds in Charlotte, NC.

"Oh, my gosh, let's go on that one!" I gasp, looking up at a spinning one. It looks like the riders lay on their stomachs, making it seem like you are flying like Superman.

I look around trying to see where to buy tickets, when I hear Gavin say, "Fuck no."

I spin around and look at him, seeing he's shaking his head while pulling out his pack of cigarettes. "What?" I ask.

"I said fuck no. I ain't getting on any rides. One, we just ate and I'll barf, and two, I don't do rides," he tells me.

"Come on, please?" I beg, looking over at Adam.

"I'm with Gavin, girl. I'll throw up if I get on that spinning deathtrap. I'm sorry," Adam says.

I slump forward, heartbroken. The whole reason I wanted to come to Kemah was to go on some of the rides. There's no way I'm going to be the dork who goes by herself. How lame would that be? It wouldn't even be fun getting all strapped in and riding it alone. A huge part of the fun is sharing the adventure with another person. I admit defeat and walk toward the exit.

"I'll do it with you," I hear called behind me.

I stop, turning slowly on my heel with a look of surprised confusion on my face. "Huh?"

"I'll go on the ride with you, but we have to go buy tickets first," Jason says, and he points to his left toward a booth with a big sign above it with ticket prices listed.

"Really?" I squeal, unable to contain my shocked excitement.

"Yeah, but just the one. You sure that's the one you want to ride?" he asks.

I spin around in a circle and make sure it's the winner, and when I see it's the only one I've never ridden at any other amusement park, I answer, "I'm sure," and then skip ahead of him to the ticket booth. After purchasing one ride apiece, we go and get in line. I don't have a clue, nor do I care where Gavin and Adam have gone. All I know is at this moment, I wouldn't want to be anywhere else. What could be better than doing one of my favorite past times with a guy I'm crushing on?

But it's so much more than a crush.

Shhh, don't ruin this moment with all the brain activity.

Okay, but don't say I didn't warn you.

Duly noted.

My heart is racing as we wait our turn. It's not a scary ride, so I know my heart rate has everything to do with the handsome man standing beside me. I don't know what to say to him; I want to break the quiet tension, but have no idea how. Thankfully, he puts me out of my misery. "I haven't been on an amusement park ride in years. Not since I went to Astroworld a couple years ago."

"Oh! I love Astroworld! My brother Tony took me there. He made me get on the Dungeon Drop...twice. That's the one ride I can't stand. I will ride any rollercoaster you can put me on, but I hate the droppy ones. There's this one at Islands of Adventure in Orlando called Dr. Doom's Fear Fall, and instead of taking you up slowly and just dropping you, like the Dungeon Drop, it shoots you up fast and bounces you down. I like that one better," I ramble.

"I'm not big into rides," he admits.

"Then why are you doing this one?" I ask, confused.

"You wanted to do it. I promised tonight was your night, and you looked so bummed when they wouldn't come on here with you, so I told you I'd do it. No big," he says with a shrug, and we step forward in the line, slowly making our way to the front.

I don't say anything for a few minutes, absorbing what Jason said. I look around at all the bright, flashing lights of the swings, the ship that goes back and forth until it finally flips over, the Rock-n-Roll Express with its loud music blasting as it slows to a stop and then starts going backward, and hear the clinking sound of the rollercoaster car as it makes its way up to the top of the wooden hill. I smell the potent aroma of funnel cake and popcorn, and I look up above us as the ride full of people fly above us, squealing and laughing as they go round and round on the big, metal machine. I don't really understand why he wouldn't enjoy this, but the fact he doesn't and yet is still willing to do it, just because I want to, makes me all squishy inside.

On a whim, I turn to face him and wrap my arms around him, giving him a spontaneous hug. "Thank you for doing this. Not only the ride, but this whole night. I've had a blast, and it's all thanks to you," I tell him.

"You're welcome," he says into my hair and rubs my back. "Plus, I felt like I owed you. That was really thoughtful of you to have a girls' night out with my mom. None of the girls any of us have dated, or even the female friends we've had for years have ever done that before."

I smile into his chest, and then only let go because the ride ends and it's our turn to get on. I skip over to an empty slot and try to figure out how to mount it. One of the workers makes his way over to us and tells us to slide up onto the padded bench on our stomachs next to each other. After lining us up, having us spread our legs a little, he lowers a padded bar and locks us in place. There is a joystick-looking thing between where our two bodies rest on our elbows. The worker tells us that after the ride rises to its full-height, we can use the shifter to make us fly high or low, and then leaves us to lock in the next set of people.

Jason immediately grabs onto the shifter. "Hey! Why do you get to control the joystick?" I ask playfully.

"I'm the man, goddamn it," he says, thickening his Texan drawl, and I giggle.

"All right. I guess since you're only here to make me happy, I'll let you play with the stick," I tease.

"I've got a stick you can play with," he says, and when I

look up at him in shock, I see he's just as surprised he let that slip out as I am. I burst out laughing as he pulls his lips in between his teeth, shaking his head. "Was that my outside voice?" he asks.

"Yup," I reply, popping the p, and before either one of us has a chance to say anything else, the ride jolts into motion.

From the ground, the ride looked fun, but not that wild. But from up here, locked into this position, it's a lot more exhilarating, feeling just like we're flying. As we rise to the very top of the structure, we see the people ahead of us start to tilt up and then down, and Jason begins to move the shifter, which makes us dip and then rise again, causing it to take my stomach. I squeal when he makes us dip again, and reach out to put my hand around his on the joystick, flying us upward once more.

The ride ends way too soon, and I'm sad when it's time to get off, not only because I was having so much fun, but because I don't want my alone time with Jason to end. We find the guys at a table, Gavin carrying on and pointing at a group of girls in Daisy Duke shorts and fur-covered boots, who look absolutely ridiculous because it's only about fifty degrees out. I stick my hands into the pockets of my hot pink hoodie and roll my eyes.

I have to admit I'm partly jealous they have the balls to wear the shorts at all. I only own a few pairs myself, opting only to wear them at home alone or get-togethers with just my family. Growing up being picked on for having toothpicks for legs will do that to a girl. Sure, it can get pretty miserable during the heat of summer, but it's better than having to deal with assholes in parking lots yelling out of their car windows at me to 'Eat a cheeseburger' while I make my way into the grocery store. Yep, that happened.

"Y'all ready to go?" Jason asks, pulling out a fresh pack of cigarettes from the front pocket of his dark burgundy wool shirt and starts hitting the top into the palm of his hand. I've seen his routine a million times now, and I say the steps in my head as he completes it.

Hit the pack in his hand ten times, then spin it around. Repeat.

Unwrap the cellophane from around the top half of the pack, ball it up, stick it in his jeans pocket.

Lift lid, and tear out the silver paper. Ball it up, stick it in the same pocket.

Take out one of the front cigarettes, flip it over, and slide it back into the pack upside-down. His 'lucky' that he'll smoke last.

Pull out another cigarette, close up the pack, stick it back into the front pocket of his shirt, and then light up.

It's probably weird I notice these different things he does, but during one of our twenty-question games, he admitted he's OCD about certain things. He has an obsession with numbers, adding, multiplying, and formulating problems in his head to calm himself down if something is bothering him. He's also super anal about symmetry. If something is off by even a couple millimeters, he can spot it. The dude doesn't even need a measuring tape. He can tell you how big something is in inches just by eyeballing it.

And then there are these routines. The cigarettes were the

first one I noticed, but he has a few more, like the steps he takes drinking a bottle of beer versus a mixed drink. After popping the top off a bottle, he can't just hold the beer in his hand; he takes a swig, and places it on the table, before picking it back up for another drink. If it's a mixed drink, he keeps the skinny straw it's served with in the glass, but doesn't actually drink through it. He uses it to stir the liquid, then bends it over the side of the glass and holds it pressed between the tumbler and his fingers. I'm sure there are endless routines he has, and I absently wonder if there is one he uses to get ready, which is probably what takes him so long before we go somewhere.

By the time I'm even conscious we're moving, we're already at Jason's truck. Back on the highway, we pass an oncoming car that has one headlight out, and out of habit, I yell, "Padiddle!" causing Jason to turn and look at me strangely. I laugh and say, "Sorry, it's a game from back home."

"What's the game?" he asks curiously.

"Well, whenever you see a car with only one headlight, you call out 'padiddle', and the first person to get three gets owed an article of clothing. So like, if I got three in a row, you'd have to take off your shirt...or something," I say the last part quietly, realizing what I'm telling him.

He chuckles and asks, "Is this one of your weird North Carolina things, like how you make a wish every time the clock either hits 11:11, or 12:34. Next thing you know, it'll be, 'Oh, look, a stop sign! Make a wish' or 'Hey! It's a Starbucks! Give me your pants'."."

I elbow him in the ribs and he grunts, making me laugh as he rubs the spot I hit like it actually hurt. "Shut up. You pick on me all the time for being from NC. First the way I say pecan, then you called me a Yankee...oh, and don't forget when your dad was raking and I called it pine straw. It *is* pine straw!" I complain.

"No, it's pine needles...Yankee," he adds.

"Ugh! It's pine needles when it's still attached to the tree, and pine straw when it falls off. And again, North Carolina is below the Mason Dixon line. I am not a damn Yankee," I growl.

"Whatever you say...Yankee."

CHAPTER Sixteen

Pulling into Jason's driveway, Gavin hops out and immediately walks over to his truck. "See y'all later. I'm beat," he claims before sliding himself into his driver's seat. With a short wave out of his lowered window, he backs out of the driveway and then heads home. *Ooookay,* he's never left without at least trying to get me to come home with him before, but I'm glad he didn't. I wouldn't want him to taint the amazing night I've had.

Adam climbs out of the back of Jason's truck and walks over to us to do the normal bro-shake with him and to give me a light one-armed hug before telling us goodnight and getting in his own vehicle and going home. Jason looks down at me, the automatic floodlights attached to his house at his back casting shadows across his face. He looks expectant, like he's waiting for me to say or do something, but I don't know what.

"Well?" he prompts.

I feel a swarm of butterflies take flight in my belly. What does he want? If I did what I really wanted, I'd freakin' pounce on him right here in the cold driveway, but I don't think that's what he's asking for. *In my dreams.* "Well what?" I ask with a nervous smile.

"I told you to pick three things you wanted to do tonight, and you reserved one. We've only done two, the movie and Kemah. So what's you're third pick?" he asks.

"Seriously? I thought I forfeited that last pick when you agreed to get on the ride with me," I say with a grin.

"Nope, that counted as part of number two, Kemah. You can choose one last thing to do tonight," he tells me.

"I can't just save it for another day?"

"Uh-uh. Told ya, babe. Tonight is your night. You gotta use it or lose it," he says with a shrug.

I laugh lightly, then try to think of something to do. I pull out my cellphone and check the time. It's a little past 10pm. It's too late to go see any type of attractions; I don't really want to go play pool; I know he won't go to a dance club, and I certainly don't want to go to another strip club. *Hmmm, what to choose, what to choose...*

"Ummm...want to go to Walmart?" I ask him.

He cocks his head to the side and furrows his brows. "You can choose anywhere you want to go in the greater Houston area, and you choose Walmart? If I was a genie, that's what you'd pick as your third wish?"

"I'm not going to ask to go where I *really* want to go," I say mysteriously, thinking 'Your bed', "but Walmart is fun late at night. You go and there's hardly anyone there, and you can just look at all the stupid shit you never have time to look at during the day. The rule is though, you gotta set a budget before you even walk into the store. If you don't, it's hard to leave there without spending at least a hundred bucks."

"Well, where is it you *really* want to go? I told you I'd take you anywhere," he replies.

I can't exactly say 'Poundtown', knowing one, he still thinks Gavin has some kind of claim on me, and two, I'm not his type and don't want to make it awkward between us by making him turn me down flat. So instead, I sing-song, "I'll never tell," while turning on my heel and making my way back over to the passenger side of his truck. I close the door behind me and see him shaking his head, still standing in the beaming floodlight. Eventually, he gets back in and we go just outside his neighborhood to the closest Walmart.

"Okay, what's our budget?" I ask as we walk through the parking lot toward the sliding glass doors of the supercenter.

"How about $30 a piece?" he prompts, and I smile over the fact he's joining me in my dumb little shopping game.

"$30 is doable. I just got paid, so let's do this," I say, all pumped to spend money on shit I don't really need.

We walk up and down aisles I've never even seen before, mostly because they're in a section I've deemed the 'man-zone'. It's that dark and mysterious place in the back of the store hidden behind a fortress wall of black rubber tires and fishing poles. I see him pick up random tools before setting them back down, moving on to the next object I have no idea what it's used for. He ends up holding onto a new stick shift knob in the shape of a red-eyed silver skull as we make our way to the entertainment department.

We stroll through the DVD aisle before coming to the end, where there's a giant bin of $5 movies. We spend a good fifteen minutes shuffling through the plastic boxes, making comments about them and asking each other if we've seen this one or what we thought about that one. Finally, he picks up one and excitedly says, "No shit! I've been wanting this one forever!"

"What is it?" I ask curiously, walking around to the other side of the bin, where he's holding up the DVD package and reading the back. I bend down around him to see the front. "*Boondock Saints*? Never heard of it."

"You've never seen *Boondock Saints*? Holy shit, one of my all-time favorites. It's a classic," he claims.

I take the box from him and read it came out just six years before, and the critics proclaimed it a 'cult-phenomenon'. "I don't think you can really call it a *classic*, but it looks interesting enough," I tell him.

"Oh, it's a fucking classic. It's badass and I'll probably watch it until the damn DVD player breaks, so it's a classic," he says with conviction, and I giggle at how elated he is over his find.

"If you say so."

"You'll just have to watch it with me and see for yourself," he says, setting off the butterflies that had finally calmed down after the conversation in his driveway.

"I'd love to," I reply quietly, and start heading toward the grocery section.

I end up coming way under budget, only leaving with two extra-large dark chocolate candy bars—one for me and one for Mr. Robichaux, who I found out loves them just about as much as I do—a milk chocolate one for Jason's mom, and I pick out a giant bottle of the sparkling Moscato wine she got me hooked on, which Jason has to buy for me. I trade him for his movie, that way we're even when we check out.

We get back in his truck with all our goodies and he drives the short distance to his house. We decide to enjoy the rest of the night by pigging out on the junk food he picked out, drinking the wine, and watching his beloved movie. By now, it's close to midnight, but I don't have to worry about letting Mark know I won't be coming home tonight, because he and Kim went to visit her parents on the east coast for the weekend.

When we enter his kitchen from the garage door, we set down our bags in the middle of the dining table and unpack everything, setting up for our vegging. I don't bother with a wine glass, instead opting for one of their large, thick plastic cups, which I fill nearly to the brim. He uses a knife to open the giant plastic tray of cold cuts, cheese, crackers, and grapes, and then grabs a beer from the back fridge. He balances the tray in one hand and carries his Shiner in the other.

After arranging two of the candy bars on the kitchen counter along with a sticky note telling the Robichauxs they are for them from me, I grab the plastic bag containing the DVD, French onion dip, and potato chips, my cup of wine, and my chocolate bar, and follow Jason out of the room. I assumed we were going to watch the movie in the living room like we usually do, but he continues walking, leading me down the hallway to his bedroom.

My heart begins to pound. Sure, I've been in here before, me and the guys hanging out and watching TV back here if Mr.

Robichaux was watching something different in the living room, but I have never been in Jason's room alone with Jason. He flips on his light and toes off his boots before plopping down in the middle of the bed. I watch nervously as he sets his beer on his nightstand and then places the party tray of snacks in front of him, at the foot of the bed. He looks up at me and asks, "You gonna stand there all night, or are we going to get this party started?"

A quick, painful-sounding laugh escapes me as I think, *Oh, there's a party in my pants right now*, before I finally propel myself forward. I sit my wine next to his beer and then begin emptying the bag. I hand him the DVD to wrestle open while I tear open the bag of potato chips. I pull the lid off the dip and then remove the clear film from the tub and place it in the center of the tray of snacks. I make my way around the bed and carefully get on, being sure not to knock over any of the goodies in front of me as he stands back up to put the movie into the player.

All set up for our veg-fest, I can't help but smile a secret smile, thinking about how I got my third wish after all.

We ate, drank, and ate some more, until all that was left was a few broken chips in the bottom of the bag. We got up a couple of times, pausing the movie for smoke breaks and to refill our drinks, but when the food was all gone and I was happily full and buzzed, I laid back on his pillow to watch the rest of the movie while he laid on his stomach, facing the screen. I teased him that his feet stunk, and he immediately got up and changed his socks, plopping back down on the bed and assuming the same position. The last thing I was conscious of was a sexy Irish accent saying, "Get your fucking rope," before I passed right out, the scent of Jason's intoxicating cologne surrounding me.

I'm stirred out of my delicious dream as I'm lifted into strong arms and held close to a hard body. I'm aware of being carried down a dark hall before being placed on the comfy couch in the living room. It's pitch dark, but he still manages to find a pillow to gently place under my head and a blanket to cover me with. I could still be dreaming, but it feels like he lingers for a while, running his fingers through my hair, tracing a line down the center of my eyebrows and over my nose, all before leaning over me to press a sweet kiss to my forehead, and then he's gone..

CHAPTER Seventeen

March 4, 2005

It's been a while since I took myself out on a date, so I wake up on Friday with a plan to go to back-to-back movies all day. I log onto Mark's computer, check out the times, and come up with a schedule. First, I'll watch *The Pacifier*, because duh, Vin Diesel, and then I'll see *Cursed* and *Boogeyman*, because I like to scare the crap out of myself, only God knows why. They are all playing at the dollar theater down on the south end of town, so maybe afterwards, the guys will want to do something.

As always, I jam out in my little blue Malibu the entire drive there, but as I'm leaning forward, looking to the left to wait my turn to hop out into traffic from the NASA Road 1 exit, I'm suddenly jarred forward, hitting my face on the steering wheel. A loud gasp leaves me, and I look up into the rearview mirror, seeing I've been rear-ended by someone in an SUV. *What the fuck?* It's lunchtime, a busy part of the day, so I'd been stopped at the top of the exit ramp for a few minutes waiting for a break in traffic. So had the cars behind me. The person behind me had straight-up rammed me for no reason!

I rub my cheekbone where my face hit the wheel, and reach across myself with the other hand to put my car in park. I glance in the mirror again to see a skinny, middle-aged brunette coming toward me from the open driver's side door of the SUV. She has her cellphone to her ear, and when I open my own door, I hear she's obviously reporting the accident to the police. After giving them the location, she hangs up and immediately starts gushing.

"I am so sorry! I don't know what happened! I was waiting to get out into traffic, and for some reason thought you had gone. I pulled forward still looking left without looking straight ahead first. I feel like such an idiot! I'm so, so sorry!"

By this time, I'm shaking, the rush of adrenaline from being caught by such surprise wearing off. She looks at my face and a look of panic crosses over hers. "Oh, my God, you're hurt! Are you okay? What happened?"

I feel sorry for her; she's obviously embarrassed by her driving blunder, and also looks really upset for having hurt me, so the lingering bit of anger I felt for being rammed disintegrates and I try to console her. "I'm all right. My cheek hit the wheel. I think it'll just leave a little bruise, nothing major."

The police arrive, and it's then I turn to look at the back of my car. The entire rear is smashed to bits. I'm surprised the trunk is still closed because of the way the metal is bent; it looks like it would have popped right open. When the policeman gets off his motorcycle, he comes over and immediately asks if there is anyone hurt. He jots it down on his notepad when I tell him my cheek is just bruised, but there is no actual big injury, and then he begins asking questions about what happened.

I've never been in a wreck before; I don't really know what to do, so I'm grateful when he tells me he just needs my license and registration, and asks the same from the woman who'd hit me. He writes up the report, first asking me what had happened, and then after I am finished, I hear him ask the woman the same questions. It surprises me when she tells him a completely different story than she had told me when she first walked up to me after the accident. She tells the police officer someone was trying to make their way around her on the exit, so when she tried to pull forward to give them room, that's when she rear-ended me. It's clear there is no other person on the ramp beside us, because it is only a single vehicle wide lane, so he gives her the same unbelieving look I give her. He then tells me to get all of my stuff I need out of the car and to call someone to come pick me up. I see a couple of tow trucks are already sitting on the side of the road, waiting to pick up my car to take it where I want it to go.

Being on this side of town, I don't want to call my brother, who is at work at this time of day, so I call Gavin hoping he'll pick up, even though he is in class right now. But after a couple of calls go unanswered, I know I have to call the only other number I have in Friendswood—Jason's house phone. I mentally cross my fingers and pray his mom answers. I'm all jittery and freaked out at the moment, and could really do without Jason picking on me for getting in an accident, even if it was completely not my fault. Plus, I think adding all those butterflies to my already frayed nerves would not do well for my psyche at the moment.

After two rings though—just my luck—he answers, surprise lacing his voice over seeing my name on the caller ID. "Hello?"

"Oh, crap. Hey, Jason. Um...someone rear-ended me on NASA Road 1. Is there any way you can come pick me up?" I ask, cringing as I wait for him to laugh at me.

"Are you okay?" he asks gruffly, and I hear movement on his end of the line.

"Yes, I'm fine. I'm just stranded with no one else to come pick me up. Can you come?

"Yeah, I'll be there in ten minutes," he says reassuringly, and then asks with more force, "Are you sure you're okay?"

"I'm a little shaken up, and my cheek hurts because I hit it on my steering wheel, but other than that, I'm fine. It was just a little fender-bender," I tell him to pacify him, because he sounds genuinely worried.

"Okay, I'm on my way." And with that, he hangs up the phone and I wait with the police officer until he arrives. I'm

172

embarrassed as hell when I become aware of the rest of my surroundings. We are on an exit ramp from 45 South, and this road is a pretty busy one, leading to not only tons of restaurants, the movie theater I was headed to, and shopping centers, but it's also the main way to get to the Space Center. There's a line of cars behind us the length of the ramp, and I breathe a sigh of relief when I see another policeman has pulled up at the tail end to start directing drivers as they back out of the exit ramp and carefully reenter the highway.

When Jason squeals to a stop on the side of the road, gets out of his truck, and takes a look at the back of my car that is now sitting on the flatbed of the tow truck, I'm shocked when he turns toward me with a look of absolute fury.

The look on his face makes me take a step back as he storms toward me. His anger is coming off of him in waves, and I'm worried he might be upset he had to come pick me up, interrupting him from whatever he was busy doing at home, until he reaches for me, his left arm going around my waist, pulling me into his protective embrace while tilting my chin up with his other hand. He turns my face to the side so he can examine my hurt cheek closely, and I'm mesmerized as I stare at his dark brown eyes taking in what is probably now an ugly bruise. He lets go of my chin and traces his fingertips gently over my cheekbone, his touch sending sparks across my flesh, making me shiver against him. His face softens as he tucks my hair behind my ear and then looks into my eyes. I can't breathe. I'm...I'm wrapped up in Jason's strong arms, unable to speak, hell—think. All I'm conscious of is the man holding me; everything else has faded into nothingness.

His voice is soft as he says, "You're trembling."

I know it probably has more to do with his presence than anything else, but I tell him, "The wreck scared me, came out of nowhere." I don't even recognize my own voice. It comes out breathy, like an imitation of Marilyn Monroe telling JFK happy birthday.

My response seems to put the anger back into Jason's system though, because he turns, still keeping one arm around my waist as he faces the woman who rear-ended me, who is standing with the police officer near the other, empty tow truck. "What the hell happened?" he asks her loudly, startling her into explaining the story she'd fed the policeman. When she gets to the part about the person behind her trying to get around her, he calls her on what we all knew is a lie. "That's bullshit. There's not enough room for anybody to try to make their way around anyone else on this ramp. You tried to pull forward to give them room? You're a goddamn liar. How about we ask them right now?"

Jason lets go of me and starts to make his way to the lifted Silverado that is behind the woman's SUV. Not yet having its turn to navigate back down the exit, the truck still sits perfectly aligned in the narrow lane. Before Jason has time to even reach her SUV though, the woman yells out, "Wait!" and he halts his furious stride, turning back toward them.

"Okay, I didn't tell you the truth. I hit her when I wasn't paying attention. I was glancing back and forth between the traffic and my cell phone, and when I saw a break, I just gunned it, not looking forward before I went," she says, ashamed.

Jason storms back over to me, wrapping his arms around me once again. "Well, thank baby Jesus there was break in traffic then, because what if there was a car coming? You could have forced her in front of the oncoming vehicle! It might've smashed right into her side. All because you weren't fucking paying attention," he says heatedly, his rage almost palpable.

"Okay, sir, calm down," the officer says, and then directs the woman to talk to the tow truck driver about where to take her car after he gets it all rigged up. Her SUV isn't nearly as damaged as my car. There's just a little dent on her front bumper. When she moves to do what he said, the policeman walks up to Jason and me. "Wow, young man. Have you ever thought about joining the force? I could really use people like you to play 'bad cop' with these lying assholes," he jokes. Seeing Jason is still too riled up to find humor in the situation, he clears his throat and says to me, "If you're sure you're all right, sweetheart, you can just follow the tow truck to the shop your insurance adjuster said to send it to. When you get there, you'll have some paperwork to fill out, and according to your insurance plan, they'll let you know if you get a rental car or not."

"Thank you, sir," I tell him, and then look up at Jason. I gasp lightly when I see he's looking down at me, almost *through* me, trying to determine for himself if I'm truly okay or not. "I'm fine," I reassure him once again. "Can we go now?"

After he takes in a deep breath, clearly calming himself, he nods, putting his arm around my shoulders to guide me to his truck. He opens the passenger door and helps me up into the tall cab, closing it after he sees me buckle my seatbelt. I use the time it takes him to walk around the front of the truck to settle myself, flexing my fingers in my lap, arching my back as far as I can before relaxing into his bench seat. My heart is racing a mile a minute, and I know it has nothing to do with the car accident anymore, and everything to do with the man who just opened the driver's side door, sliding his muscular frame behind the wheel. I watch the sinew under the scorpion tattoo on his forearm work as he twists the key, starting the ignition.

We follow the tow truck to a collision center at a Chevy dealership about ten minutes away. The entire process takes about two hours, filling out paperwork, going through insurance policies, and all that jazz, but by the time everything is taken care of and it's time to leave my Malibu in their hands, I'm sitting pretty in a brand new 2005 burnt orange Nissan Murano, fully covered by insurance until my car is all fixed. I've never driven an SUV before, but this thing is *nice*.

Jason stands outside the driver's side, his corded muscular arms balancing him as he leans in the window to talk to me. "Well, you're all set. They said it should take about three weeks to get it fixed, so when they call you to come pick it up, you tell me and I'll come with you to make sure they didn't do a shit job."

"Yes, sir," I agree with a grin. "Hey, thanks for coming to

my rescue. What can I do to thank you?"

"It's all good. You don't have to thank me," he says, looking down at his booted feet as they shuffle the gravel of the parking lot.

"No, seriously. I want to do something for you. This has taken hours. Let me at least feed you. I'm starving," I insist.

"All right. I could really go for a hot dog," he tells me.

"For real? I'm treating you to grub and you choose a damn hot dog?" I raise an eyebrow at him.

"I fucking like hot dogs," he scoffs.

"Okay, okay...I'll meet you at James Coney Island off 45," I say, and he stands up, taps the top of the SUV, and I see him walk toward his truck.

CHAPTER Eighteen

March 12, 2005

I pull into Jason's driveway and wait in my rental car for Gavin to come out of the house. When I look up, he's coming from the backyard instead. He makes his way around the front of the vehicle to the passenger side, where he opens the door and sits inside next to me. He looks down to his lap, where he twists his gawdy gold nugget ring around his finger, looking like he's trying to find the right words to say.

After a few silent minutes without even him greeting me, I can't take the awkwardness anymore and finally ask, "What's up?"

"I don't think we should see each other anymore," he says with no emotion in his voice. I had a feeling coming over here this was what he wanted to tell me, but I'm curious...

"Okay, can I ask why?" A panicky feeling starts to slowly simmer inside my belly, along with a sudden sense of dread creeping up the back of neck.

"I just don't have feelings for you the way a guy dating a chick should. That, and I don't get the sense you feel that way about me either," he says honestly.

"When did you come to this conclusion?" I ask.

"I was just in the shop with the guys, and they asked me what I was doing with you. It made me realize that we aren't going anywhere; it's been fun and all, but I know you're not the person I'm supposed to be with, so what's the point?"

Since when does he and his friends talk about serious stuff like the girls they're dating? I have mixed feelings as I sit here wrapping my head around what's happening. I am not upset in the least about Gavin and me not casually seeing each other anymore. I'm just scared to death about what this could mean for the friendships I've made.

And, of course, not seeing Jason.

He picks that exact moment to verbalize what I was dreading would happen. "I don't think we can be friends. It would be too weird trying to be friends with a chick I've slept with. That's just a line that can't be erased once it's been crossed."

"Okaaaaay...well, that sucks, because I really love hanging out with you and the guys—"

"That's another thing," he cuts me off, more venom in his voice than I've ever heard there before. "I don't want you coming around here anymore. Adam, Jason, the

Robichauxs...they're all mine. They're *my* friends, and I let you come and spend time with them, but they're mine. So now that we aren't together, I don't want you coming to hang out."

With that, he opens the passenger door, gets out, slams it closed, and makes his way back from where he came around the side of the house. I stare in shock at the place where his retreating back disappeared, and slowly, achingly, a sob from the depths of my cracked-open heart comes bubbling out of me.

I don't know how long I sit there bawling my eyes out over being told I was to never see not only Jason again, but his family too, who I have grown remarkably attached to in such a short period of time. By the time I'm conscious of the fact I'm still sitting in my rental in the Robichauxs' driveway, my face is covered in tears and my shirtsleeves drenched in snot. It's not my most attractive or sanitary moment, I'm sure, but as I back out onto the street, a sense of rebellion washes over me. Who the hell does that Jack-off think he is, telling me my friends are "his" and I can't hang out with them anymore? Fuck him! When I pull out of Friendswood and onto 45 north, I am determined to keep Jason and his family in my life.

CHAPTER Nineteen

March 19th, 2005

I psyched myself up to call Jason's house phone, crossing my fingers this time that it *would* be him who answered. I haven't talked to any of them in a week, and I brace myself to be turned away. I mean, I would understand if he chose Gavin over me. They've been friends since their early high school years. If given an ultimatum of his best friend's friendship or hanging out with a chick he's only known for two months, well then it'd be silly of me to think he'd pick me.

The phone rings, and my heart stops when I hear his deep Texan drawl answer, "I was wondering if I'd ever hear from you again."

He sounds happy to hear from me, not like he's gearing up to tell me to never call him again. "Hey, um...well, your guard dog told me I wasn't allowed to come hang out with him or y'all anymore, so I kinda thought you wouldn't want me to."

"Wait, what?" Jason asks harshly.

"Uh...Gavin said I wasn't allowed to see y'all anymore. He said that you and your family belonged to him, and I wasn't to come around anymore," I say, surprised he didn't know about this.

"That motherfucker. I'll kill him. Kayla, of course you can come hang out with us. I mean, so there's no hostility, it'd probably be best to do it at times he won't be around, but you...you're one of my best friends. I love spending time with you. He has no say over who I can and cannot hang out with. Fuck him," he says heatedly. "When he came back to my dad's shop after talking to you in the driveway, he told us you'd thrown a fit and said you never wanted to see any of us ever again."

"What? Are you serious? He told me I wasn't the one for him and so there was no point in me coming around anymore. Then he got out of my car and stormed off. I was so stunned I didn't even say anything!"

God, I am so glad I called. Jason would have been left thinking I was some bitch who never wanted to see him again, and his family...*fuck!* "Jason, please tell me he didn't tell your parents the same thing. Oh, my God, your mom... please tell me he didn't tell her I did that!"

He shushes my panicking and tells me, "No, babe, I

haven't even seen him since that day, and my parents left on a cruise a couple days ago, so they have no idea what's been going on."

I could cry I'm so relieved. After how sweet, generous, and loving his family has been to me, it would kill me if they thought I would have pulled such a shitty move. "Oh, thank God."

"Hey, do you want to come over and watch a movie or something? I don't know about you, but I've been bored out of my mind not having to school you in pool and poker all week," he asks teasingly.

"Ass. I'll be there in an hour," I reply and hang up, jumping up from my bed, a surge of adrenaline making me dance around my room like a crazy person for a minute. I'm in the middle of shaking my ass in the mirror when I notice my appearance. Dear lawd, I look like a homeless person. My matted hair is sticking up in some places and glued to my scalp in others. I'm in my ratty pajama pants I've been living in for the past three days, and I'm pretty sure that smell is coming from me, not the turtle cage. I grab my phone and hit redial.

"You okay?" he answers, sounding worried.

I laugh, knowing he was probably thinking of when I called after my wreck. "I'm fine; I haven't even left yet. Make that closer to two hours. I look like something my bird pooped. I'm gonna take a shower and stuff before I head down. Okay?"

"Sounds good. That'll give me time then to figure us something out for dinner," he says.

"Awww, you gonna cook for me, home skillet?" I've had his cooking before. He's surprisingly really, *really* good at it.

"Yeah, I'll throw something together. Take your time. Don't get rear-ended." And with that, we hang up and I do pirouettes all the way to the bathroom, doing an arabesque as I bend over to turn on the faucets in the shower. Wow, I'm so giddy I've broken out my ten years of ballet skills I haven't used in about five. I better calm down or I'll probably hurt myself.

After showering, blow drying my hair, and putting on a little makeup to hide the fact I've been hiding in my cave for a week, I walk over to my closet to pick out what I want to wear. My new pink t-shirt, for sure, but as I pull out the Bui Yah Kah bag it's still sitting in, I see inside is also the pair of white linen shorts Kim bought me. She forced me to try them on in the store, and after she came into the dressing room with me—since I wouldn't come out—she said they were perfect and got them for me, even though I insisted I'd never wear them. She told me they would be in my closet 'just in case I realized I'd die from heat exhaustion in Texas if I tried to wear jeans in the summer'.

It's the beginning of March and it's already hitting the mid-eighties. We won't be leaving Jason's house, and it'll be just the two of us, and I don't think he'd ever pick on me for my skinny legs, seeing how he learned how self-conscious I am about them after one of our rounds of twenty-questions. He may be a broody ass, but he'd never purposely hurt my feelings, I don't think. Decision made, I pull out both the pink shirt and the white shorts, snap off the tags, and get dressed. After a few spritzes of my Lucky You perfume, I grab my purse, set the house alarm, and head out to my car.

Jason's garage door is open when I pull in, so I knock on the side door just inside it. I hear him yell, "It's open," and make my way into the kitchen. The vision before me stops me in my tracks. Jason, in a black wife beater and jeans, has a dishtowel thrown over his shoulder, and is steadily stirring a yellowish liquid inside a measuring cup. There are two different pots going on the stove, and I see the oven is on too.

"Hey, can you grab the salmon out of the oven please? I can't stop stirring or the hollandaise sauce won't turn out right."

"You know how to make hollandaise sauce?" I ask quietly, still not moving.

"Yeah. Woman, oven. Unless you want burnt fish, which even my sauce won't fix," he tells me, lifting his chin in the direction of the oven.

"I don't even know what hollandaise sauce is," I admit, setting my purse down on the kitchen table and grabbing the oven mitts. I pull the salmon out and see it's cooked to perfection...at least, it *looks* like it's cooked to perfection. I have no idea how to cook fish. It certainly smells good. It's topped with minced garlic and pepper, and the aromatic mixture is making my mouth water. I sit it on the silicon pot holder on the counter, and turn to see him trying to lift the lid off of one of the pots on the stove while still holding the whisk he was stirring with.

I walk over next to him and say, "Tell me what to do. I suck at cooking, but I can follow directions."

187

"The potatoes are done boiling. Just grab them off the heat and dump them in the colander in the sink for me," he says.

Still wearing the oven mitts, I do what he said, draining the potatoes and then putting them back into the pot. "Now what?"

"The butter and milk are in the fridge. Grab the hand mixer out from the cabinet under the microwave and mash the potatoes," he instructs.

I hesitate for a moment, but then get out the ingredients he said and the hand mixer, and after looking at the appliance like a foreign object for a few moments, I finally give up all pretenses. "So, yeah. Never made mashed potatoes before."

He looks up at me like I've grown a second head. "You've never made mashed potatoes? How can you be American? Like...never?"

"Nope. I've made the boxed kind that has handy dandy directions on the back, but never, like, *real* potatoes," I confess.

Apparently satisfied with the sauce, he sits it down next to the stove and pulls the dishtowel off his shoulder, using it to wipe his hands before walking over to where I stand holding the mixer away from me like it's going to bite me. He takes it out of my hand and pulls the drawer open next to my hip. He grabs the two metal doohickeys that stick into the machine and clicks them into place, looking up at me with an expectant look I suppose is him asking if I've got it. I nod, and then he takes a spoon from the same drawer before closing it.

He digs out two heaping scoops of butter, adding it to the pot of drained potatoes. Then he takes the jug of milk and adds enough that it comes about halfway up the white, boiled cubes. He pulls the salt down from the cabinet above our heads and sprinkles enough to lightly coat the top, and then plugs in the mixer. He watches me as he places the metal spinney things in the center of the potatoes, and then flips the switch on. It starts up, and I watch as the chunks turn into a perfectly whipped concoction I know is going to taste delicious. He flips the mixer off and then pushes the button that disconnects the potato-coated prongs from the plastic and hands them to me. He smiles when I lick it like cake batter, pointing toward the sink when I'm done tasting it. They are damn good.

I walk over to the sink and rinse them off before opening up the dishwasher and placing them in the utensils rack, and then rinse the colander while I'm at it, placing it in too and then close it up. I spin around to find Jason tasting a green bean over at the stove. I stroll over to him, and watch as he blows on a bean he pulls out of the pot with a fork, his lips pursing together to cool off the garlicky-smelling legume. Instead of eating it himself, he holds to the fork out to me, and I lean up to take it between my teeth.

It's the best freaking green bean I've ever had. I don't know if it's because Jason cooked and fed it to me, or if it's because it's just that good, probably a mix of the two. He turns off all the burners and tells me to grab two plates from the cabinet. When I bring them over to him, he moves around with masculine grace, filling our plates with mashed potatoes, green beans, and then a healthy slab of flaky fish. He sets the plates down at the dining table and asks what I want to drink. "Is there any wine?"

He gives me a look that asks, *Are you kidding?* before moving to the back fridge to pull out my pink Moscato, along with a bottle of beer for himself. I hurry to the cabinet to grab a wine glass, choosing to be classy for our nice dinner he's made instead of drinking from a plastic cup.

After the wine is poured, and the beer is opened, we settle in to enjoy this amazing looking food. Before he takes a bite, I stop him by placing my hand on his tattooed forearm. "Thank you for cooking for me. Sorry I'm worthless in the kitchen. I'm a microwave queen," I tell him.

"No problem. I love to cook, so it's no big thing," he replies with a crooked smile.

He picks up his fork and starts to dig into his fish, but I stop him once more when I ask, "Hey...where's that fancy holiday sauce you made?"

"Hollandaise...and good call. I woulda been pissed when I went to clean up and saw I forgot I took the time to make the real thing," he says, standing up to go grab the saucepan from beside the stove. He places it on a potholder in the middle of the table, and then spoons some out on top of his salmon.

"So what is this sauce?" I ask, looking at the thick, yellow concoction.

"It's basically a butter sauce. I guess they just wanted to give it a different name to make it sound fancy," he jokes.

"It's the shit. Try it."

Never one to turn down a new food, I spoon some out of the saucepan and put it on my plate instead of directly on my fish, just in case I don't like it. I don't know why I doubted him though, because as I dab a forkful of my flaky salmon into the sauce and place it in my mouth, I can't help the groan that leaves me, closing my eyes to better enjoy the flavor explosion in my mouth. "Sooooo good," I moan, and open my eyes to see Jason watching me with a smirk on his sexy face.

We eat our dinner in comfortable silence, finishing every morsel of the perfect meal before cleaning up the kitchen together, our movements like a choreographed dance as we wash pots, wipe surfaces and leave everything in the rack to dry.

I follow Jason out the back door after grabbing the cigarettes out of my purse, and it's not until I'm sitting down in one of the patio chairs, feeling the cool weatherproof fabric against the bare skin of my thighs that I remember I'm in shorts. The whole hour I've already been here, I had forgotten about my self-consciousness. Sure, I'm not what Jason goes for; I'm not what he finds beautiful, but around him, I'm comfortable in my own skin. Maybe it's a good thing I'm not what he finds attractive, because I know it doesn't matter. Nothing I can do will make me his type, so I don't have to worry about impressing him with the way I look; I can just be me.

"So what have you been up to this week?" he asks, lighting his cigarette and leaning back in his chair.

I don't want to sound like a total loser, admitting I've done absolutely nothing this week but go to school, work, and then home, so I embellish by saying, "I had a ton of papers and projects due at school this week, and they needed me to work some extra shifts at the dealership, so I've been pretty busy. What about you?"

"I haven't really done much of anything. I went and played in a 9-ball tournament a few nights ago, but that's about it," he says.

"How'd you do?" I ask.

"I did all right," he says, and in Jason-speak, that means he probably kicked ass. I smile at him knowingly. "So what movie do you want to watch?"

"Well, I fell asleep before the end of your Boondock Saints. You want to watch it again? You said you could watch it over and over," I remind him.

"Sure," he replies, putting his cigarette out in the ashtray and then standing to make his way over to the door. I take one last drag off of mine before snuffing it out and going inside.

About ten minutes into the movie, after having gotten comfortable on his bed, I feel a tension I just can't shake. I want to talk to him, but I can't find the courage to say what I need to get off my chest. Suddenly, I have an idea, and it may seem cowardly, but fuck it. I pull my cellphone out of my purse sitting on the floor beside his bed and type him out a message in the notepad. I would send it to him as a text, but one, I don't have his cell number, and two, I heard him tell Gavin his parents took texting off his plan after he racked up a $300 bill. I hand him my phone for him to read what I wrote, and then he erases it and types something back. We hand the phone back and forth between us, holding a silent conversation as the movie plays before us.

I'm glad you let me come over, even though Gavin said I wasn't allowed.

This is my house and my family, not his.

Can I tell you something?

No.

Asshole.

I hear him chuckle as he types.

Of course you can tell me something.

The only reason I kept dating him in the first place was so I could come hang out with you.

I know.

You know?! How did you know?

You didn't look at him the way you look at me.

Oh.

Can I tell you something?

I never tell you no.

True. When he was thinking about breaking it off with you, I only told him he should because I couldn't stand thinking he had any claim on you.

Really? But why?

I hear him take a deep breath and sigh before he types something out slowly and hands me back the phone.

He's not good enough for you. Shit...I'm not good enough for you. And I doubt I would think anyone in the world would be.

What are you talking about? I'm not even what you like. No matter how much I eat, I'm not going to get even close to what you go for. You saw those pics of my mom and the rest of my family. I'm stuck like this.

Babe, I don't go for big girls.

I almost break my neck as my head spins around to look at him after I read that last message. Which I read ten more times. He has a smirk on his face as he watches the TV, not even bothering to look at me.

What the hell do you mean you don't go for big girls? You've only brought around girls two, three times my size...your email address and screen name is NOMAX4ME! All the stories y'all have told me about you "going hogging"... ??????

It was all a joke. Well, not really a joke. It was a plan.

Plan for what? To be a freakin' asshole? To make me look stupid and you guys laugh at me behind my back?

No, babe. It was to make you not like me. But it apparently didn't work.

I don't understand.

Gavin always reeled in the girls with those fuckin blue eyes, but then the sec he opened his dumbass mouth, it would break whatever spell he'd have on them. That's when I'd swoop in and pick them up. I had to learn how to talk, learn some game, because I'm seemingly unapproachable. He'd keep whatever shallow chick would stick with him just for his looks, and I'd end up with the girl who fell for my game. Yeah, we're dicks, but it is what it is.

I think about what he's written me, letting it sink in for a little bit, but the whole "plan" thing isn't quite clicking.

So what does that have to do with you pretending to only like larger women?

I was trying to be a good friend. The last couple of girls Gavin really liked and brought around, they ended up blowing him off and gunning for me. I thought if I told you I only liked women of a certain size...which you definitely are NOT...then it would turn you off and you wouldn't even consider wanting me.

Wow, are you seriously so cocky you thought you had to put on chick repellant?

Hey now, don't forget. Who just confessed they only dated my friend so they could hang out with me?

He's got me there.

Whatever.

Can I tell you something?

No.

You can't tell me no. And even if you could, I'd tell you this anyways, even though I shouldn't. I came up with that plan before he even brought you over the first time, because he kept talking about you. Knowing Gavin can't keep a girl with his looks alone, I tried to make you hate me, or at least not do anything that might attract you away from him. But when y'all came over while I was fixing my truck and I laid eyes on you the first time, it turned into more than warding you off for my friend. I was trying to protect you too.

Protect me? From what?

From me. You were so beautiful and cute, and when you tripped in my driveway and dropped the F-bomb...I don't know. You affected me. I had never even met you before, and you affected me. You were this tiny little thing with a great big smile, and then the mother of all cuss words came out of that sexy mouth...it caught me off-guard. Especially because you screamed innocence. I was trying to protect you from me.

Jason, there's nothing you need to protect me from when it comes to you. You're amazing, and sweet, even if you do try to come off as a dick. You can pretend to be this big tough bad boy, but I see through it.

That's where you're wrong. You have it backwards. I am the bad guy. You just have a way of making me want to be...different.

I look over at him again, gazing at his profile as the lights from the TV play across his face. He's so incredibly sexy. I can tell he's aware I'm staring at him, taking in every one of his features, but he doesn't fidget or say anything; he just lets me have my fill, completely comfortable with being admired. This is confidence, much different than the cockiness he always likes to portray, and it turns me on that he doesn't try to distract me or interrupt my perusal. I could just stare at him for hours, at those amazing dark chocolate brown eyes surrounded by the thick, long eyelashes, or the perfectly shaped mouth I've been dying to kiss since the second I met him.

In the end, it's me who ends the game of chicken, breaking my view to take a deep breath, drawing on his confidence, trying to steal some for myself so I can type him out another message, something I'm scared to death to ask him. Fuck it.

I want you to try.

My hand is shaking as I place the phone in his, and my heart is pounding hard in my chest as I watch him look from the TV down to the cell, then his finger hit the button to close out the text. When he swings his legs over the side of the bed and stands, I'm confused, and then mortified as my eyes follow him as he leaves the room.

What have I done? Oh, my God, I shouldn't have told him that. Maybe I can lie. Maybe I can tell him I meant I want him to try to be the good guy I believe he is. I know it would never work though. He always knows when I'm lying, always knows when I'm hiding something. What do I do? Where did he go? Should I leave?

As all these questions run through my mind on repeat, I'm about to get out of the bed when Jason reenters his room, shutting his door behind him.

"Wh-what are you doing?" I stutter, suddenly very, very nervous.

"I went to make sure the house was locked up," he explains as he makes his way over to the other side of the room, reaching up to pull the string on the blinds to make them lower all the way to the bottom of the window.

"Oh, well...do you want me to go? Are you ready for bed? I know it's getting late, so I'll head home," I ramble, leaning over the side of the bed to find my shoes. I grab and line them up to stick my feet in them, but as soon as I stand up, Jason's only inches from me. I hadn't even heard him move from the window because my heart is beating so loudly. I gasp in surprise at seeing his dark features up so close, stumbling back a step.

He reaches his hand out to steady me, his tattooed bicep flexing with the movement. God, what I'd do to feel those arms wrapped around me.

"Say it."

His words startle me, and my eyes lift from his arm to his almost-black irises. "What?"

"Say it, babe. I read the words, and I know exactly what they mean, but I want to hear you say it," he says in that delicious drawl.

"I...I..." Jesus, I'm a nervous wreck. I can't make the words come out. It's a mix of embarrassment that it's never happened before, fear of him rejecting me or not being good enough for him, with a hint of excitement thrown in to add to the adrenaline pumping through my system at not only the proposition we've presented each other, but the fact his grip on me is burning my skin, setting the rest of me on fire.

"And not only do I want to hear you say it, I want to hear you beg."

CHAPTER
Twenty

My heart has never pounded so hard or fast in my life. I feel like I might hyperventilate. My breaths are coming in short, quick bursts, and I have to make a decision before I pass out from the fight or flight instinct taking over my body. Do I stay and fight my fear, suck up the anxiety and just put it all out there what I want him to do, facing it all head-on, or do I run? Stay and potentially embarrass the shit out of myself, or go back home and wonder what could have happened here tonight had I stayed?

I close my eyes for a moment, allowing the heat of his strong grip to soothe me, consciously taking a deep breath and letting it out slowly to calm my nerves enough to give him my response.

Opening my eyes and looking into his, my voice comes

out shaky but sure. "I want you. I want you to try to make me c-come." The last word is stuttered, but only from having to speak my wishes out loud, which I've never had to do before.

"You've said it now, but before you actually get it," he closes the space between us, making my entire body feel like it just went up in flames, "I'm gonna make you beg me to *let* you come. I won't just get you there; I'll make you have to hold it off until you plead."

His confidence is intoxicating. He seems to truly believe he can give me what no other man has been able to. He knows the truth. He knows that no guy has ever been able to make me orgasm. He's the only person I've ever told my secret to, and now that this is happening, he'll be paying close attention. He sees straight through my lies and embellishments. He'd know it in a heartbeat if I were to fake it. Plus, I've promised myself I never would again. Not only does he believe he can get me there, but he thinks he can control my body to listen to his demands. I want to believe him. I want to give myself over to his sureness and let him take care of me. He truly thinks he can do it, so by all means, I won't do anything to hinder him.

"Okay," I breathe, and as soon as the word is expelled from my lips, his are crashing down on mine with such force, it knocks me back a step, but then my prayer is answered, and those hard, sculpted, inked-up arms wrap all the way around me. I'm surrounded by him as he consumes me, those almost-femininely shaped lips feeling nothing but pure male as they work against mine, which open to him as he presses his tongue into my mouth.

I let out a long, relieved groan as the mystery is finally solved. He tastes just as sexy as I imagined, if not more. The mix of cigarettes, Shiner Bock, and Jason come together to be a delicious concoction that instantly makes my panties flood with arousal. All I'm breathing in is the scent of his heady cologne that still affects me like a drug or a spell, making my body roll against him like a cat wanting to be petted, begging for more.

I've never been kissed with such ferocity before, like he can't get enough of me, the same way I feel about him.

CH♠PTER

Twenty-One

I can't tell if I'm actually moving or if I'm just mentally floating until my back makes contact with the wall next to Jason's bed. I'm pinned between it and his solid body, barricaded in by his rock-hard biceps, cocooning me in until I am aware of nothing but him. His denim-clad knee moves between my bare legs, and he presses his thigh upward until he rubs against my white linen shorts-covered center, making me whimper as his tongue thrusts against my own. He's devouring me, making my heart pound with both excitement and maybe a little bit of fear at his intensity.

There is nothing tentative about his touch, nothing like the normal first time of being with a new lover. He doesn't bother gauging my reactions with cautious caresses. He knows just what to do to send me reeling, and he doesn't worry about asking permission to do it. He is in complete control of my body, playing it like a savant, already aware I would never tell him no. I give myself over to him, putting my trust into his capable hands, believing he'll do what he says he will and make me feel the way I've never felt before, feel the *things* I've never felt before.

His hands leave where they were pressed on either side of my head against the wall, and they come to rest at my throat. My heart thuds with alarm for a second, never having been touched in such a dominant way before, until the gentle stroke of his thumbs along my jaw soothes it away. The stroke moves lower, tickling down my neck, over my collarbone, separating to travel around the outsides of my breasts, sending a shiver up my spine, making me moan into his mouth.

My skin breaks out in gooseflesh and his caress move down my sides until he finally stops to grip the bottom of my pink V-neck t-shirt. Somehow, even in the hypnotic state he's put me in, my self-consciousness breaks through. My hands land on his, gripping them tightly to keep him from pulling my shirt up. I usually keep my top on, which guys don't seem to care when I let them skip over second base and head straight to third.

He stops kissing me, and I move forward to retrieve the connection we lost, but he stands up to his full height, bringing his knee out from between my thighs. I feel cold from the sudden distance.

"Let go," Jason demands.

"I...I just want to keep it on," I tell him, not able to meet his eyes.

"Let...go." His tone leaves no room for disobedience, and I lighten my grip on his fisted hands. "Good girl, now put your hands above your head and don't move them."

"Jason, I—" Panic clogs my throat for a moment before I squeak out, "Can we turn off the TV so it's not so bright in here?" I look around his body and nod toward his television set, which now just shows the menu screen of the DVD we'd been watching.

When my eyes meet his, he must see how completely terrified I am, because in a softer voice he tells me, "I want to see you. There is nothing about you I don't find perfect."

My natural reaction to shake the uncomfortable feeling quaking through me is to make a joke. "Up until about ten minutes ago, you had me believing you only like thick girls. There is nothing about me *that Jason* would find perfect."

He doesn't find my joke funny. He doesn't laugh or even smile. Instead, he leans into me so close I instinctively turn my head to the side, and whispers into my ear, "It's your long legs I think about wrapping around me when I jack myself off every night. It's your small but beautiful cherry-topped tits I imagine sucking on—the perfect mouthful—as I come all over my hand. Let go of my hands, put yours above your head, and don't...move."

Taking tiny breaths in and out, I keep my face turned away as I do as he commands, removing my grip from his once again and then slowly placing them above my head, resting them against the wall. He lifts my top until his palms connect with my waistline, and it feels like I'm being branded. His touch burns my flesh, and as he slides upward, dragging my shirt along with it, I don't feel the cold chill of embarrassment I had been dreading. He blazes a trail up over the band of my pretty light-grey lace racer-back bra, and his touch is so searing that even when he glides his fingertips over my armpits to work the soft cotton the rest of the way up my arms, it doesn't tickle. I don't even flinch. He's melted me to the wall.

He doesn't pull my shirt all the way off, instead leaving it around my wrists to give me something to grip onto. I clutch it like a lifeline as he caresses his way back down the path he just scorched until he rests his hands on my ribcage. He keeps them there as his lips find mine again. And I don't realize he's done this purposely to help me grow acclimated to his touch until I'm squirming, trying to get him to move them closer to their eventual targets. It's not until a whimpered, "Please," passes through my lips that he finally gives me what my passive aggressive body had been begging him for.

His rough fingertips glide across my skin until they meet in the middle, directly in the center just below my rapidly pounding heart, between my breasts. With a practiced movement, he pulls the clasp away from my body and the sides in opposite directions, unhooking the front closure of my racer back bra.

As the squeezing pressure of the elastic around my lungs releases, so do the butterflies that had been confined to my chest, allowing them to fly south into my belly, and much lower places as well.

Touch me.

The cups of my pretty lace bra just dangle beside my uncovered chest.

Touch me, I plead to him telepathically.

I feel so exposed. He's not close enough. His lips are still working magic against my own, but I'm well aware of what is happening from my neck down.

Nothing.

No other part of him is touching me, and it's making me absolutely mad.

Touchmetouchmetouchmetouchme. TOUCH ME!

I can't take it anymore.

Something inside me snaps.

I lunge.

My small frame wraps around the solid wall of muscle in front of me, my much smaller body connecting with his at full-force, not making him budge an inch. But as he feels me finally set myself free, bringing our bodies flush with each other, he leans forward and slams my back into the wall with a growl that sounds like a mix of both relief and ferocity.

He rips his mouth from mine and I gasp for breath. Aggravated, I work my shirt from around my wrists and throw it to the ground, and as he kisses a path to my ear, he groans, "So fucking sexy."

At his words, I turn wild trying to get the goddamn bra off my shoulders. I arch my back to get it from around me between my back and the wall, which presses me further into him, making him curse into the side of my neck. He grinds his hips into me, and I'm now coherent enough without his distracting kiss to feel his thick, rock-hard erection through his jeans.

His arm wraps all the way around my hips as he lifts me, and my arms automatically lock around his shoulders as me carries me to his bed. When we reach it, he spins us until it's my back that lands on the mattress as he comes down on top of me. I don't have time to think before his scruff-covered face nuzzles the soft skin of my breasts, and then he does something no guy has ever done before—he worships them.

"So soft." He traces the slight under-curve below my nipple with his tongue, his breath giving me goose bumps and instantly hardening the tips. "Smell so good." He gently runs his nose down the center between my small mounds before scraping his whiskers across the delicate flesh. "Want to eat you." The difference in textures, the sound of his deep drawl, and the actual words he's saying is building something in my core. I'm not even conscious my hips are grinding against him until he says, "I bet you're so fucking wet for me right now," and then finally takes one of my nipples into his mouth and brings up a hand to massage my other breast.

I don't know what one would call the sounds escaping me as he devours me, making me come unglued. Long gone is the nervous feeling that had threatened to ruin everything only minutes before. Even as his hand starts to make its way down my ribs, over my butterfly-filled stomach, to the hook and zipper of my white linen shorts, I feel nothing but need as I help him work them over my hips and down my legs until I can kick them all the way off.

I lie underneath him in nothing but my light grey lace

panties that had matched my bra. I reach for the hem of his shirt, and he allows me to pull it up his muscular torso. He then sits up on his knees to pull it over his head.

Oh, dear Jesus.

More of his perfect flesh, than I've ever seen at one time, greets me. Rippled muscles, smooth, tan skin, a light dusting of chest hair, tattoos everywhere. That's all I have time to take in before he lowers his dark head once more and kisses a trail from my sternum down until he comes to the top of my panties.

"Everything about you is so girly, pretty, and perfect... right down to your lacy underwear," he tells me, and I can't make out whether he's making fun of me or what until he adds, "I've always wanted a girl like you."

My heart swells from the sweet words, and it dances a giddy rhythm as he begins to slide my panties ever so slowly over my hips. I look down and my eyes lock with his; our mutual stare never falters as we hold our breaths as the lace leaves the tips of my toes. Finally, he breaks his gaze, and I can almost feel it as his eyes skim down my entire body until they come to rest at the apex of my thighs.

Thank you, sweet baby Jesus, I am a hygiene Nazi. At least I know when it comes to *that* part of myself, I have nothing to worry about. And when he lets out a muffled groan, I know he greatly appreciates it too.

Just like he did between my breasts, he runs the tip of his nose over my bare mound and I can feel the cool air shift as he inhales. I shiver as his hot breath hits me when he whispers, "So fucking perfect." He takes his knee and separates my legs, making room for the rest of his muscular frame to lie between them.

He doesn't even give me a moment to second guess anything. The next thing I feel is the long, purposeful slide of his tongue from the very bottom of my pussy to the hood of my clit, and I immediately shudder with the pure perfection of that first intimate lick. And when I hear him moan against me, "Even better than my fantasy," before repeating the glided path of his hot, wet mouth, my eyes roll back and my hands clutch his sheets.

His tongue takes a slow perusal of my most secret place, dancing the tip from side to side from the very top all the way down to my perineum, even taking a moment to tease between the outer and inner lips. I can feel every slight movement he makes, everything more hypersensitive than it's ever felt before. When he moves his hand from where it was gripping my thigh to wrap around my leg and then uses his thumb to pull the thin hood from my clit, my toes curl, and I hold my breath, waiting for what I know is going to be the most intense feeling I've ever had.

But it doesn't come. He waits, holding me open; I can feel his hot breath on my sensitive skin, but the contact never comes. I'm still holding my breath and every muscle in my body is tense, and when that scary feeling of lack of oxygen finally hits and I empty my lungs with a loud whoosh, *that* is when he finally places those magical plump lips around my clit and sucks me into his mouth.

"Oh, dear fuck," I half-groan, half-scream, rolling my hips up to get even closer to his face. He locks his strong arms around my thighs and holds me still, forcing me to take what he's giving me, not allowing me to move away when it starts becoming overwhelming. He switches between long licks with the flat of his tongue and sucking on the bundle of nerves, not allowing me time to focus long enough on one sensation. It's both incredibly arousing and highly aggravating, but I'm so out of my mind with pleasure that it takes me a moment to realize there's a stirring deep, way deep in my belly that I've never felt before, not even by myself.

I concentrate all of my attention on the feeling, locking in on it like a heat-seeking missile. My breath comes out in sharp pants, and when he finally stops switching between the different movements of his talented mouth and steadily focuses fast, direct swipes of his tongue against my clit over and over, that feeling builds and then snaps, and stars explode behind my eyelids. My body implodes, curling in on itself, my legs drawing up, my top half folding forward, and my hands go to his buzzed head.

I'm not aware that every curse word in the English language leaves me as I spasm. All I'm conscious of is Jason's continuous torture of my oversensitive clit. His arms lock even more firmly around my hips as I try to get away from him, and when I realize I won't be able to escape his grasp, I take a deep breath and try to calm myself, forcing myself to give into the sensation instead of fighting it.

When he feels me relaxing back into his touch, he lets go of my left leg with his right arm and brings it underneath him, and that's when he fills my pussy with two fingers, gliding in easily, thoroughly soaked from his wet mouth and my own arousal. I bite my bottom lip and moan, enjoying what I didn't know was exactly what my body craved.

But soon, it's not enough. I need more, and not just his fingers. My hips working against his hand and his mouth, I reach down to his shoulders and try to push him away. When that doesn't work, I lift my top half off the bed and reach under his arms, tugging him. Of course I don't move him an inch, but he gets what I'm asking and allows me to pull him up my body.

He kisses a wet path from my bare mound, across my hips, up my stomach, stopping at my chest to pay homage to each breast, across my collarbones, up my neck, and by the time he reaches my lips, almost all of the dampness that had been on the lower part of his face has been wiped clean. Only a slight hint of my scent still lingers as he presses his lips to mine, giving me the slowest and sweetest kiss I've ever received in my life.

He still has his jeans on. The rough fabric rubs against the soft skin of my inner thighs. I reach down and begin unbuckling his belt, and then unbutton and unzip the fly. He kisses across my jawline and then buries his face in my neck, where I feel him breathe me in. I smile, remembering I put this perfume on specifically because I know he likes it. And I feel his hot breath hiss out against my throat as I finally reach into the front of his pants and grasp him through his underwear.

Dear Jesus. No way. There's no way that's going to fit. Are you kidding me? It's like all the cock God forgot to give

Gavin, he put as extra on Jason's. The thought makes a giggle bubble up from my chest and erupt from my mouth. I feel Jason freeze above me, and he slowly pulls his face from my neck as he hovers over me, looking down into my face with a questioning look.

"That is not the sound a guy wants to hear when a girl reaches into his pants and grabs his cock for the first time," he says quietly, one side of his mouth quirking.

I press my lips together, pulling them into my mouth and bite down on them, trying to hold in the laughter that wants desperately to escape. He lifts an eyebrow at me, and I shake my head quickly, closing my eyes as my body starts to quiver from keeping myself from laughing.

"Babe," he says, and I open my eyes. "Da fuck are you thinking about, woman?"

The image of a bearded man wearing white robes with a baker's hat and an apron on up in the clouds making penis-shaped cookies fills my head, and I absolutely lose it. I let go of his huge dick and cover my mouth, letting out the laughter I had been trying to keep clamped down. When tears start to roll down the sides of my face and into my hair, I look up at him and wheeze out, "I'm sorry! But there is no fucking way that's going to fit!"

He slightly sags with relief, his head hanging loose for a moment before he looks up at me with a breathtaking grin. "Fuck, you can't do that to a man," he growls, and then reaches across the bed to pull open his bedside table's drawer, pulling out a condom.

"Oh, um. About that. Um...well, you see. Uh. I'm allergic

to condoms," I stutter out. "I mean regular ones. If...if I had known there ever even was a chance in hell this could happen, I would have bought a pack of the non-latex kind I have to use, but um...yeah. I didn't think you uh...wanted me."

"What would happen if I use this?" he asks, holding up the condom between two fingers.

"Um, well...I'd sorta...swell shut. And then you'd have to give me a big dose of Benedryl," I confess, embarrassed.

He slumps with disappointment, and I suddenly want to cry for having to tell him no. "I'm sorry, Jason," I say, my voice trembling.

His head jerks up and he looks into my eyes, seeing the tears filling them, but no longer the kind from laughter. "Hey, it's not your fault. Don't cry, baby," he whispers, leaning down and kissing me. He reaches his hand up to cup my face as he deepens the kiss, and suddenly I'm not thinking about God making penis cookies or my latex allergy anymore.

Throwing caution to the wind, I whisper, "I'm on birth control," and I feel him pause. I press my head into the pillow to pull away from his face enough to see his expression, and I see the thought process cross his every feature. He knows I would never lie to him, and he knows I'm not the type of person who would offer this up to just anyone.

"I'm clean. I just went to the doctor—"

"Two weeks ago, I know. I remember when you told the guys. It came back all clear," I interrupt his reassurance.

"You sure?" he asks.

"More sure than I've ever been about anything," I tell him.

And that's the end of all conversation. He devours my mouth in an earth-tilting kiss, making me groan in the back of my throat. I reach down and shove his jeans and underwear down his hips and as far down his muscular thighs as I can stretch without having to disrupt our kiss. Then pulling my legs up to hook my big toes in the waistbands, I tug them the rest of the way down his legs as I straighten mine. He chuckles against my mouth, and says, "Now that's talent," before I feel him kick the last of his clothing the rest of the way off.

It's then that it hits me. Jason Robichaux is making love to me. The man I've been secretly pining over for the past three months, the one who makes my heart race every time he walks into the room, the one who always takes care of me and comes to my rescue, subtly letting me know how he really felt about me, but I was too clueless to realize it—yeah, that one. It's a dream come true.

The passion I feel for this man consumes me, and my body starts to move against him in a way that is purely instinct, beckoning him to make me feel whole. I feel him reach between us as he aligns the head of his thick cock with my entrance, and I unconsciously tense, bracing myself for the pain I'm sure will soon come. He leans his whiskered face over to my ear, his hot breath soothing me as he whispers, "Relax, baby. Let me take care of you."

He uses his hand to move himself up and down my slit, coating himself with my plentiful wetness. Barely dipping the tip in before moving out and up to tease my clit with the velvety head, he coaxes me to loosen my muscles so the next time he dips inside, he slides slightly farther in, making me gasp with pleasure. "That's it. Let me in," he murmurs, taking my earlobe between his teeth and sending me into an all-over body shudder.

All tension leaves my body, and Jason times it perfectly, using my slight distraction to plunge the rest of the way inside me. It takes my breath, leaving my lungs empty but the rest of me feeling fuller than I've ever been before. There is no pain, just the feeling of being consumed, overtaken, surrounded, and filled up by the intoxicating man above me.

And then he sits up and begins to move. Long smooth strokes in and out as he sets a rhythm I know will take me places I've never been. I'm still sensitive from the orgasm he gave me with his mouth, the first orgasm I've ever been given by another person, and the realization that I will always know he was the one to give it to me starts that funny feeling deep in my belly once again. I look down at where our body is joined as he pumps in and out of me, and then my gaze slides up the tattooed rippling muscles of his torso and then over to his drool-worthy biceps, the muscles flexing as he holds his weight up on braced arms. I slide my hands up his forearms, over those bulging biceps, across his rock-hard shoulders, and graze my fingers up the back of his neck and into his buzzed hair. I pull him down to my lips and say against them, "I feel it."

He knows exactly what I mean, because he lets out an almost feral sound as he slams his mouth down on mine and starts pumping into me, his hips pistoning, rolling on the upward stroke so his length caresses the magical place at the top of my inner wall, and then arching his back as he pulls back out to drag the head of his cock against it. It's creating wave after wave of sensations, making my entire body feel flushed and chilled all at once.

He sinks down onto his left elbow and trails the fingers of his right hand down my neck until he reaches my left nipple, pinching and plucking it between his thumb and middle finger until I'm whimpering, and then he dips his head to soothe it with a swipe of his tongue. His hand continues lower until he slides it around to my back, going further still until he cups my ass, squeezing roughly, all the while pumping into me, keeping up that infallible pace. He hikes my leg up farther, bringing my knee up to where it rest almost at his armpit, locking it in place between his strong arm and his solid torso as he grinds his hips.

My breath starts its shallow pants once again, and before I know I'm even close to the edge, I'm taking a running leap, base jumping off the cliff. I take in a lungful of breath and prepare to break glass with the shriek that wants to escape me, but it's cut off as he catches it with his mouth, stealing it with his delicious kiss as he continues his relentless thrusts. My pussy tightens around his cock, milking him as my muscles ripple around him. I've never felt anything like it before, and all I can do is dig my fingers into his biceps and hold on for dear life as the sensation takes over my whole body.

And then I'm being moved. I feel him carefully slide out

of me before he begins maneuvering me. He sits back on his haunches before sitting me up and turning me over on my stomach. He keeps my legs together before lying down on top of me, entering me inch by slow, torturous inch from behind. When he's fully seated inside, stretching me and touching me in places I didn't realize I had, he uses his hand to pull my hair back away from my face and behind my ear so he can whisper into it, "Now cross your legs."

My brow furrows. I've never even heard of this position before, and I've read a lot of damn romances, and not to mention every issue of Cosmo for the past five years, but when I do what he said and cross my legs at the calves, he moves above me and it sends me spinning, and when he slides his hand underneath my stomach, and then farther down until he can circle my clit with his fingers, I cry out with the overwhelming sensation that wracks my body, making me writhe against him, pressing my ass back into him.

A few seconds more and I'm screaming into his pillow as he loses all control. He uses a knee to separate my legs, grabs hold of my hips and pulls me up until I'm on all fours, and then he slams into me, driving into me with ruthless thrusts, his balls slapping my clit and his front beating my ass with every plunge, ripping another orgasm from me and making me collapse down on my elbows as he keeps hold of my lower half.

The ripples last forever, until finally, after one...two...three last slow, purposeful thrusts, he growls as he comes, filling me with his hot, shooting seed, and then his forehead hits the middle of my back as he folds himself around me. His panting breath, his sweat-glazed skin touches every inch of me, cocooning me as I come down from the rollercoaster ride we just experienced together.

A few moments later, he slips out of me carefully, and I'm grateful for his gentleness because after what he just put my body through, I'm sore in places I've never been sore before. I barely have the strength to unfold my legs and stretch them out behind me, lying down on my stomach as I feel him move off the bed. He opens his bedroom door and I watch him pad across the hall, giving me the perfect view of his fantastic ass. I've never really admired a man's butt before, but damn. *Dat ass.*

He disappears into his bathroom, and after hearing water run for a few minutes, he returns with a warm, wet washcloth, which he uses to softly press against my tender center. I'm in awe as he cleans me up, especially as he leans down to press a sweet kiss there when he's finished. And just like that, my infatuated crush on him turns into something so much more.

I'm in love with Jason Robichaux.

CHAPTER Twenty-Two

Kayla's Chick Rant & Book Blog
Blog Post 4/9/2005

It's been three weeks since that very first time of making love with Jason. Three weeks I've been going to see him nearly every day, mostly cuddling up in his room, watching movies, vegging out, and ending the night with one last cigarette in his driveway, where he gives me a hug goodbye and tells me to drive safe.

He's taught me so many things in that bedroom, things I didn't know about my own body. Ever since that first time, we've had to be extra careful though. His parents came home from their trip, so we've had to be quiet and time our trysts after we know they're in bed asleep at the other end of the house.

It's been amazing. The best three weeks of my life.

And yet...

Y'all tell me what you think in the comments below. I'd love to hear what you think.

After we've made love and it's time for me to make the drive home, Jason seems...shuttered? Closed off a little? I don't really know how to explain it. Maybe I'm making it up in my head, just being a silly, paranoid girl, but it's almost every single night he does this. After getting redressed and heading out to his driveway, we sit on the cement and lean up against the closed garage door as we share our 'after-nooky cigarette' as we call it. It's mostly quiet; we don't really speak much during this time, and instead of being the comfortable silences we share during the day, it's kind of awkward.

When we first hooked up, his parents weren't there, so he had me stay the night with him, holding me through the entire night. But then, the first time we did it after they came back, I tried to give him a kiss goodbye by my car, and he ended it quickly, giving me just a swift peck before sending me on my way. At first, I chalked it up to him being tired. It was about three in the morning, after all. Maybe he was in a hurry to get to sleep.

But now, three weeks into this...relationship?...and it happens every single night we see each other. Oh! Also, while we're sitting there, I try to make plans to see him again, a simple, "Do you want to hang out tomorrow?" And he never, NEVER gives me a straight answer. It's always, "We'll see," or, "Let me see what I've got going on." I mean, he always ends up calling me the next day and telling me to come over, but why won't he just make it a plan? A date?

A date. Speaking of dates, he's taking me on our first real one tonight. When I asked him the night before last if he wanted to do anything this weekend, he gave me a "I'll let you know," gave me my normal hug—not kiss—and then closed my car door behind me. But then I received his call this morning, telling me he has something special planned for me and to dress up. This is new territory for us. I've been trying not to let myself get my hopes up, but I can't help the thoughts that float through my head like, *Is he going to ask me to be his girlfriend?* or *Does he want to let other people know we're seeing each other?*

From an outsider's perspective, you'd never know we're sleeping together. During the day, around his parents and Adam, and even Gavin a time or two, who was pissed at first that I was hanging out with "his" people, but got over it when Jason ripped him a new one while I hid a beaming grin, we just look like a guy and a girl who are really close friends. Best friends, even. Jason and I had spoken briefly before his parents got home, in between making love in his bed and a ferocious romp on his bathroom counter, where he spoke delicious and dirty things in my ear as he forced me to watch us in the mirror... Le sigh...

What was I saying? Oh, yeah, we spoke briefly before his parents came home, and he told me he'd rather not everyone know we were sleeping together. He said he liked how his mom was with me, and that he didn't want that to change. He was scared that her opinion would change of me if she knew I was having sex with him. It kind of hurt my feelings at first because I thought he meant she'd think I was some kind of slut, but he corrected me, saying she thinks lowly of people who sleep with *him*. Period.

This stunned me. Mrs. Robichaux shows nothing but love toward her son. Yes, sometimes it's a tough-love approach, which he's definitely deserved in the past from the stories I've heard, like when they kicked him out of the house and he had to live in a van in the Baybrook Mall parking lot, but she's never anything but loving. From what I've gathered in what little he's let me in on, he's gone to therapy since we was little for various issues. He chalks it up to abandonment issues from being put up for adoption, but with a family like the Robichauxs, I can't help but think it's something else.

Does she know about his sexual past? About his involvement with the stripper, or the swingers' club? Is that why he thinks she'd look at me differently? Would she think I'm into all that stuff? She's a great lady with a wild sense of humor and can have a potty mouth at times, but she's also a devout Christian, goes to church every Sunday, bible study, in all sorts of groups in her church, and volunteers for every event they hold.

So when I began asking myself these things, I could see why he wouldn't want me to let his parents in on the fact we were seeing each other as more than friends. I wouldn't want her to associate me with something she would most definitely find dirty. It just hurts my heart that Jason feels this way. If he's feeling even a fraction for me what I'm feeling for him, it's sad to think he believes he can't share it with his mom.

He saw the way I reacted when he told me he wanted to keep us a secret, and to make me feel a little better, he came up with a plan. He said any time we were hanging out together with other people, and he was thinking of me or wanted to touch me in a more-than-friends sort of way, he would give me a wink. He told me any time he'd catch my eye and send me that secret message, to know that he was thinking about holding me, or kissing me, or—his words—fucking me against various flat surfaces.

And boy, those long, dark eyelashes of his have been getting a work out. Nearly every time I look up at him while we're smoking on his back porch, or eating dinner at his dining room table with his family, or even watching a movie in his living room with them, he catches my attention and gives me a wink, and a warm feeling washes over me and I give him a secret smile. I live for those winks.

Wow, I just realized how long this post is. Sorry for writing you a novel this time, but thanks for any advice you leave me! I'll let you know what the 'special plans' were in my next post!

<3

'Dress up,' he said. 'I've planned something special for you,' he said. As I look at the piles of clothes spread out across my bed, floor, and top of my dresser, I want to kick Jason's ass for putting such pressure on me. Where is he taking me? What does he consider 'dressed up'? The only thing he let me in on was wherever we are going, we're going alone, just the two of us.

I've got my outfit narrowed down to either some really cute tight black pants with a one-shouldered red satin top, or a little black dress I picked up a few days ago with Kim. After being with Jason for the past few weeks, and him telling me how much he loves my legs, my confidence in the way my body looks has grown enough that I went out and bought a couple pairs of shorts, a jean skirt, and now, the little black dress I'm trying on now.

I step into it, and as I zip up the bottom, turning to look over my shoulder into the mirror to see the open back, I smile as I replay his words while I got dressed the next morning after our first time together.

And don't think I didn't notice your shorts, babe. Those are fucking hot. I don't know why you hate your legs. I love them. They're different than everyone else's. Beautiful. Perfect. They go on for miles, and I can't wait for the next time you wrap them around me.

Decision made, I grab my bottle of black raspberry vanilla

lotion and start slathering it onto my legs, making sure there's not a dry spot in sight. I dance around in a circle as I spray the matching body spray into the air, letting the mist land on me where it will.

I go into my bathroom, hike my skirt up and crawl up onto my sink. Looking into the mirror and seeing my red lace panties staring at me, I realize I have no idea how to act in a dress. *I'll have to be careful tonight,* I think as I sit Indian-style on my bathroom counter. I reach behind me and pull open the top drawer, which holds all my makeup and a pair of tweezers. I lean close to the mirror, making sure my eyebrows are perfect, none of my French heritage peeking through between my two brows, and then I take my time doing my makeup. I do it a little heavier than I normally do, going for a smoky eye and a natural lip.

I hop off my countertop and do a little wiggle as I pull the skirt back down into place, and then I run my brush through my hair one last time. I hustle into my room and grab my small, blood-red clutch and slip my feet into my nude pumps. I truly suck at walking in heels, but for some reason, if I had to, I could run in these puppies. They aren't super tall, and don't have a platform, and they're extra bendy, so I don't look like a baby giraffe learning to walk like I do in other heels.

I've told Mark and Kim about my date tonight, so they've been fairly warned if they wake up and I'm not here in the morning. A girl can only hope, right? I get in my car and slip in the new CD I made on my brother's computer, and as the techno beat of Paul Oakenfold's "Ready, Steady, Go" comes on, I giddily wiggle in my seat and head toward Friendswood.

I pull into Jason's driveway and then pause. I'm confused about what I'm supposed to do. If he's wanting to keep us a secret, then how am I supposed to walk into his house all dolled up and his parents not realize he's taking me on a date? Has Jason even thought that far ahead? Well, I don't want to look stupid just sitting out here in my car, so I get out and start toward the garage door. Before I even get there, the door opens and Jason steps out, closing the door behind him.

My step falters and I stumble to a halt, whispering, "Motherfuck," under my breath, just as I had the first time I saw him in this very spot. He looks freakin' amazing, especially as he gives me that wicked smile when hears my reaction to seeing him. He's wearing dark grey pin-striped pants, and a jet-black button down long-sleeved shirt. He's got on shiny black shoes and as he turns around to lock the door behind him, I see he's accessorized with bright silver cufflinks, which matches the tiny hoop in his left ear. When he turns back around, I notice he's holding a CD.

He makes his way toward me and grabs my hand, walking me to the end of his driveway. He wraps his arm around me and buries his face in my neck for a brief moment, where I hear and feel him breathe me in for a second before telling me to stay right here. I watch him take off in an easy jog until he vanishes around the side of his house, and then a minute later, his mom's little convertible silver BMW appears from where it's kept in his dad's shop.

He pulls around and stops in front of where I stand at the end of his driveway, and then hops out to run around to the passenger side to open the door. He makes a sweeping gesture with his hand, and I give him a smile as I walk over to him, giving him a quick kiss on his cheek before sliding into the seat. He closes the door behind me and then gets back into the driver's seat. "You ready?" he asks, pressing the button to put the soft convertible top down.

"As ready as I can be without knowing where we're going," I reply, grabbing a hair tie out of my clutch and braiding my hair quickly into a side ponytail over my shoulder. He gives me that drop-dead gorgeous grin again before putting the car in gear and taking off, throwing me back into the leather seat.

My heart is pounding by the time we merge onto 45 South, and I watch nervously as he lets go of the steering wheel with one hand to pull out the CD he'd been holding when I first arrived. He slides it into the player and cranks up the volume to be heard over the rushing wind and sounds of the busy highway. My eyes go back to the road as I clutch at the armrest, digging my fingers into the smooth black leather. When Paul Oakenfold's "Ready, Steady, Go" starts to play, I can't help but laugh, a tiny bit of the tension leaving my body.

"I just made a CD with this song on it too," I tell him, peeling my eyes from my surroundings to look over at him. He glances at me and gives me a wink, and that warm feeling fills me once again. He pulls onto the next exit ramp and then onto the feeder. The traffic light barely turns yellow and he slows to a stop. This is unlike Jason, who likes to speed through the very end of yellow lights, smacking the ceiling of his truck and yelling, "It's was orange; I swear!"

"You totally could have made that," I say, raising my eyebrow at him.

He doesn't say anything, just looks over at me as he rests his hand on the stick shift, his knee bouncing a little to the beat of the techno song. The sun has set and the highway to our left blocks the light from the restaurants and stores on the other side of the road, so the only light around us is from the red light we sit at, and a few street lights. It causes shadows across his handsome features as he continues just to watch me, not saying a word.

My brow furrows and I smile. "What?" I ask, turning to look to my right to see if he's actually looking at something past me, but there's nothing there, just the thick wooded area, one of the only undeveloped spots off of 45 South.

I turn back around to face him again, and he's still watching me, and that's when the light turns green. Instead of looking toward the road, he shifts into first gear and hits the gas, his eyes still locked on mine. I nervously glance at the empty road ahead of us and then back to him as he changes into second gear. His eyes dart purposely from my eyes, down to my lips, and then back up to my eyes as he cocks his brow and shifts into third, giving me a sexy smirk.

"Jason. Are you being serious right now?" I cry, looking back to the open road to see he's staying perfectly centered in the lane. I shift back to his face and yell, "Stop doing the 'drive and stare', Jason! This is not *The Fast and the Furious!*" as he moves into fourth.

He chuckles, probably amused that I know he's recreating Paul Walker's flirtatious move from the movie, and then finally tops out at fifth gear, raising his hand to press a button on the stereo for the next song to play. He then reaches over and lays his hand halfway up my left thigh, sending tingles down to the tips of my toes and directly up my skirt. He finally breaks his stare and looks forward, and when the song begins to play, so do his fingers.

My brow furrowing, I look down at his hand on my leg, watching his fingers dance across my smooth tan skin as he plays the notes perfectly to Coldplay's "Clocks". The piano solo in the beginning is beautiful, one of my favorites I've listened to over and over since it came out, and since I took piano lessons for four years when I was younger, I know his keystrokes would be accurate. I'm mesmerized, both charmed and shocked by this innocent but extremely sexy move he's just laid on me.

His family has an upright piano in their living room, but I had no idea Jason knew how to play. As his fingertips continue to play the tune against my sensitive flesh, I grow more and more turned on, the thought of this gorgeous, tough, muscular tattooed man knowing how to play the piano sending me into a heart-palpitating frenzy.

When the song ends and his warm hand comes to a rest on my leg once again, there is no longer a single thought in my head wasted on road safety. I unbuckle my seatbelt and throw myself over the narrow center console, circling my arms around his neck and pulling him closer to me to plant a kiss on his delicious pouty lips. He smiles against my mouth, and I open my eyes to see he is still watching as he drives, my head tilted at an angle so he can see ahead of us.

I deepen the kiss, my tongue stabbing into his mouth, like a needle injecting pure lust as I try to convey how much passion I feel for this man. I unwrap my right arm from around his neck and place my hand on his left thigh, sliding it briskly up to cup his rock-hard bulge through his dress pants. He groans into my mouth and then pulls his head away from me, saying, "Even I can't handle driving when you do that. Sit back, baby. I promise to take care of you tonight, but first, let me do something special for you."

I smile, squeeze him through his pants, and give him one last gentle kiss on his lips before sitting back into my seat and putting my seatbelt back on.

A few minutes later, we arrive somewhere I've never been before. Jason walks around to the passenger side, helps me out of the car, and places my hand in the crook of his elbow, escorting me inside. When we walk inside, to the left is a row of about ten pool tables, in the middle is a huge bar that runs the entire depth of the room, and on the right are tables and booths. It's a classy billiard hall, and it looks like they serve food too.

"Would you like to play or eat first?" he asks, turning toward me.

"Let's play. I'm not quite hungry yet," I tell him, nodding in the direction of the pool tables. He agrees and guides me to the bar, where he gets our set of balls and orders us drinks. I don't recognize what he gets us, but when the bartender returns with some opened green bottles of beer with salt around the necks and limes sticking out of the top, I give Jason a questioning look.

"Just trust me," he says, and grabs the bottles after handing his credit card over to open a tab. I grab the rack of balls and follow him to one of the open pool tables. I place the tray in the middle of the table and continue to follow him when he makes his way over to a small table with two chairs against the wall. He sets the bottles on the table and then pulls one of the chairs out, gesturing for me to sit. I thank him and take my seat, watching as he slides into the opposite one.

"This is Dos Equis. It's a Mexican beer, and when it's served with the salt and lime, it gets rid of that taste you don't like. I'm determined to find a beer you'll enjoy, and if you don't like this one, then I don't think one exists," he proclaims.

Every time he's bought a different beer in the last few weeks, whether we went somewhere or he brought a pack to his house, he's made me taste it to see if I liked it. So far, I've tried Shiner, Budweiser, Bud Lite, Coors, and Michelob, and all of them have been disgusting. I'm just not a beer girl.

He slides one of the bottles to himself, and after he pulls the lime from the neck, squeezes the juice into the drink, and then shoves the peel back in, my brow furrows as he sticks his thumb into the hole, turns the bottle upside down, and then turns it right side up before sitting it down in front of me. I feel my core clench as I watch him suck the salt from his thumb.

"Try that," he commands, and then proceeds to do the same routine to his own beer.

"Now that it's got your cooties all over it..." I trail off with mock-disgust.

"Woman, just drink it. You flip the bottle to make the lime go to the bottom, so it doesn't block the opening. Besides, you've had a lot worse things in your mouth." He smirks, shifting his eyes down to his lap and then looking back up to me with a heated smirk.

"All right, all right." I give in and pick up the beer, letting out an overdramatic sigh, knowing the drink is going to be gross. Seeing him grab up his bottle and licking a little bit of the salt off the neck before taking a swig, I do the same, and then take a tentative sip.

Holy shit! It's not nasty! The saltiness mixes with the sour of the lime, making the beer taste almost sweet. I look down at the bottle, reading the label and seeing the two golden Xs I'd seen before on neon signs at bars and clubs. I glance up at Jason and see his sexy grin before returning the drink to my lips for a less cautious mouthful.

"Well, this one doesn't suck," I admit. "Good job, even though God only knows where that thumb has been." I raise my eyebrow at him before standing and walking over to the pool table to set up the balls.

He rolls two cues across the table next to us, checking to make sure they are good and straight, and then comes over to my side, handing me one. I stand to the side of our table while he breaks and calls stripes. After taking his next couple of shots and then finally missing, I pick which solid I'm going to aim for, and get into position. That's when I feel his hard, hot body come up behind me.

He molds himself to me, his muscular left arm stretching

along my thin one to move my hand holding the front end of the stick a little farther back, also using his fingers to tweak the way I'm grabbing it. Instead of wrapping around the cue, I now have it balanced between my thumb and the knuckle of my pointer finger.

"I've always wanted to do this to you, ever since the first time we went and played," he says low in my ear, sending chill bumps down my arms. "Now in your mind, draw a line from the pocket to the ball, and wherever that line would come out the back end of the ball, that's where you want to hit it with the cue ball." His deep voice vibrates inside his chest against my back, and I can barely concentrate on not grinding my ass against his hips, much less the shot.

"You okay?" he asks, and I can hear the smirk in his voice. "You're trembling."

"I'm fine," I reply, clearing my throat and spreading my feet a little farther apart to get lower to the table. *Concentrate, Kayla*, I tell myself. I'd kill to impress him, loving the feeling that swells inside me the way he looks at me when I beat him at a hand of cards. I focus between the pocket and the solid blue ball in front of me, drawing the line in my head like he told me to, and then zeroing in on the back of it at a spot a little to the left of its center, I strike the white ball gently. It hits the blue ball directly where I wanted it to, and it slowly rolls across the green felt until it falls easily into the corner pocket.

I feel Jason's right hand squeeze my hip and pride swells inside me, along with the inferno deep in my belly. I turn in his arms, placing my butt against the table, and grin up into his face. He smiles before placing a gentle kiss on my lips and reminding me, "Next shot."

We play a couple of games, him guiding me through some of my turns, teaching me different things like banking, which I never get the hang of, and jumping the cue ball, which I couldn't quite make it do. I do, however, sink a lot more balls than I ever have before. Jason is a good teacher.

I've managed my way through two Dos Equis, and I don't know if it's because I'm not used to drinking beer itself, or if this brand has a lot of alcohol content, but I'm already feeling a little buzzed. We decide to gather up our rack and move to the other side of the bar to eat. I order a big plate of Texas cheese fries, topped with bacon and chives, and he orders a Philly cheesesteak, minus the onions and peppers, along with another round of our beer.

"So I've been thinking about getting another tattoo," I tell him. "It's backwards though. I know where I want it, but I don't know what to get."

"Where do you want it?" he asks, taking a pull of his beer.

"Behind my ear. I've seen a couple pictures of tattoos there, and it's adorable," I reply, dipping one of my fries into the ranch dressing in front of me.

"Know what I just realized?" he prompts. When I quirk my eyebrow up in acknowledgement, he jokes, "You have a heart tatted on the back of your neck, and I have a spade on my arm. We're two suits short of a deck of cards."

"Our tattoos always seem to match up in freaky ways, like remember when we saw Constantine?" I take a sip of beer and tilt my head at him. "Weird coincidences."

"I don't believe in coincidences," he states.

"What do you mean?" I ask, loving it when I can actually get him talking.

"I believe in fate. I believe everything happens for a reason. Even the smallest things that may seem coincidental, I think it's all part of a big plan," he confesses.

"Wow, I didn't picture you as the predestined type," I remark.

"There's a lot you don't know about me, babe."

The tone of his voice makes it sound like he just might be ready to finally let me in on things he's never been willing to share, things he's always brushed aside, changing the subject when I'd ask about them. So I venture, "I wish you'd tell me more about you, the stuff you always try to avoid." Doesn't he know by now there's nothing he could tell me that would scare me away?

He sighs, seeming to war with himself, and then he abruptly stands and makes his way over to the bar. I watch as he leans into it, crossing his arms over the shiny wood as he tells the bartender what he wants. When he returns, he's carrying two shots. One is what I have come to happily know is a Buttery Nipple, and the other is a dark brown liquid that looks like it would make me vomit just by taking a whiff of it.

"Okay, confession time. I trust you more than I've ever trusted another girl before, so I'll tell you anything you want to know. But if I'm going to reveal all, I'm not going to be able to do it sober. There's fucked-up shit I don't even want to remember, and much less tell the girl who looks at me like I hung the goddamn moon. But you asked for it, so bottoms up, babe," he commands, raising his shot glass in the air.

Lightly clinking his with mine, we tap the bottoms on the table, and then shoot our drinks. I chase mine with a swig of my beer, and the mixture makes me shudder. Not a good combo. I settle back into my seat and nibble on another cheese fry, waiting for him to start.

"God, I don't even know where to begin," he says, more to himself. "Well, how about I just start with what my therapist says is what controls my whole line of thinking, which leads me to react in certain ways not...normal to other people?"

I nod, accepting everything he's willing to tell me.

"In my mind, there is a set of what I call 'principles'. It's just a set of guidelines I live by, and if people don't follow what my mind has deemed acceptable to these principles, I don't react...nicely," he hedges.

"Okay, stop right there. You're not going to scare me off, Jason. Stop trying to sugar coat and pussy foot around," I tell him.

He slouches down for a minute, staring at his beer bottle a moment as he twirls it around, and then straightens, seeming to gather the courage to confess his demons. "I almost stabbed a guy at McDonald's once, because he called me a motherfucker."

I look at him, not flinching in the slightest. He must not realize yet that I'm the most nonjudgmental person in the entire universe. "Why just 'almost'?" I ask.

He looks startled, not expecting this to be my reaction to what he believes is some unforgiveable event. "I, uh...Gavin and I were there, and this dude from school was there, and he was just talking shit. I gave him fair warning. I told him if he didn't stop fucking heckling us, something bad was going to happen, and that's when he called me a motherfucker. I stood up, flipped the whole goddamn table over, and whipped my pocket knife open. If it wasn't for Gavin, I would be in jail right now for murdering the son of a bitch."

"Well...you did give him fair warning," I concede. He blinks at me a couple of times. I'd laugh if I wasn't worried he'd stop talking. "Confession time of my own. I dated this Army guy once; he was twenty and had already been active duty for three years. He had been a part of some really bad crowds as a teenager, gotten into some terrible trouble, and they told him he had a choice either to join the military, or he'd have to be put in juvie until he turned eighteen, at which time he'd be transferred to real jail. He'd been in trouble before, but what landed him in this time was he curbed someone. Do you know what that is?" I ask him.

"Yes, I know what that is. Hell, I've never done that to anyone. That's fucked up." He flinches.

"Yeah, well, he also had a damn good reason to do it, seeing how the dude had pulled a gun on him, not knowing he was a black belt in Kempo. But my point is, three years later, that messed-up little asshole was working his way up as one of the best snipers in the Armed Forces. People can change," I insist.

"It's actually funny that was what they gave him the option to do. After 9/11, my two buddies and I went and signed up for the Marines. Wes," he points to his black sleeve-covered arm, indicating the memorial tattoo there, "and Larry ended up going for it, but again, I ended up getting fucked. I specifically signed up to be Intel. Larry and I got the highest scores in the country on our ASVAB tests, and were automatically qualified to enlist for whatever jobs we wanted inside the Marines. They guaranteed us the jobs we picked when we signed the contracts, but when we went that last time to finalize everything, it turns out the fucking recruiter had lied to me. There were no spots open in Intel, and he was hoping I'd get on the bus anyways, with the hopes I'd let them put me in whatever slot they needed a body. I told him to go fuck himself. It was the goddamn principle of it."

"It's a good thing you didn't go," I say quietly. He cocks his head to the side, silently questioning my reasoning. "I mean, one, I wouldn't have met you, and two, if you would have gone, you probably would have stuck with one or both of your friends if you could, right?" He nods. "Well, what if it was Wes you would have stuck with?" I look down into my French fries, hating the thought of never having met Jason.

"People gave me so much shit after that. They taunted me, saying I was just being a pussy and was scared to go over there. I kicked their ever-loving asses. It wasn't that though. Even if they would have told me a spot opened up in Intel, I wouldn't have taken it, because the fact of the matter is that motherfucking recruiter tried to get one over on me." He shakes his head.

"You still haven't told me anything that's so bad you've been avoiding talking about it since we met," I sigh. "Here I was thinking you had some deep dark secrets, and really, it was all just for show. You're fake mysterious. I want a refund." I grin. His lips twitch, fighting a smile. He really thinks whatever he's done in his past is unforgiveable, when really, he's just stuck to his guns and not let anyone fuck him over without them paying for it. "What else?"

"I have this...anger. No one, especially me, has been able to figure out where it comes from. You know my family. You know they're the greatest people on the planet, but for some reason, when I hit about twelve years old, I just got mad. That's when my mom started obsessively trying to figure me out, what was 'wrong' with me. We tried out all sorts of therapists, doctors, church counselors, teachers... I went from being diagnosed depressed, to ADD, to OCD, and all sorts of stuff. I was put on antidepressants, then Ritalin, and some other crazy stuff that made me a zombie. Every different person gave us a different diagnosis, and none of them were right. When I was old enough, I started self-medicating, hanging out with some not-so-great people and doing every drug under the sun. That's when it went from just self-destruction, to being a little shithead and an asshole to my parents. It eventually led to them finally kicking me out.

"This was before the whole Marine snafu, and Larry, who had gotten in a fight with his parents, decided to kick himself out of his own house, and we lived in a minivan in the mall parking lot for a couple of weeks. That's when I hit rock bottom. It was exactly what I needed, and I finally went crawling home with my tail between my legs. They didn't let me into the house right away. I had to earn it. I lived in Dad's shop for a while, upstairs above where we keep Mom's Beamer. I still go up there to this day when I need to cool off," he confesses.

"Did you ever figure it out?" I ask.

"No. I mean, I've been able to tamp it down some. I have a little more self-control than I used to, but that's a very, very recent thing," he replies, and the way he says it, added to the way he's looking at me gives me the impression it has something to do with me. The thought warms me.

"I'm still not impressed. I thought you were going to tell me something like you're in the Witness Protection Program as a deal for outing your sidekick after robbing some bank that led to a bunch of hostages getting offed or something." I shrug.

"Um, morbid much?" He chuckles. "All right, there, woman. Challenge accepted." He straightens in his seat. I grin, knowing he's about to try his best to rattle me. It's not going to happen. Not only did I grow up with three big brothers who got in enough trouble to give my mom gray hair by the time she was forty, I grew up in a town full of soldiers. Put a bunch of testosterone-filled alpha men in one place and it's always a pissing match of who-did-the-worst-stuff. Call me jaded, but not much fazes me. I've pretty much heard it all.

"Larry and I used to hang out of his Buick and bash mailboxes," he proclaims.

"Child's play." I wave my hand at him dismissively.

"We got kicked out of school for setting a dumpster on fire with fireworks at our high school."

"Lame," I say in a bored tone.

"Gavin and I had to spend a night in jail for public intoxication when we were caught drinking inside one of the new houses being built in my neighborhood."

"Losers."

"I stole a bunch of jewelry and money from a bedroom at a house party," he confesses quietly.

"Was it a friend's?" I ask, thinking that was kinda messed up.

"Nope, it was the asshole who called me a motherfucker at McDonald's," he says with a smirk.

"Dumbass should've locked the doors." I shake my head.

"I punched a cop once," he whispers, leaning across the table.

"What did he do to deserve it?" I question, realizing a pattern. Everything Jason did, it was actually called for. He just acted on what people wished they could. Sure, it wasn't a good thing, but it also wasn't the worst. He was a real-life vigilante of his own principles.

He grins mischievously. "That one was by accident. I was at a club and we dog-piled this dude who was bad-mouthing the Marines, and the cop tried grabbing me from behind. I didn't look before I swung. Oops."

This makes me burst out laughing. "Did you get in trouble?"

"Nah, thankfully the cop was the brother of one of my friends, and when we told him what we were fighting about, he let me off with a pat on the back. He was an ex-Marine." He chuckles.

We grow quiet for a few moments as we finish our food and beers, and when the waitress comes by, Jason asks for a dessert menu. When she returns with it, he orders the one chocolate item available, my favorite, chocolate mousse pie. He also asks for two more Dos Equis, even though I tell him it probably won't go very well with the sweet dessert. He doesn't care.

She serves it a few minutes later, setting it between us with two spoons. When we're halfway through it, after I've moaned and groaned with pleasure during every bite, he says out of nowhere, "You're kind of amazing."

"What?" I mumble with my mouthful of gooey chocolate.

"There's no shaking you, is there? I could tell you I kidnapped someone and turned them into my sex slave and you wouldn't bat an eyelash, would you?"

I cough. "Actually, yes, I would, but it would be out of jealousy. I read a book like that once and it was the hottest thing ever."

He shakes his head at me. "See? I've never met a girl like you. I didn't think one like you existed, one who could accept me the way I am, accept all the shit I've done in my past. Like I said, I don't believe in coincidences."

"Why, Jason," I say in an exaggerated southern belle accent, "are you saying we were fated to be together? I do declare!" I make a joke, because I'm not sure if this is what he's really saying and don't want to freak him out if it's not.

"I believe we were at least meant to meet and know each other. I mean, you have no idea what I'm feeling right now, having let all of that stuff off my chest. I feel like I could fucking fly right now, all this weight lifted off me. Add in the tattoos...and not to mention I'm the only one who's been able to get you off...several times in fact," he says the last part quietly, his beautiful dark eyes gleaming at me over the table. "Way too much to be coincidence."

My heart leaps in my chest. I feel like I could float away myself, having trouble believing this isn't a dream right now, with Jason verbalizing everything I could ever hope he'd say to me. I've felt these things for a long time, even before I really knew much about him. I felt this connection to him I could never explain. A pull...a link...whatever you could call it, he felt like home to me.

CHAPTER
Twenty-Three

Kayla's Chick Rant & Book Blog

April 24th, 2005

I'm so sorry I've been offline for so long, peeps. I've just been so busy trying to balance school, work, and spending as much time with Jason as possible, that my blog has suffered. I haven't even had time to read that much, except for what I sneak in at work, when I'm not napping on my desk. Thank goodness my door has one of those button code lock knob-thingies and I'm a light sleeper. I can pass right out, and as soon as I hear someone punching in the code, I snap up with papers in my hand like I've been filing the whole time.

If it weren't for those little catnaps, I'd probably be walking around like a zombie. As soon as I get out of school, I go to work, and when I get off when we close, I go down to Friendswood, where I hang out with Jason and his family, who still don't know we're together...well, I say together, but we're still not official. He hasn't asked me to be his girlfriend yet. Ugh. Anyways. Then, I drive my happy ass back home around 3am and sleep until it's time to go to school at seven.

Thank God, the semester is almost over. I'm finishing up my US History paper as soon as I publish this blog post, and then for the next week, I'll be doing my finals in my other three classes.

So I just wanted to update y'all, and let you know I haven't died since I've never gone this long without posting before. I'm just a busy girl! Next review will be of the Karen Marie Moning book I'm reading, *Kiss of the Highlander*. Holy hell, peeps. I might have a new favorite! Stay tuned. ;-)

CHAPTER Twenty-Four

May 7th, 2005

I survived another semester of college and managed to get all As and Bs. Don't ask me how. I'm just glad I'm naturally good at writing essays and could pretty much bullshit my way through Computer Science class.

As a job well done, the Robichauxs have sent Jason, Gavin, and me on an overnight trip to Galveston. At first, I didn't think it was a good idea. I mean, Gavin knows Jason and I hang out a lot, but he doesn't know we're together without a title. He doesn't know we've slept together either. When you're around someone you're seeing, you act differently with them than you would just a friend, even a best friend. You look at them, casually touch them, and just all around move differently around them. How the hell will I be able to hide all of that? It's easy with his parents, because I wouldn't be groping their son in front of them anyway. Plus, I'm only around them for short periods of time, like dinner, before Jason and I are off to do something on our own. But this weekend, we'll be with Gavin 24/7.

Jason assures me we'll be fine though, so I'm going to trust him and just follow his lead. Right now, we're in line in Jason's truck to board the ferry boat from Galveston to Bolivar. As always, I'm riding in the middle between him and Gavin.

We've been waiting in this line for nearly an hour, but listening to the guys crack jokes is entertaining enough to make the wait not so bad. When it's finally our turn, Jason follows a man in a neon yellow vest's hand gestures, guiding him to drive directly onto the boat to park snuggled with all the other cars on board. This is wild to me. We're in a truck... on a boat.

When the ferry is full, I watch in the rearview mirror as the back raises slowly right behind us, kind of like a giant tailgate. I catch Jason smiling at me out of the corner of my eye, and I playfully stick my tongue out at him, knowing he's wanting to pick on me for being such a small-town girl as I view everything through my wide eyes in my fascinated face.

Once the ferry starts moving, the guys open their doors, leaving me with a confused look on my face as the hop out of the truck. Gavin shuts his door, and Jason sticks his head back in and asks quietly, "You comin', babe?"

"Where are we going?" I slide across the bench seat and out his door as he holds it open for me.

"We're going up to the top. You can stand up there instead of just sitting here in the truck," he explains.

I follow him as he maneuvers between all the vehicles until we make it to the center of the boat, where a metal door leads to a set of steep, shallow stairs. He gestures for me to go first, and I feel him playfully poking my butt cheeks as I carefully climb the steps, making me giggle and swat at him with the hand not gripping the railing.

When we come out the heavy door at the top, straight faces are back in place like we weren't just flirting up a storm. We spot Gavin at the very front of the ferry, leaning over as far as he can to look at the water below. Jason sneaks up, grabs his back from behind, hollering out a growl and making Gavin jump a foot off the ground.

"Holy shit, fucker!" Gavin exclaims, punching Jason in the arm. Jason cackles as he rubs his bicep, and I have to keep myself from drooling as I watch his muscles flex and stretch. *There is just something about those tatted arms...*

"So what do y'all want to do first when we get to Bolivar?" Jason asks.

"I say we go to the nude beach," Gavin says, waggling his eyebrows.

"Nude beach? There is no nude beach. Isn't that only in Europe or something?" I ask, a little panicked at the prospect of being dragged along to one.

"Nope, there's one here called Crystal Beach. You're not allowed on it unless you're at least topless," he tells me.

I can't tell if he's joking or not, so I look to Jason. I'm surprised to find emotion there...I'm not quite sure how to describe it. It looks a little like pissed-off, maybe jealous? So if he's jealous of Gavin talking about taking me to a nude beach, then that means there really is one, right? The expression quickly disappears as Gavin turns his attention toward him with a mischievous grin on his face. "I'm down for whatever," Jason says with a shrug.

I look between the two, back and forth a couple of times before I finally shout, "Hell no! I am not going to a nude beach! First of all, no one is seeing my itty bitty titties. Plus, the only people who go are old people with saggy...parts. Choose something else."

Gavin bursts out laughing and confesses there isn't really a nude beach on the island. I glance at Jason and see his smirk, so that quick glimpse of jealousy I saw before must've been over just the simple thought of me going to one, or maybe of Gavin seeing me naked.

"There's really nothing on the island I wanted to do. I just knew Kayla had never been on a ferry before, so thought we could take the short trip. We can always just turn around and go straight back," Jason suggests.

"Yeah, let's do that. I'm getting pretty hungry," Gavin agrees.

"Oh! Can we go to that Greek place? What is it called? Olympics something." I hop up and down. "My brother took me there a long time ago, when I was like fifteen. It had the *best* gyros."

"Nah, they tore that place down a while back," Jason

shoots me down. He glances at Gavin over my head, but before I can turn to see the exchange, he continues, "We had a hurricane a couple years ago, and it demolished all that stuff on the seawall."

"Oh no! That sucks. I loved that place," I pout. "I don't care then. I'm not picky," I say, leaving it up to them to decide where we go. I'm just along for the ride. I lean against the railing, looking down and watching as a couple of seagulls and a pelican fly along in front of us, occasionally swooping down to grab whatever was swimming near the surface of the water.

I hear the boys talking, but I don't strain to hear them over the roar of the ferry's engine and loud lapping of the water as we slice through it, and soon it's time to return to the truck. Driving off the ferry, we make a U-turn and get into the short line waiting to board it once again. I'm glad we won't have to wait another hour just to cross the water back to Galveston. We make it onto the very same ferry, and this time, we go up and sit on one of the benches in the smoking section to pass the eighteen-minute crossing.

After driving along Seawall Boulevard, we soon pull into a strip mall, and when we park in front of a restaurant, I look up and see Olympia Grille. My head turns abruptly and I look into Jason's laughing eyes. I use the back of my hand to smack him in the belly, and he doubles over his steering wheel, pretending I knocked the wind out of him. "You guys just love fucking with me, don't you?" I say with annoyance, but I soon break into a grin as we all get out and enter the Greek restaurant.

After finishing up all our gyros at the Greek restaurant, we picked up a couple of six-packs, a bottle of vodka, and orange juice from the liquor store on the strip, and then headed here. The three of us are sitting on the balcony of the beach house Jason's parents rented us for the night. We all put on our bathing suits, but haven't made it down to the actual beach yet. The bright yellow two-story house on stilts is right on the beach, and occasionally, Gavin will lean over the railing to yell down to scantily clad girls laying out in the late afternoon sun or walking along the water. He's tried several times to get Jason in on checking out the 'hot chicks', but Jason just chuckles and shakes his head, enjoying his beer and cigarettes as he chills out in one of the lounge chairs.

Jason has been winking at me constantly, making it hard for me not to laugh as he lets me know without speaking that he's thinking about me in a not-just-friendly way. When

Gavin isn't looking, Jason catches my attention, eyeballs my bikini, then looks up into my eyes with a wicked glint in his before sending me a wink and turning away. It's the least self-conscious I've ever been in a bathing suit before, and it's all because this man makes me feel like the most beautiful girl in the world.

I've been struggling not to drool ever since he came out of the bathroom wearing his white board shorts and his black wife beater, his naturally tan skin and tattoos calling out to me like a beacon.

"So are we going swimming, or what?" Gavin says from the railing, wiggling his fingers at a group of girls as they walk past our beach house.

"I don't get in the actual water, but I'll go lay out while you two go in," I say, lighting up a cigarette of my own and then taking a sip of my Screwdriver Jason made me.

"What do you mean you don't get in the actual water?" Gavin asks incredulously.

"I mean, you see all that wet stuff that keeps getting really close to us before it's sucked back out? Yeah, I don't get in that," I tell him, shaking my head.

"Well, why not?" He looks confused.

"I don't do sea creatures. I don't do seaweed touching me, and I don't do sticky water that'll make me itch after the sand glues to it." I shudder.

"Oooookay. Let's grab our shit and go down there, and you can just chill on a towel or something. You ready," he aims at Jason.

"Yeah, sure," Jason replies, standing and taking hold of

the cooler handle next to his lounger.

I walk over to him and fold up the chair, carrying it under one arm, wrap my beach towel around the back of my neck, put my pack of cigarettes between my teeth, and then grab my drink in my empty hand. I nod at Jason before heading to the wooden steps that lead directly down to the sand. I hear him chuckle as he follows, and I try not to squeal when I feel him pull at my bikini bottoms. He leans down to me and says, "You had a letter in your mailbox."

I burst out laughing. My pack of cigarettes launches from my mouth, and I'm pretty sure I would have fallen down the flight of stairs if Jason's massive arm didn't wrap around my waist, steadying me before my drink even has time to slosh around in my plastic cup. As fast as his arm appeared, it's gone, but it leaves behind a searing heat where his skin had touched mine.

I continue down the stairs, planning on coming back to find my lost smokes, and when I set all my stuff in the sand, I turn around and run right into him. He holds the pack out to me, apparently having picked it up for me. "Do you really not go in the water at all?" he asks quietly.

"Not at all. The only natural body of water I get in is the lake behind my house back home, and that's only because the fish are little and the water is so clear I can see them, and because my dad clears out the greenies in the swimming area," I tell him.

"Greenies?" He smiles.

"You know, the slimy plants that are in lakes? Greenies." I shrug, unfolding the lounge chair.

He turns and starts toward the water, but not before teasing me over his shoulder, "Yankee."

"I'm not a damn Yankee!" I yell after him, and I see him shake his head as he jogs the rest of the way out to where Gavin is wading into the ocean.

Something cold hits my stomach, making my abs twitch. Before I can even open my eyes from the catnap I was taking while laying out, I'm being lifted into strong arms. But when I do open them, they're not the arms I love being wrapped in. They belong to the dickhead currently running with me toward the rolling waves of the Gulf Coast. "Gavin! Don't you fucking dare!" I squirm, trying to escape what I know he's about to do. It would probably hurt falling from his six-foot-plus height, but it would be the lesser of two evils than being thrown into the godforsaken water. I kick and scream, and finally lean toward his chest and bite into the tan skin of his pec, but I'm too late.

He hollers out in pain as my teeth sink in, but I'm already hovering over the water. When he launches me in the air, all I have time to do is take a deep breath, hold my nose, and clamp my eyes shut before I break the surface, going completely under. I scramble to the surface, instantly going into panic mode when I feel things tickling against my legs.

My face finally makes it out of the water, and I gasp and cry out at the same time, my heart pounding in my chest as fear and misery wash over me. Some part of me is conscious Gavin is just standing there laughing at me, and as a wave sucks me back under, all I can do is pray he will realize his joke is far from funny and will pull me out. Being the daughter and sister of four sailors, you'd think I'd love the ocean, or at least be good at swimming. Nope. I'm flailing, not able to tell which way is up or down.

When my lungs start to burn and I feel like I'm literally about to drown, I finally feel arms wrap around my body and tug. I suck in a lungful of breath as soon as I can, clinging for dear life to the person holding me, and as I hear his deep whisper in my ear, I know I'll be okay and let out a relieved sob. "Shhh, I've got you, baby. I've got you." Jason doesn't even flinch as my claws dig into his flesh. I bury my face in his neck as he carries me out of the water, every inch of me trembling as he walks us to the lounge chair and sits down with me in his lap.

Everything that's happened in the last few minutes hits me even stronger than the wave that just took me down, and I suddenly burst into tears. Jason mumbles soothingly to me as he rubs my goose bump-covered skin, running his hands up and down my legs and then in circles on my back. He uses his fingers to wipe the wet tangled hair out of my face, and then leans forward to press his cheek to mine, rocking me like a child. He lulls me into calmness until I'm almost asleep, worn out as the adrenaline leaves my body.

I hear someone approach, but before they reach us, Jason's livid growl rumbles in his chest against my ear. "You need to get the fuck away from me right now, motherfucker."

"What the fuck, man? It was only a joke. How was I supposed to know she couldn't swim?" Gavin asks defensively.

"She told you straight up she never goes in the water, and

yet you threw her in against her will. Thank fuck I was coming back from getting more beer, or you would have just stood there fucking laughing while she drowned. You couldn't see she was panicking?" Jason's body is tense, as if he's getting ready to attack, even though I'm still curled up in his lap. I wrap my arms around him more tightly, and I feel his muscles loosen marginally.

"I thought she was just messing around!" Gavin insists.

"You need to back the fuck away before I rip your goddamn head off, and I mean right the fuck now," Jason orders. I've never heard him so angry before. I would never want to be on the receiving end of his wrath if just his words and tone can spark such a sense of foreboding.

"Seriously, dude? She's fine. What's your problem?"

"My problem is you should've kept your motherfucking hands to your goddamn self. She's not some fucking little plaything," Jason seethes.

Oh no. Oh no no no no no.

"What is this really about?" Gavin questions.

I dig my nails into Jason's back, trying to get his attention, bring him out of his fury so he won't blow our cover. I wouldn't care if Gavin knows Jason and I have been together, but I know Jason will regret blowing up and letting it out this way.

"I will say this one time, and then I don't want to see your face for the rest of the night. When someone tells you no, it fucking means no. You don't make a joke out of it and do what you want anyway, hoping just to ask for forgiveness later. You don't take advantage of people when they're vulnerable, forcing them into doing something they don't want to do when their defenses are low. It's the fucking principle," he growls the last part.

"You and your dumbass principles," Gavin grumbles not-so-quietly.

And thar she blows.

Jason stands abruptly but has the mind to turn around and place me in the lounger gently. When he turns, I see his back flex and he seems to swell with his rage. He prowls up to Gavin, his intensity crackling in the air between and around the two men. "What did you say?" he challenges. "I'm not quite sure I heard you correctly. Can you please repeat the words that just came out of your motherfucking mouth?" His tone is menacing. I haven't seen this side of Jason. It's scary, and it's kind of mind-boggling to think this is the same man who was just cuddling me after rescuing me from the water.

"Are you really wanting to fight me right now?" Gavin asks incredulously. He lifts his arm and gestures toward me. "Over *her?*"

"Did you not hear what I said? No, this isn't just about her. It's the fucking principle." He punctuates the last word with a shove to Gavin's chest.

I stand up on shaky legs, ready to jump between them like an idiot, but I don't have to. Gavin doesn't engage. He throws up his hands and backs away, apologizing to Jason, and then to me over his massive shoulder. This is not a pussy move. Oh no. For once, I think Gavin has half a brain. It would be absolutely stupid for him to even think about standing up against Jason right now. He looks like it would be physically possible to do exactly what he threatened, ripping Gavin's head off with his bare hands.

Jason stands there all puffed up until Gavin enters the beach house, and then he turns, shaking his head as he storms back over to me. He's coming at me so hard, I take an involuntary step backward, and I know he sees it and it affects him when he looks up into my face with confusion. He halts, stopping a few feet in front of me, and then he slumps. He drags his hand over his scruff-covered face, visibly trying to regain control over himself, and when his eyes meet mine, they are full of remorse.

"I...I'm sorry you had to see me like that." He puts his hand out and approaches me like I'm a skittish cat. I'm not afraid of him; just the way he was coming at me before, I didn't want him to accidently knock me down since I'm standing on legs that belong to a newborn foal. To ease some of his worry, I don't wait for him to reach me. I eat up the distance between us with one lunge and mold myself to him, rescuing him from his inner turmoil the way he just saved me from the swirling waves.

His face lands in its favorite spot at the side of my neck, and even though we're still dripping wet, sticky, and covered in sand, we wrap ourselves around one another like each other's soft, familiar, warm, and comforting security blanket.

Kayla's Chick Rant & Book Blog

May 13th, 2005

I just got off the phone with Jason. He's busy helping his mom organize the attic tonight before she and her hubby leave in the morning for their own weekend in Galveston. When we got back from ours, we told them how great the beach house was they rented for us, so they decided to book it for themselves.

Speaking of that weekend, after Gavin disappeared inside the rental, he wisely called Adam and had him come pick him up. I felt a little bad that he didn't get to enjoy the getaway the Robichauxs sent us on to celebrate the end of our semester of school, but at the same time, I was glad to fully enjoy the time alone with Jason. Plus, the asshole nearly drowned me, so serves him right.

Something happened to us that weekend, something binding. We didn't do anything for the rest of the time we were there besides cuddle up in the master bedroom's king-sized four-poster canopy-covered bed, making love several times, only coming out for food, which we'd brought along with us to save money instead of eating out for every meal. I'm so glad we'd done it for another reason though: a very naked Jason for twenty-four hours straight.

Jason and Gavin made up a few days later, with Gavin making a smartass comment about 'bros before hos' that almost got him punched in the face in the middle of the man-hug he was sharing with Jason. That's when it finally dawned on him there was more between Jason and me than we let on.

He didn't seem to care much, not that we explain the extent of our relationship to him. We left him thinking we were just friends with benefits. Technically, I guess that's what we really are. But it feels like so much more. I feel like we were put on this Earth for each other, and he told me he feels for me something he's never felt for anyone else before. Combine that to how he said he trusts me more than any girl he's ever met, and I believe he's feeling the same things I am. To me, love is what happens when you mix trust, your heart, your soul, and sex. Sure, you can 'love' just about anyone, but I'm talking about *love* love. Like the forever kind and I really think that's what I have with Jason.

He told me he has something special planned for me at his house tomorrow and to show up around four. I think I'll finish reading my Michele Bardsley advance review copy she sent me. Ahhh, the perks of being a book nerd.

CHAPTER
Twenty-Five

May 14th, 2005

This is it. I know it. This is when Jason is finally, *finally* going to make it official. I dance in my driver's seat the entire drive down to Friendswood so enthusiastically, that by the time I pull into his driveway, I'm breathing heavily and kind of exhausted. My heart pounds I'm so excited, giddy with the possibility of being able to say I'm Jason Robichaux's girlfriend.

Hi, I'm Kayla, Jason's girlfriend.

Hey, I'm Jason's girl.

Oh, nice to meet you, this is my girlfriend Kayla.

Hey there, let me introduce you to my boyfriend Jason.

Oh, ya know, just going to hang out with Jason, my boyfriend.

I feel like I'm in high school again. I want to break out a notebook and practice my signature as Mrs. Kayla Robichaux and draw hearts and flowers around it. I want to turn the page and play MASH, and see how many kids we'll have, if we'll live in a mansion, and what car we'll drive.

Notebook...school supplies...college...*classes!* Oh, hell, so much to do. I gotta sign up for another semester. Should I take classes this summer, or just wait until the fall? I wonder what Jason has planned. If he's not planning to do a summer semester, maybe I won't either, that way we can spend more time together. Or maybe I should anyway? I don't want to smother him. I don't think Mark and Kim would be cool with me staying with them longer if I'm not actually going to school.

Shit, I gotta talk to them. I never planned to stay longer than just the one semester. What if they tell me I can't live with them? I'll have to find somewhere else to live. Maybe I could move closer to Friendswood so I won't have to drive so far every day. Then I could enroll at the school down here that Jason goes to.

Oh, my God, how cute would we be going to classes together? And then we could study late into the night at IHOP. He's been thinking about getting his own place. Maybe we could get one together. My heart skips a beat at the thought. I know I'm letting my imagination run wild right now, and I'd never voice any of this aloud, but I can't help it. Things have been so perfect with Jason. I know he's the one.

He's been so open about how he truly feels about me; I feel confident he's ready to take our relationship to the next level.

I turn off the ignition after taking a deep breath and let it out as I step out of my car. I make an effort to settle myself as I walk into his garage and knock on the side door. His mom's SUV isn't in its bay, and I smile to myself at the possibility of him having something special planned while his parents are in Galveston for the night.

He opens the door and I can't help myself. I step up to him and immediately wrap my arms around his neck, pulling him down to me to kiss him feverishly. I feel his hands at my waist as he caresses the bare skin of my back. I'd worn my cute Hollister short-shorts and a teal crop top since it's so flippin' hot out. The kiss goes on forever, and I enjoy the feel of his erection pressing into my stomach as he gives me one final peck on the lips before he pulls away. "Well, hello to you too," he says, and then walks into his kitchen.

When I walk in, he's already plated food and set the table. He gestures for me to take a seat, and then grabs a glass of wine off the kitchen counter he must have poured before answering the door.

He comes over to the table and sits down, placing the wine in front of me. "You trying to get me drunk?" I tease, picking up the glass and taking a sip.

"Something like that," he says, and takes a drink of his beer. "Dig in." He points to my plate, and I look down and see he's grilled us some steaks and made green beans and baked potatoes to go with them. He's even sautéed me some onions and mushrooms, knowing that's my favorite way to eat a steak. I pick up my fork and knife and cut into the beef, and it's cooked exactly how I like it, perfectly seared on the outside and pink on the inside. I stab a slice of onion and a mushroom, along with a bite of meat and lift it to my lips, the smell instantly making my mouth water and my stomach growl. He watches me as I try the first bite, and I see him smile before my eyes roll back and I moan in appreciation. *So fucking good.*

Our meal is mostly quiet. I'm excitedly waiting for him to bring up the conversation I'm dying to have, but in true Jason form, I know he's going to torture me and make me wait until the last possible moment. *Damn him and his surprises.* Regardless, I smile to myself; I always love his damn surprises.

We finish eating and I help him clean up the kitchen before we head outside for a smoke. Again, we barely speak. This game he's playing is making me anxious, causing me to smoke another cigarette as I put out the last one. Why doesn't he just go ahead and spit it out? Is he nervous? I know he hasn't been in a real relationship in a very long time, but shit. We've been close and sleeping together for nearly three months. The only thing that would really change is the fact that people would know.

The tension inside my body is building to a fever pitch, and I'm about to blow a gasket and just yell for him to spill it already, when he puts out his cigarette and stands. He reaches between my fingers and takes mine, putting it out in the ashtray before taking my hand and pulling me to my feet. He tugs me along with him to the door, through his living room, down his hall, and into his bedroom, where he closes the door behind him. I turn around to face him, and before I can make a sound, he crashes his lips down on mine, wrapping his strong, tattooed arm around my back to catch me from the force of his demanding kiss.

I can barely catch my breath. He gives me no time to inhale as he alternates between deep licks of his tongue and rough presses of his pillowy lips to mine. Suddenly, I hear him growl, and the next thing I know, I'm landing with a bounce in the middle of his bed and his heavy body is coming down on top of me.

CHAPTER Twenty-Six

His intensity is like nothing I've ever experienced before. If he wanted to make this night something special, one I'd never forget, then he's doing a damn fine job. He grinds his pelvis into mine, his thick erection pressing into the hot hollow between my legs, making me moan. He takes the opportunity to lick into my mouth, and the familiar taste of Shiner, cigarettes, and Jason fills me. The way he's moving against me, if he doesn't stop, I'm going to come before he even gets me naked. I find that thought amusing, seeing how before this all happened with the amazing man above me, I was never able to reach my orgasm, and now I have them almost every night.

Over and over, he's satisfied my body, taking me above and beyond anything I ever thought I could feel. He takes my hands and places them both over my head, holding them in only one of his, and I gasp as he uses his other one to slide up my shirt and up under the cup of my bra to pinch my nipple. It causes my hips to jerk upward, and he hisses in a breath when our centers collide. I wonder for only a second if I've hurt him, and then my worry flies out the window as he glides his hand down my stomach to snatch the snap closure of my jean shorts open. He pulls down the pathetic excuse for a zipper—it being only about an inch long since my Daisy Dukes are super low rise, showcasing my hipbones, which he normally loves to lick and nibble, driving me crazy since he's so close to where I need him to be.

He somehow works the skin-tight denim over my hips and down my thighs, low enough to where I can work my legs the rest of the way out of them. He presses himself against me once again. With me only in my black thong, I feel the outline of him through his jeans clear as day. His cock behind the zipper of his jeans rubs right against my clit, and the way he's devouring my mouth, taking my breath away, makes me see stars. My breath comes out in pants and he continues to thrust against me, making me whimper and shake my head.

I don't want to come yet. I want him inside me. But he carries on with his assault on my now tender lips and my soaking wet pussy. My tiny thong is doing nothing to contain my arousal. I can feel I've drenching the front of his pants as he grinds into me. I fight against his hand holding mine above my head, but he's just too strong. Finally, all I can do his cry out into his mouth when I can't hold out any longer as he forces me to come. I shudder and convulse, and he doesn't let up, even as my body goes limp beneath him.

All of my strength is completely depleted, and I can only lie there as I feel him reach between us to undo his jeans. He kicks them off, along with his underwear, and I quiver helplessly as I feel him hook his finger in the crotch of my thong and pull it aside. "So fucking wet for me, baby," he whispers against my neck as he dips his finger inside me. Even the stroke of just the one finger makes me gasp because I'm so sensitive after the orgasm he just gave me. I open my eyes and look up at him as I feel him pull his hand away from my pussy and I see him bring it up to his mouth to lick my wetness from his finger. "Mmmmm, I'll never forget how good you taste," he says against my ear. I want to tell him he never has to worry about that, because I'm his to taste for the rest of his life, but the words leave my brain as he moves my thong out of the way once again, and without warning, he thrusts his huge cock inside me, balls deep.

My breath leaves me in a silent scream; I can't even make a sound. The force of his claim on my pussy is so overwhelming I lose all sense of where and who I am. I become the sensations he's pounding into me, only aware of the dizzying, tumbling, spinning feeling that's consuming every sense I own. There is no more bed beneath me; we are no longer in his bedroom, in his house, in his neighborhood, fuck, even in this universe. I am delirious with pleasure, reaching a level I didn't even know existed.

As he pistons his hips into me, still holding my arms above my head, he uses his hand to clamp it over my mouth, and it's not until then that I realize my throat is raw. I hadn't even been aware I was screaming. He places his palm high enough to block most of the oxygen from my nose as well, and before I start to panic, I see he's doing this purposely, calculating the measurement of air to allow me as he continues his assault on my pussy.

That's all it takes. My eyes clamp closed. I take as deep a breath as I can force behind his hand, and my body convulses. Then I'm falling. I'm weightless, detached from everything. I'm so out of my mind I even imagine I'm floating above our bodies, looking down at Jason as he thrusts into me without relenting. After a few more minutes of hovering in what I've absently realized is subspace, something I've only read about, but have never experienced, he growls as he delivers one last punishing plunge of his cock, coming violently as he shudders against me, bringing me back into my body and making my world tilt.

He rests his forehead against mine as we catch our breaths, removing his hand from my mouth to slide his arm beneath my neck, holding me tightly. He runs the tip of his nose up one side of mine and then down the other, making my heart clench at the tender movement. Instead of dreading our 'after-nooky cigarette' like I usually do, fearing the normal closed-off way he acts after we've made love, I'm excited. I soak in the loving way he's caressing my face, looking at me like he's trying to memorize my every feature. He leans down and kisses me sweetly as he finally carefully pulls out of me.

I allow myself to relish the way he cleans me up, taking care of me, instead of the way I usually can't enjoy it, since I'm always worried about the way he's going to act once he's finished and we get dressed. He presses his gentle kiss to my lower lips, and then takes my hand to pull me up.

CHAPTER
Twenty-Seven

We get dressed in silence, my heart pounding with excitement, not anxiety of shuttered Jason. As I slip my feet into my flip-flops, he steps up in front of me, circling his arms around my waist to pull me to him as he buries his face in the side of my neck, breathing me in like he loves to do.

He's never been so affectionate afterwards. I can't help but let the giddiness bubble inside me, knowing he's about to ask me to make our relationship official. He pulls back to kiss me, lingering against my lips, and I feel his hands rubbing up and down my back, lulling me into a comforted state, calming my nerves a little. He takes my hand once again and then guides me out to the driveway, where we sit in our usual spot against the closed garage door. We each pull out a cigarette, and I turn my face toward him so he can light mine.

He's silent for so long I'm afraid I've misjudged what today was going to be—the day I officially become Jason's girl —but then he turns to me and threads his fingers through mine. I look down at our entwined fingers, and then up into his beautiful dark brown eyes. I take a deep breath, and listen as he begins to speak.

"I can't tell you how much I've enjoyed our times together. There's no one I've ever been able to open up to so honestly before, who hasn't judged me or tried to change me. You're my best friend," he says, and then slumps down a little, looking down at our hands as he runs his thumb over the back of mine, sending tingles up my arm.

"You're mine too, Jason. It's so different with you, not having to hide things, telling you everything without having to worry about being embarrassed. I love...being with you," I tell him, catching myself at the end, not wanting to jump the gun and be the first one to say I love you.

"I love being with you, too, and that's what makes this so hard." He drops my hand and picks up his pack of cigarettes, pulling another one out and lighting it. He turns his body back around, closes his eyes, and then leans his head back against the garage door as he blows out his smoke.

My brow furrows. What does he mean, 'that's what makes this so hard'? How can loving being with each other make it hard to ask me to be his girlfriend? "What do you mean?" I ask quietly, and then let out a nervous laugh.

"You going back to North Carolina," he replies, still not looking at me.

"What are you talking about? I told you I have to choose whether I'm going back home or staying for another semester of school," I say, my voice trembling as my heart pounds, making sickening icy tendrils start to rise from my stomach.

"That's just it," he says, and finally turns to look me dead in the eyes. His voice is monotone, but stern when he adds, "There's no reason for you to stay in Texas. There is nothing keeping you here. You need to go home, back to North Carolina."

I stare at him for a moment; I have no words. I can literally feel my heart hammering against the wall of my chest before it feels like it completely stops. This is not happening. This is not how today was supposed to go. Why is he saying these things to me? I have every reason to stay in Texas, even if my only reason is him.

"There *is* something keeping me here. I *have* a reason to stay," I manage to whisper. Does he not realize I want to stay for him?

"No...you don't," he states, the tone of his voice making it perfectly clear he knows what I want, but that I'm not going to get it.

I feel the nauseating chill inside me rise up into my tear ducts, filling my eyes with the sting of tears. "Why did you bring me here tonight?" I choke out. Why did he make me such a nice dinner, and then practically brand me with the way he fucked me, holding me and making me feel cherished afterwards, when he knew he was about to end it all? My breath quickens as I begin to panic, reality crashing down on top of me.

He speaks words that would later haunt me for years to come. "I wanted us to have one last time together. I wanted to have you one more time, knowing it was the last time, so I could savor it. It's time for you to go back home. I'm not going to be your reason to stay in Texas."

With that, my heart that had frozen in my chest splinters. The crack grows, slowly making a jagged, painful circle around the center before the two ends meet, and then it explodes into sharp shards, cutting into my lungs and stealing my breath. One of the strident pieces travels even deeper, slicing into my soul and making it scream out in pain inside me, knowing its mate is throwing it away, rejecting us, telling my breaking heart it doesn't want us. I feel like I'm dying, but all I can do is stare at Jason. How can he be doing this to me? After...everything.

"I thought you were going to ask me to be your girlfriend," I murmur. "I thought...I thought all of this was a date you'd planned to make it special...and you...you're telling me to leave? You had me drive all the way down here thinking everything was great, made me dinner, and th-then made lov—no, *fucked* me, practically fucking marked me as yours..." I trail off, my mind flashing back to when he said he'd never forget my taste, the way he studied my face like he was committing it to memory. "Why? Why are you doing this? Why don't you want me to stay?"

"Kayla," he snaps, and it's not his tone that feels like a slap to my face; it's the use of my real name. He never calls me Kayla, only 'babe'. "We're twenty and twenty-one years old. Where do you think this was leading? You knew I didn't want anything serious. Fuck, you gave me enough shit for my POF page to know I only wanted casual encounters. You want to know what NOMAX4ME really means? It means the number of women I've been and will be with. There's no maximum. I already broke my rule and fucked you more than once. You want something from me I'm not ready for. Will never be ready for. I'm not the settling-down type."

His harsh words slash at me. He's never been so cruel toward me before. The strikes hurt, but nothing he can say will make me believe what we've shared meant nothing to him. He's trying to hurt me, trying to push me away. "Jason, I know what we feel for each other is real. You can't convince me, after the things we've done and the things we've told each other, you don't feel what I'm feeling.

"This is pointless. I'm not going to argue with you about it. I'm fucked up. I'm not the one for you. You deserve someone who will treat you like gold, who will settle down and be the one to give you everything you want and need. Yeah, I feel something for you, but it doesn't change the fact that we," he gestures between the two of us, "will never happen. There will never be an *us*."

I've tried my damnedest to hold it in, but I can't any longer. The dam bursts and my face is flooded with tears. He looks at me blankly, my anguish seeming to have no effect on him as he stubs out his cigarette and stands.

I've been hurt after a breakup before. It sucks. It's a mix of pain, embarrassment, sadness, and even a little bit of fear of what will come. But this? I've never felt this before. My heart is more than broken. It's shattered beyond repair. Those lethal shards did their damage to my insides and then melted away, leaving an endless black hole in its place. My soul clutches at its wound as it stands and takes one last valiant leap toward its mate, only to fall into the gaping pit that was my heart, spiraling down, down, never to feel its fated companion's closeness again.

I try one last time to break through to him, but all that comes out is a whispered pitiful, "Please."

He rests his hands on his hips, looks down to the ground, and shakes his head. "Go home, Kayla," he mutters, and I know he doesn't mean my brother's house.

He's right about one thing. Without him, I have no reason to stay in Texas.

End of Book One

ACKN♠WLEDGEMENTS

Ever since I was a little girl, I wanted to write fairy tales. I got my love of reading from my mom, Ava, and then it just exploded in the fifth grade thanks to my favorite teacher, Mr. Watson, who would read to us every day after lunch. Thanks, you two, for teaching me I can go anywhere I want, even while just sitting still.

Jason, my soulmate, my husband, my best friend, my lover, the father of my children, my *everything*: Right now, you have a lot of people really wanting to do you bodily harm, but I've tried to make it perfectly clear that I got my Happily Ever After; they just have to read to see the long, sometimes torturous journey it took for us to get here. God put us on this Earth to be together forever. We know that for a fact now. Thank you for supporting me no matter what, and for even being my hottie cover model. I love you more than coffee.

Speaking of coffee: Dunn Bros. If you know me at all, you know that Dunn Bros Coffee in Friendswood, Texas is my little Heaven on Earth. It is owned by a marvelous woman named Benette, who is so kind and generous that it makes you want to scream at the top of your lungs how great she is. Thank you, Benette, along with Houston, Austin, Nam, Andrew, Amanda, Shawna, Stephanie, and Dusty, for keeping me caffeinated and fed, and for giving me a place that makes me feel like I'm being hugged as soon as I walk in the door. This book would not have been written without your haven.

As I was sitting at Erin Noelle's table—my Twinnie—at a signing in Houston while she had gone to do her infamous cartwheels, a woman came up to me and started raving about how much she loved my work. I quickly corrected her, telling her I wasn't Erin, and that we get it all the time that we look like sisters. But she told me, "Oh, no, I know who you are. You are Kayla the Bibliophile. We aren't friends on Facebook, but since we have mutual friends, when one of them commented on a post you had made of just one paragraph of your book you were in the process of writing, I made a mental note to keep an eye out for it."

Now, at this time, I had literally written seventeen pages. I had recently gotten my editing job with Hot Tree and had put my book on the backburner. When I told her this, she said to me, "I know you don't know me, but just from that one paragraph, I have to read this book. Please, pick it back up and finish writing it. Even if it takes forever, please, you gotta write that book." If it weren't for this epic, shocking, heart-stuttering moment, this would have never happened. My friend will never know how much that short conversation meant to me. The next day, I opened my document for the first time in six months and I busted out 3,000 words, and through Facebook and desperation, I found Kylie Sharp, letting her know I was writing again, all thanks to her.

Then there are the women who have been rooting me on since I got that initial kick-start:

First, there was Anni, who lived through these "stories" with me. I'm sure a part of the reason she wanted me to write it was because she'd get her own character in a book, but I know the true reason was because she knew I had to fulfill my dream in life of becoming an author. No one has been here longer than you, woman, and I love you like the sister I never had. You make me be brave.

Second, there was Crystal Reynolds. As I was editing her book, Until Trevor, our first time working together, we made an immediate connection, saying we each got one half of the same brain. If the voices in her head weren't talking to her, they were talking to me. We work magic together. When I told her Jason and my story and how I was trying to write it as a romance novel, she told me to go for it. "Just put your fingers to the keys," she'd tell me. "Even if it's just for one hour a day, keep writing." Took me forever, girl, but I finally did it.

Next, there were my besties, Jamie Vest, Sara Ferguson, Danielle Jamie, and even Kristin Williams, who isn't really a big reader, but has read my entire book, because she knows everyone in it. Y'all kept encouraging me, motivating me, telling me to keep on going. Of course there have been some "Ewwww!" moments, seeing how y'all are friends with Jason and I wrote explicit love scenes, but you never stopped rooting for me.

Then there's JC Cliff. Even thinking the woman's name makes me go all mushy and emotional. I have never met a person so willing to do absolutely ANYTHING for me than you.

Let me tell y'all a little fun fact. My cousin Mary (love her to DEATH) is a huge reader of romance, and her best friend had written a book and was looking for an editor. Knowing that's what I do, Mary referred her to me. JC can be a tough cookie. Sometimes, self-admittedly, she comes off as more than a little blunt. She knows what she wants, and she won't settle for anything less. Me, being happy-go-lucky, goofball Kayla, you wouldn't think we'd get along very well. On the contrary, we balance each other perfectly. Even though she doesn't get my reference, I call her the Meredith to my Cristina. We are a match made by fate, and I know we will always be loyal friends who work together to make phenomenal things happen.

Thank you for teaching me this side of things. No complaints, no brush-offs, no nothing. When I need you, you are there, no questions asked. And thank you for formatting my book! I love you so much!

There is a woman in this book world who doesn't even need a second name. Someone says Kathryn, and you know exactly who they're talking about. But just in case, she's Kathryn Falk, founder and owner of Romantic Times Magazine, aka RT Book Reviews. She's the Queen of Romance, and the most fascinating person on the planet. She plans to live to be 120 years old, and I pray she succeeds, because now that I have her in my life, I never want to think about her ever not being in it. Working for and with her has been an experience I never want to end.

Instead of encouraging me the way my friends were, you issued me a challenge. You told me, "Write your book, Kayla, and you'll sign at RT." It's every author's dream to sign at RT Booklover's Convention. You knew what it would take to kick my butt into gear, and now look! You have a mind like no one I've ever met before, and I could sit and listen to your stories for hours. You could take the most skeptical person in the entire world, have one conversation with them about Mercury in its retrograde, and make a believer out of them. I sure do now! I've already learned so much from you, and I can't wait to see what else that endless knowledge of yours will teach me!

My League of Extraordinary Writers, almost named "The HAGs" (Houston Authors Guild, hehe!) Erin Noelle, TK Rapp, Sierra Cartwright, and Kathryn Falk, we make quite a team. I'm so glad I have such an amazing group of women to see in person, who are as passionate about our book world as I am. Our Readers and Writers RoundUp is going to be epic.

Heather Lane, another fated friend. Five years ago, I went to college with her sister in law, and seeing we were mutual friends, Heather fangirled out on me, being a loyal follower of my blog page. She was even too nervous to contact me, making Tina, her SIL, introduce us! We have gotten so close over such a short amount of time it's insane. Thank you for blowing up my texts, FaceTime, and messenger, (but not the phone calls; you know I hate that shit hehe!), riding my ass about finishing this book. You are the one person who messaged me every single day, asking for more words. You NEEDED more words.

And to get more words, you took stress off me by helping Sassy Sara and I keep up with my blog so I could write.

And then you made my book trailer.

I still cry nearly every time I watch it. I've been told that's normal for any author, but since this is my real story, my TRUE, honest-to-God story of my real life, seeing it played out like that is otherworldly. If anyone needs a book trailer, you contact Heather at Book Obsession Production. I swear on Jared Leto you will NOT be disappointed.

KD's Betas. OMG, girls. Y'all are freaking awesome. I pray I name everyone, so here goes nothing: Jennifer, Toski, Chrissy, Stacia, Kali, Danielle, Mandy, Lisa, Theresa, Rhonda, ML, Vanessa, Hayley, Celena, Amy, Racheal, Vanessa, Carrie, Kolleen, Teri, Jill, Carol, Kim, Kristen, Joya, and Jordan. If I've left someone out, I'm so sorry. I've gone through every email and message in our group and I think I've got all of you!

Becky Johnson. What can I say? I was a blogger who you met by word of mouth, and then you gave me my dream job. You're the best boss in the world. Literally, the world, seeing how you live on the other side of it…in Australia of all places. What would I do without you? Thank you for editing my book and making me feel like it's going to be something special. Your pride in me really means a lot, and I cannot wait to squeeze you in October.

Jamie's Uncle Arthur: You're, like, my biggest fan. You're so adorable in your fandom. I REALLY don't want you to read my book, and you sorta promised you wouldn't, but thank you for rooting me on to realize my dream itself. Anyone would be lucky to have you on their side!

Thank you, Zar, Erin Noelle's hubby, for playing "the other man" on my cover. I could tell you really didn't want to do it, but you're a fantastic friend who gave in anyways. Now, I have the best looking cover on the planet!

Thank you, Mike Fox, my photographer extraordinaire in Pearland, Texas. You...you are the best, not only for your beautiful work, but for your humor, you brilliant ideas, and for a certain referral I will appreciate for the rest of my life. All of my photos you do are fantastic, but what you captured for the cover of my book is perfection. And you're wife, Angi, is pretty damn cool too.

For all my author, blogger, and reader friends who have supported me along the way, thank you. Your likes, comments, shares, and retweets are more than this girl could ever ask for.

Saving the best for last: my daughters, Josalyn and Avary, thank you for still loving me, even when I needed to work. Thank you for making me feel like I'm still a good Mommy, even though a lot of times you have to eat quicky meals for dinner and the house is a wreck. You never fail to want to give me love, kisses, draw me beautiful artwork, or tell me "crazy" stuff, even when I look like I've crawled out of a cave. I hope, instead of thinking I was busy too much of the time, you look back and take from this to fulfill your dreams. Whatever you want to do, just do it. Finish it. Work hard until you get it done. You and Daddy are my number 1, but I pray that one day, you will see too that you can have it all.

About the Author

KD Robichaux wanted to be a romance author since the first time she picked up her mom's Sandra Brown books at the ripe old age of twelve. She went to college to become a writer, but then married and had babies. Putting her dream job on hold to raise her family as a stay at home mom, who read entirely too much, she created a blog where she could keep her family and friends up-to-date on all the hottest reads. From there, by word of mouth, her blog took off and she began using her hard-earned degree as a Senior Editor for Hot Tree Editing. When her kids started school, and with the encouragement from her many author friends, she finally sat down and started working on her first series, The Blogger Diaries, her very own real life romance.

Made in the USA
San Bernardino, CA
19 July 2017